GREGORY BASTIANELLI

SNOWBALL

This is a **FLAME TREE PRESS** book

Text copyright © 2020 Gregory Bastianelli

FLAME TREE PRESS
6 Melbray Mews, London, SW6 3NS, UK
flametreepress.com

Distribution and warehouse:
Marston Book Services Ltd
marston.co.uk

Thanks to the Flame Tree Press team, including:
Taylor Bentley, Frances Bodiam, Federica Ciaravella, Don D'Auria,
Chris Herbert, Josie Karani, Molly Rosevear, Will Rough, Mike Spender,
Cat Taylor, Maria Tissot, Nick Wells, Gillian Whitaker.

The cover is created by Flame Tree Studio with
thanks to Nik Keevil and Shutterstock.com.
The font families in this book are Avenir and Bembo.

Flame Tree Press is an imprint of Flame Tree Publishing Ltd
flametreepublishing.com

A copy of the CIP data for this book is available from the British Library.

3 5 7 9 8 6 4 2

HB ISBN: 978-1-78758-348-1
PB ISBN: 978-1-78758-347-4
ebook ISBN: 978-1-78758-349-8

Printed in the UK at Clays, Suffolk

GREGORY BASTIANELLI

SNOWBALL

FLAME TREE PRESS
London & New York

For Rhonda, whose love warms my heart
on a cold winter's night

PART ONE
'TWAS THE NIGHT
BEFORE CHRISTMAS

CHAPTER ONE

A snowplough trudged along the narrow turnpike lane, trying to keep up with the onslaught of wet heavy snow piling up on the road in thick drifts. *Hell of a way to spend Christmas Eve*, Toby Hodge thought as the blade of his plough burrowed through the piles of white. The wind whipped snow across his windshield, blades thwacking back and forth, useless as crusty slush built up along the edge of the wipers and the sides of the glass, narrowing his view of the road before him.

Damn! He could barely see the road. Hadn't he just gone down this way not more than an hour ago? The storm was piling the snow up faster than he could keep up with it. And where the hell were the other state ploughs? He hadn't seen anyone else on the highway for a while. He tried raising the other trucks on the two-way radio, but got nothing but static. The storm wreaked havoc with communications. Damn. New Hampshire hadn't seen a blizzard like this since '78, and that was over forty years ago.

Fitting, Toby thought, considering this was to be his last run of the winter. Nell had kept telling him to retire the week before Christmas, giving them time to enjoy the holiday season before their big move to Florida. But no, Toby knew how short-staffed the Department of Transportation was this time of year, and offered to work right up to the day before Christmas. Then they'd have one day to enjoy the holiday with their children and grandkids before the trucks came to pack everything up for their relocation.

Then this shit had to hit. He had watched the reports all week. Everyone was predicting it would be a big one. He remembered '78. God, that seemed so long ago. He was young, the kids young. Evan was only a baby that year. Now he was grown and had given Toby a couple of mighty fine grandkids. Not bad considering his son had been a high school dropout whose life got derailed by drugs. But Evan turned his circumstances around and Toby felt blessed about that.

Seeing your child suffer in life aged you. And if that wasn't enough, Old Man Winter decided to rear his ugly head and give Toby one last blast to remember him by.

No way he'd soon forget this. One more slice of misery to kick his ass. God, he wouldn't miss this. Not one bit. If only this night would end. He'd probably miss the grandkids opening gifts tomorrow because he'd still be out here on the turnpike, trying to clear the lanes for all the holiday travellers. Toby hated the thought of missing the little ones in the morning. This would be his last Christmas to see that. After that, he and Nell would never set foot up north this time of year. That's the thing he'd miss the most about moving to Florida – seeing the grandkids on Christmas morning. He'd wanted one last moment of that, and this storm had ruined it. He should have listened to Nell and retired a week earlier. She was always right. He just hated admitting it.

Don't think about it, Toby told himself. *Get through this nightmare and it'll be over with.* Soon he'd be lazing in the sun on the fishing boat, casting for stripers or bluefish; piña coladas at the tiki bar and all-you-can-eat buffets every Saturday night. No more shovelling, no more ploughing, no more frozen fingers and numb ass cheeks. Just sun, sand and surf.

But now the only waves coming at him were white and the snowplough struggled against the tide. Hadn't he just cleared this section? How the hell could it be snowing so damn fast? He dropped a gear and looked down at his speedometer. He was barely doing thirty. Toby was surprised he could even move the thick snow at that speed.

He looked up from his dashboard just in time to see the brown shapes in front of him.

"What the——" he yelled before slamming on the brakes.

Reindeer?

He looked into his driver's side mirror, which was encrusted in snow. He hadn't noticed if there were vehicles right behind him before he hit the brakes, and though visibility was horrid, he could see no sign of headlights.

Was anyone crazy enough to even be out on a night like this? No, just him. He was the only idiot, Nell would say. If he could get the damn radio to work, he'd call the station and tell them to shut this stretch of highway down. It was already nearly impassable, and his plough wasn't helping much. More than anything he wanted to be home, even suffering the admonishing his wife would give him. How many times had she told him? Enough for sure.

Nell was always the reliable one. She knew best. That was one sturdy woman he had married those many years ago. He knew Nell was readying their house for his return from this dreadful night, snow-blowing the driveway and shovelling the walk to the front steps. She'd keep stoking the fire in the woodstove, more than likely bringing in extra wood from the shed. She wouldn't be just sitting on her ass waiting for him to come home. And that would be in addition to all the baking she'd be doing for the big day tomorrow: pies and cookies. That woman would not stop. And when he did finally get home tonight (more likely tomorrow morning), she'd have him sit and relax by the fire and bring him a mug of steaming hot cocoa with a dash of peppermint schnapps. Even though she herself would have suffered through a rugged night, she'd make damn sure he was comfortable when he got home. *God bless that woman*, Toby thought. No way would he have made it this far in life without her by his side. And she didn't expect much in return. Just the comfort of knowing he was home.

Now if he could only get there.

Toby looked beyond the windshield, rubbing the frost from the inside with a gloved hand, flakes of frost peeling off and dusting his dashboard. There was no sign of the deer. He swore he had seen them. Several. Bucks too. He saw antlers, he was sure of it. What the hell were they doing running around in this shit storm? Toby eased down on the clutch and shifted into first gear. The plough lurched forward, and then stopped. He lifted the blade, brought it back down, pressing on the gas. The truck didn't budge. The snow he saw in the path of his headlight beams nearly reached the top of his plough blade.

This can't be, he thought. *It couldn't have built up this fast.*

He shifted the gear into reverse, glancing again at his side mirror for headlights, and then tried to back up. He felt the wheels spin. He tried going forward but got only a couple feet before slipping sideways.

In more than forty years of ploughing he had never gotten stuck. A rig this big, weighing this much? No way the wheels should be spinning or sliding.

Toby slumped down in his seat, thinking. Maybe if he released some sand and spread it around the tyres. He didn't want to get out in this mess, not with that pelting snow and swirling wind. He was comfortable in his seat with the blast of hot air blowing on him through the dashboard vents.

He grabbed the radio handset. "Hello, base! This is P-12. Can anyone hear me?" He sensed the anxiousness in his voice. If they could hear him, they'd probably be laughing at him. Nothing but static spat out of the speaker.

"Damn!"

Toby grabbed a flare from the glove box and shoved it in his pocket. He pulled on his fur-lined winter hat tight over his ears and reached for the door handle. The wind ripped at him as soon as he opened the door, almost tearing it from his grip. He stepped onto the ice-crusted runner and slipped, falling onto his back in the snow. It was good so much snow had built up on the road, otherwise the fall might have hurt badly. As it was, only his pride stung.

He struggled to get up. *Way too old for this*, he thought. *If Nell could only see me now.* The grandkids would certainly have a laugh, and that thought brought the only smile to his face so far this evening. He shut the truck door and walked toward the back end. The wind whipped snow around his face, icy pinpricks jabbing his cheeks. He couldn't see very far beyond the truck. The path he had just ploughed along the highway was getting swallowed up quickly. He thought he could make out lights from vehicles in the distance coming this way.

"Shit!" he said. He took the flare out of his pocket and pulled the string. It burst into a bright red light and he tossed it into the road behind his rig. They couldn't be moving very fast in this. He hoped they'd see the flare in time.

Toby knew approximately which mile marker he was at on the turnpike, which meant it was a few miles between exits, one of the more desolate stretches on the highway, with nothing but woods lining both sides. No easy way to get off. Nobody should even be on it on a night like this.

He unlatched the shovel attached to the side of the truck.

With the wind howling like a freight train, he could barely hear himself think. But another sound joined the night.

Someone calling for help.

He turned toward the front of the truck, the direction the sound was coming from.

It had to be his imagination. The wind screeched too loud to hear anything else. But it came again, a low moan. Someone hurt? Out here?

No. It was a trick of the wind. It just sounded like a person's cry.

But it compelled him enough to walk toward the front of his truck and around the wide plough blades. Ignoring the snow pelting his now-numbed cheeks, he stared out to where the headlight beams ended, cut off by the swirling snow and dark night.

A figure stood in the road.

Motionless.

Wet snow stuck to his eyelashes and he wiped it away with one gloved hand, the other still gripping the shovel. It was still there. A tall, stout figure.

"Hello?" Toby called, his voice sucked away so that he couldn't be sure the person had heard him.

He climbed into the snow on the road in front of him, sinking up to his thighs. He struggled to lift each leg and plant it in front of him. When he got a few feet closer, he realised what he was looking at.

A snowman.

What the hell? he thought. *Is this some kind of joke? Who the hell would build a snowman in the middle of the turnpike?*

There was no mistaking it. Three round balls of snow piled on top of each other. Branches for arms stuck out of the sides of the middle section. A black top hat perched on the head, tilted forward so Toby couldn't see the face. A red-and-white scarf wrapped around the neck, its ends flapping in the wind.

With everything he'd been through this miserable night, this senseless act irked Toby the most, and he felt like smashing the damn thing with his shovel.

He gripped the handle and took a step forward.

Then the snowman's head rose, tilting back as its face came into view. Beneath the coal-black eyes and long crooked carrot nose was a black mouth grinning with two rows of sharp teeth.

Toby froze in his tracks, bringing the shovel up against his body defensively, his heart thudding in his chest.

He turned to run, but his feet were stuck. He pulled at his legs until the snow finally released its grip. Toby stumbled through the snow, like wading through wet cement. He didn't dare look behind him, because he knew if he did, he'd see that deranged snowman lurching after him.

What the hell?!

The snowplough was only a few feet away, but the snow made his efforts so slow, he didn't think he'd be able to reach it. He tossed the shovel aside, as if losing the excess weight would help. His arms swung wildly, trying to propel him forward through the thick snow. Cold air sucked deep into his lungs, preventing him from screaming. He could hear a swooshing sound from behind.

He slipped and fell into the road beside his front tyre. Scrambling, he got up and grabbed the handle of the driver's side door. It was at that moment when he finally glanced behind him.

Toby saw nothing but the swirling snow.

He opened the door and climbed up into his seat. He slumped back, releasing an exhausted breath, only to continue panting. He removed his gloves and saw his hands were shaking.

A mirage? he wondered. Toby knew tired drivers sometimes hallucinated. Highway hypnosis they called it. Was that what had happened to him? He had been ploughing for nearly twenty hours straight, and at his age—

Crack!

A branch smacked against the driver's side window, causing him to jump. The long branch split into three thinner ones, like fingers on a misshapen hand. It scraped down the glass, etching narrow cracks, as if trying to claw its way in.

No, Toby thought. *This can't be.*

He punched down on the door lock and moved to the middle of the bench seat. He shut the headlights off. *Maybe it won't see me,* he hoped.

Crack!

The branch came down again, this time on the windshield before him. The three twiglike fingers bent, digging at the glass.

It can't get in, Toby told himself. *The glass is too strong. It won't break.*

The branch pulled away from the windshield. Toby peered out the glass, looking around all three sides of his cab. He didn't see anything.

A strange sound came, faintly.

Toby turned off the truck's engine and listened. It sounded like it was coming from under the truck's hood. A scraping sound. It was getting closer.

Then he realised it was coming from the vents in the dashboard.

CHAPTER TWO

Eight vehicles eventually caught up to the snowplough stuck in the right lane of the turnpike. The first one to reach it was an SUV and the driver didn't even see the plough in the darkness till it was almost too late, the flare's glow now buried in snow. With its lights off, the big orange rig was hidden in the darkness of the night, camouflaged by the swirling snow.

It was fortunate none of the vehicles were able to move very fast on the snow-covered highway. When the driver of the SUV realised the plough was stopped and hit his brakes, the vehicle turned sideways and slid to a stop. That caused the eighteen-wheeled tractor-trailer behind it to jackknife, despite how cautious the experienced trucker behind the wheel was being.

Once that happened, the rest of the vehicles on the turnpike ground to a halt. Stacked up in line behind the eighteen-wheeler was a coupe, a luxury sedan, a hatchback, a minivan, an RV and a station wagon bringing up the rear. There was simply nowhere to go. The snow continued pounding the area, building up and beginning to bury their vehicles. So there the occupants of the vehicles sat.

And waited....

CHAPTER THREE

Eventually, some of the drivers got out of their vehicles and walked forward to see how bad the situation was. Graham Sawyer stepped from the sedan into a torrent of wind and icy snow pelting his face. From the car behind him came a young kid in a ski vest and winter cap, one hand raised in an attempt to shield his face from the elements.

His arms must be cold, Graham thought, never having understood the point of a winter vest. Graham himself only had on a leather bomber-style jacket. He had picked up his best friend from Logan Airport in Boston and hadn't really expected to step out into the elements. His fingers were already growing numb in his leather driving gloves.

The young kid, who barely looked in his twenties, said something, but the words were snatched by the wind. Graham just nodded and the two of them moved forward in the snow. As they passed the coupe, its driver rolled down the window. Graham could feel the heat pouring out of the vehicle and got his face close to steal some warmth.

"What the hell's going on?" asked the driver, a middle-aged man in a suit and tie. Folded on the seat beside him was a dress coat.

Someone else not dressed for the elements, Graham thought. He guessed no one had expected to be dealing with this.

"Don't know," Graham shouted into the man's open window, still enjoying the warmth on his cheeks. "That's what we're going to check out." Was the man an idiot? Did he think they knew anything?

"Well, I ain't getting out in this shit," the man replied. "Let me know what you find."

The man put his window up before Graham could respond. It didn't matter. The fellow didn't look like he'd be much help. Graham and the kid continued trudging forward through the snow. It was hard to breathe with the wind pressing against his face. His lips felt numb, and snot ran from his nose. He wiped it away on the sleeve of his jacket, hating to do that. *This sucks*, he thought.

It was dark on this stretch of the highway, no lampposts, and nothing but woods on both sides. Not a house or building in sight. The tall pine trees that lined the highway looked like snow-covered mountain peaks with jagged ridges.

As Graham made his way around the jackknifed tractor-trailer, he glanced back to make sure the kid was still with him. He was keeping pace, but a few feet behind, rubbing the arms of his sweater under the vest. The wind still blew in his face, frustrating Graham that it could blow in every direction he looked.

On the other side of the tractor-trailer, he saw an SUV stuck sideways in the middle of the turnpike. Two men were outside it, and as he got closer, Graham saw a heavy black man in a dark winter coat, a fur-lined hood surrounding his round brown face. He was talking to a tall middle-aged man whose neatly trimmed beard was caked with frost.

"What's it look like ahead?" Graham asked the duo, straining his neck to view beyond the SUV, though the mist coughed up by the swirling snow prevented seeing more than a few yards.

"There's a snowplough up ahead, just sitting there," the bearded man said. "No lights on or anything. Thought I was going to slam into it."

"You were going too fast for this crap," the black man said, irritation in his voice.

"I was fine," the bearded man said. "I've got good traction and tyres on this." He indicated his vehicle. "But that damn plough screwed me up."

"Has anyone checked it out?" Graham interjected.

"We were just going to," the bearded man said.

The black man shook his head. "Don't matter. Ain't no one going anywhere. This road is done. And," he said, pointing at his tractor-trailer, "that ain't moving."

Graham looked back at the jackknifed truck. He had to agree it didn't look like it'd be able to move. So that meant no going forward for those behind it, and he doubted there'd be any chance to turn around. The road behind them was only getting worse. Hopefully more ploughs would be coming this way.

Man, this really sucked. His spirits sank. On Christmas Eve at that. Trying to be a good friend and pick Clark up at the airport, and now look what it had led to. His wife, Natalie, had been against the whole plan. Let him take a bus, she had told him. He should be home with the kids, not prancing about on Christmas Eve, especially with the storm brewing. He had checked the forecast, but thought he would be a bit ahead of the worst of it. And he was, until Clark's plane was late getting in, and the traffic out of Boston was worse than he'd expected. It looked like she'd be putting the girls to bed without him. Damn.

"Tried to raise someone on my CB," the trucker said. "Can't get shit. Nowhere on the bands."

"I tried making calls too," the bearded man said. "Useless."

"Yeah," Graham said, looking up at the sky. "I'm sure the storm's knocked out the cell towers. Let's see if we can find anything out."

The four of them marched through the snow, the trucker in the lead with a flashlight, the kid bringing up the rear. Graham thought about telling him to go back. His arms must be freezing. He wasn't sure what any of them could do anyway. But maybe the plough guy could tell them something if he was still in touch with the DOT office.

The dark orange hulk of the plough truck was encrusted in snow. No lights on, its engine not running like those of the other vehicles. *Strange*, Graham thought. How was the driver keeping warm? Graham was freezing, his fingertips stinging. He kept squeezing them, but they felt like icicles.

The trucker scanned his light over the driver's side window. The cab was empty. Graham saw cracks in the glass. *Had that been caused by the storm?* he wondered. He looked at the trucker, who returned a quizzical glance and shrugged.

"Where the hell is he?" the bearded man yelled, peeved.

The trucker drew his light to the turnpike lane ahead. There was no semblance of a road, just a long stretch of white, interrupted by peaked drifts.

"Told ya," the trucker said. "We ain't going nowhere." He directed the light to the other side of the median where the southbound lanes couldn't even be seen. "Strange," he said. "We're all going this way. Ain't nobody headed the other way.

"Hadn't thought about that," Graham said, surveying the scene. "Odd."

"Why would he abandon his plough?" the kid shouted into the wind.

Graham almost forgot he was there; the kid had been so quiet.

"Maybe it broke down and he walked out," the bearded man proposed.

"Ain't nobody walking out in this mess," the trucker said. "Besides, he would have left his hazard lights on."

"And why did he shut his engine off?" Graham asked, though he didn't expect an answer.

"This just don't make sense."

Maybe the plough had broken down, Graham thought. He stepped onto the runner and opened the door to the cab. He peered in, aided by the beam from the trucker's flashlight. More cracks were spiderwebbed across the windshield. The keys dangled from the ignition; a thermos perched next to the driver's seat.

Graham leaned forward, getting ready to climb into the cab and... what? Maybe try to see if it started. The trucker might be better off trying, being more experienced with big rigs. Graham placed his hand on the driver's seat for leverage.

It was wet.

He looked at his gloved hand. Even with just the dim light from the flashlight, he could see his glove was splotched with red.

Blood?

Graham looked perplexed at his hand. Something wasn't right. They were stuck in a storm, that was all. But something had happened here. Suddenly the numbness his body felt from the winter cold was joined by another state of frozen: fear.

He leaned back out of the cab, noticing a red smear along the air vents on the dashboard, dripping down onto a puddle of blood on the floor mat.

CHAPTER FOUR

Dean Hagen loosened his tie as he sat in the rented sports coupe behind the tractor-trailer stretched across the road. He had been cranking the heat full blast earlier and now was too warm in the cramped car, even considering the miserable conditions of the night. Though he had shut off the heat more than an hour ago, he was still sweating.

What a bitch this night was, he thought, squirming in his seat. He had taken a last-minute flight from Alaska after the phone call from his mother. His father had slipped on some ice and cracked his hip and was now in intensive care at the hospital. Then the rental company gave him this piece-of-shit car to drive in this fucking storm. A sports coupe? But they didn't have anything else left, so he was stuck with it. And stuck was the appropriate word. Though judging from the disabled tractor-trailer truck in front of him, he could have been driving a tank and it wouldn't have mattered on a night like this.

Even the roads in Alaska hadn't been this bad this winter. He had been on a consulting assignment for the past two months there, winnowing out the expendable employees at a manufacturing plant. It was what he did and he was good at it, getting rid of people, and he got paid very well to make businesses run more efficiently.

People at the firms he encountered always fell into two categories: those who ignored him and made no eye contact, hoping he'd not know who they were, even though he had all their files; or the people who went out of their way to interact with him, telling him about their kids or ill parents they took care of, trying to get sympathy from him. It made no difference. It came down to job importance and what could be done without. Not so much what, but whom. Only Dean's wife understood how his job affected him.

Dean hated that it had to be done at Christmas. It soured his mood. He pushed for a delay till after the holidays, but the owners of the plant wanted it finished with before Christmas, so two days ago Dean had turned in his recommendations and the owners signed the termination notices and handed them out. Christmas was going to suck for a lot of people there.

And now it was sucking for him. Would someone come to help on the highway? Did anyone even know he and the others were trapped out here?

The guy he had talked to earlier had stopped on his way back to his car and informed Dean of the situation up ahead: an abandoned snowplough and no way to get through the road. Things were really bad if even the snowploughs got stuck.

There was something unsettled in the man's face that didn't sit well with Dean. Something about him didn't look right, as if the guy knew more but didn't want to say.

But Dean didn't keep his window down long enough to hear any more. He knew he needed to keep warm. It could be a long night. Sweat trickled down the back of his neck. He was warm enough now so he took off his suit jacket and loosened his tie some more. God, it had actually gotten really hot in here. Whatever he thought of this piece-of-crap car, the heater sure worked well.

He cracked the window a tiny bit. Some snow blew in, but the cool air actually felt good. Dean shut off his windshield wipers. What was the point? The snow quickly blanketed the windshield, darkening the interior of the car.

Dean undid his tie and took it off. It felt like it was choking him, making it hard to breathe. He also undid the top couple buttons of his shirt. That felt better. The air from the opening in the window cooled him off a bit.

He wondered how his dad was doing. What a hell of a thing to happen right before Christmas. Dean never came home this time of year, usually always on the road somewhere. For some reason, companies liked to downsize this time of year. Cut loose the slack before feeling obligated to hand out holiday bonuses.

Summer was the only time he returned to see the folks and spend some time lying in the sun at the beach. *Hot like this*, he thought, as he removed his vest and tossed it on top of his suit coat on the passenger seat beside him. He cranked the window down a bit more, paying no heed to the snowflakes drifting in and melting on the warm vinyl interior.

Dean undid the buttons on his shirt cuffs and rolled up his sleeves.

Damn, it was still warm in here.

CHAPTER FIVE

Kirk Britton sat behind the wheel of his hatchback, trying to remember something.

He held his girlfriend's hand, which was surprisingly clammy. His gloves and winter cap were on the dashboard by the heating vents drying, the snow caked on them melting, forming little rivulets of water that ran down the dashboard.

It was temperate in the car, and the numbness in his arms had finally gone away. He had taken off his ski vest and thrown it on the floor of the back seat. It was soaked from the wet sticky snow. The sleeves of his sweater were still damp, but he was getting more comfortable. He kept the heater on for Sonya's sake. She was scared. He could see it as he looked into her dark brown eyes, which had grown moist as she looked on the verge of tears. The warmth inside the car gave her some comfort from the ferocity of the storm outside.

"We'll be okay," he said, squeezing her hand.

She looked at him with those sad eyes and tried cracking a smile. *That's my girl*, he thought, smiling back. He turned the windshield wipers on again, and they struggled to push the wet snow away before returning to their resting place when he shut them off. Kirk did this every few minutes to give them some visibility into the world raging outside their car. It helped keep them from feeling claustrophobic.

As he gazed at the stranded vehicles in front of him, he couldn't help but wonder if seeing what lay ahead of them made the situation seem even more hopeless. Maybe it would be better to let the windshield stay covered. But no, that made the car feel like a coffin, so every few minutes he hit the switch. He noticed he had to do it quicker each time, because the snow was building up faster, which meant the storm wasn't slowing down any, only getting stronger.

"Think of this as an adventure," he said.

"I didn't need Christmas Eve to be an adventure," she replied, and it came out almost as a giggle.

Kirk was worried she'd get hysterical. That wouldn't be good trapped in the confines of the car. He'd seen her get like that before a big midterm or final exam. It wasn't pretty.

He wished he could slide up closer to her, but the console between the seats provided a barrier. He leaned over as far as he could and with his free hand brushed the wisps of brown hair from where they clung to her cheek.

"I'm sorry I got us into this mess," he offered.

She pouted. "It's not your fault."

But it was. They should have left the campus as soon as winter break hit, but he had told her that he couldn't get out of his work schedule. He drove the Zamboni for the campus rink and the college hockey team hosted its annual holiday tournament, which didn't finish till last night. He told her that he'd got stuck with the ice-making duty for the game. That was a lie. He'd actually volunteered to work the tournament, making up a story about having the shortest commute home for the holiday, so he got the gig. He'd lied to her because he couldn't tell her the real reason. It was a worthwhile lie. She would know soon enough, but for now, the reason was hidden in his suitcase in the back of the hatchback.

And because of him they were snowbound on this turnpike, heading to her parents' for the holiday. Kirk had planned a big surprise for Sonya on Christmas morning, and now it looked like it might not get here. At least, not in the way he intended.

He hit the windshield button again. The motor of the blades whirred as the wipers pushed the snow. What it cleared off the glass was forming a wedge of ice on either side of the windshield, narrowing their view with every stroke. At this rate, the wipers would become useless and their visibility diminished.

For now, Kirk could see the big sedan in front of him, the vehicle belonging to the guy he had gone with up to the front of the road jam. The man had been awfully quiet after he had checked inside the snowplough, barely saying a word on the way back to their cars. Something was bugging him.

Of course, Kirk couldn't talk to Sonya about that. No need to worry her any more than she already was. Nothing had been accomplished by going outside, except Kirk nearly froze his arms off. They concluded that they were stuck and going nowhere and there was nothing to do but get back in their vehicles and wait for help. He looked at his gas gauge –

plenty of fuel to keep the car running and warm, so that wasn't a problem. Still, something someone had said before they'd split up and returned to their vehicles had resonated in the back of Kirk's mind. He just couldn't remember what it was. It had seemed important.

"What if no one comes for us?" Sonya asked, inching closer to him.

Kirk laughed at the ludicrousness of the question. "Of course someone's going to come," he said. "They have to check the roads. They'll know people are travelling on the highway. Another plough is bound to come by. They have to keep trying to keep the roads clear."

"I just wish the phones worked," Sonya said. "I wish I could call my parents. They must be worried to death."

He stroked her hair again. He couldn't help but agree with her, but there was nothing they could do. The storm had knocked out any phone service. He glanced behind at their belongings behind the rear seat, specifically at their snowshoes. They had planned to do some snowshoeing on Sonya's parents' land. They lived in an old farmhouse surrounded by more than fifty acres, and they were going to explore it. Kirk had met Sonya in the outdoor club at college and they shared a lot of the same interests. They soon fell in love – well maybe him first, but her eventually. They only had one semester before graduation and beginning the next chapter in their lives.

"I have an idea," Kirk said, and saw the hopeful look in Sonya's eyes. "We could put our snowshoes on and try to hike our way out of here." He raised an eyebrow for emphasis, as if wanting to be praised for coming up with a solution.

Sonya's eyes widened. "Are you crazy?" Her gaze turned to the windshield, her mouth agape. "Look at it out there. We'd die before we got very far. And where would we even go? There's nothing but woods. Do you even know how far it is to the next exit? I have no idea. I can't even tell where we are, and I've been travelling this way most of my life."

She didn't need to say that much to show him how ridiculous his suggestion was, and he felt dejected. But he wanted to be heroic and strong for her. She might not be able to make the walk out of here, but maybe he could alone. He'd hate leaving her here in the car, but if he could find help…. She turned to him and placed a palm on his cheek. "It's sweet of you to try," she said, leaning forward and pressing her lips against his. They were surprisingly warm. "I wish we could get closer."

He glanced behind them. "There's a blanket in the hatch. Let's get in the back seat and cover up under it. We're probably going to be here awhile, might as well get comfortable."

"I like that idea," she giggled.

They climbed into the back seat, and Kirk rummaged around in the hatch area, pulling a wool throw blanket from beneath one of their suitcases. It had their college mascot of a cougar and the school's logo on it. He unfurled it and draped it over them. Sonya sidled up beside him, pressing her body up against his, and they lay back on the seat. He pulled her close and slipped an arm around her shoulder. She rested her head on his chest.

"Much better," she whispered with a sigh.

He smiled. This felt good and right. He hoped it would always feel like this.

In the front of the car, the snow piled up on the windshield.

Kirk still tried to remember what it was he was forgetting.

CHAPTER SIX

Shelby Wallace sat behind the steering wheel of her minivan, silently cursing her ex-husband. It was because of him that she was stuck in this storm, and even though her vehicle hadn't moved in a couple hours, she still gripped the wheel tight, her knuckles almost as white as the snow piled up on the windows. Her children in the back seat had opposite responses to their predicament. Luke, who was eight, exhibited excitement, as if they were on some great adventure. His sister, Macey, two years older, pouted with frustration, a hint of fright seeping through her tense eyes.

Shelby related to her daughter's emotion, but didn't want to show the kids her own fear. She was the parent and needed to keep on a brave face for their sakes. She tried to find some Christmas music on the radio to distract the kids, but only static poured out of the speakers, the storm disrupting whatever stations were in the area. The music would have been a blessing. Instead, the whining from the back seat of the van frayed her nerves even more than the storm. It was all she could do to keep from screaming at them.

"Can I go outside?" Luke asked in a squeaky voice.

"No!" Shelby said. "It's really bad out there."

"Can I at least put the window down? I can't see anything."

"You'll let all the cold air in," Macey said, shocked that he would even suggest the idea.

"Leave the windows up," Shelby shouted back, casting her sternest look at him in the rearview mirror. She wished the kids would just fall asleep. But it was hard enough getting kids to sleep in all the excitement of Christmas Eve, never mind being trapped in a raging blizzard.

"Will Santa still come if we're not home in time?" Luke asked with genuine concern.

"He's not going to come at all if you don't keep quiet," Shelby yelled, regretting it as soon as the words left her lips. It wasn't the kids' fault.

No, it was their dad's. He was supposed to bring them home after spending the day with them. Shelby was going to have a relaxing day home alone, wrapping presents and getting everything set up for Christmas morning. But Nelson had called, telling her he couldn't bring the kids home. He'd had a little too much celebratory drink. Of course. She shouldn't have expected anything different. His drinking had been what drove them into divorce court in the first place, and here they were three years later, and it was still her burden to deal with. She was furious and let him know it on the phone. It wasn't fair. Of course he treated her like she was overreacting. That was always his response, that she got too worked up about things that were no big deal.

But this was a big deal. He was supposed to bring the kids home, and now she had to go out in a storm to retrieve them. He suggested they just spend the night, that she shouldn't go out with the weather this rotten. But Shelby damn well wasn't going to let him enjoy waking up on Christmas morning with the kids. That was her right; she'd made sure it was written into the divorce decree. And she wasn't going to let this storm stop her.

And now she felt like crying, because she was in a big mess and she didn't know what to do. It didn't look good for getting home in time for Christmas morning and she could feel the tears building up behind her eyes, ready to unleash. But she couldn't let the kids see her cry. She had to be strong. So she turned the despair into the rage she felt toward Nelson for causing her to be in this mess. She gripped the wheel even tighter.

This had a chance to be worse than the last Christmas she spent with Nelson. That was when his drinking really pushed her to the limits. Macey had been having horrible sneezing and sinus problems. About a week before Christmas, the doctor determined it was caused by severe allergies, specifically pine trees. Shelby realised their Christmas tree had to go, but Nelson argued against it. Another six days he had said – Macey could last. But Shelby couldn't stand her daughter's red eyes, stuffy nose and headaches. Shelby was removing the decorations from the tree one night when Nelson came home from one of his drinking bouts with his poker-playing buddies in the neighbourhood.

"What the hell are you doing?" he had yelled at her as she laid out the ornaments on the coffee table. She explained to him exactly what she was doing and why. Macey was upstairs and too congested to even come down to the living room.

"Stupid!" Nelson yelled. "Six more fucking days!"

"Don't yell, she can hear you." But Shelby knew once he was in this condition, anything she said would only aggravate him more.

"Why the hell bother taking the decorations off?" Nelson yelled. "Just throw the damn thing outside just like it is."

"My mother has an artificial tree she's going to bring over tomorrow. I'll just redecorate it then."

"Hell no! If I can't have a real tree, I don't want no fucking tree at all."

He pushed her aside and grabbed onto the trunk of the tree, lifting it off the floor, water from its stand spilling over the carpet, needles dropping everywhere, a bulb clattering to the floor.

"What are you doing?"

"Getting rid of the tree," he yelled, carrying it toward the front door. "Just like you wanted." He opened the door and heaved the tree outside, ornaments and all.

He glared at his wife, as if proud of what he'd accomplished. "Problem solved," he said before slamming the door shut, a smile on his face.

The memory of that day made Shelby shiver.

She kept both the front and back windshield wipers going so she could see some of the highway. Behind her was a large vehicle, she couldn't tell what, maybe a box truck or something. Ahead of her was a hatchback, nearly half-buried in the snow that was piled up to its bumper. She saw shadows moving around in the back seat of the car and wondered what its occupants were doing.

CHAPTER SEVEN

Kirk Britton and Sonya Tackett snuggled beneath the wool blanket, waiting for rescue. Her body next to his warmed his heart as well as his flesh. The engine was running and he kept the lights on so emergency personnel could see their car when they came. When they eventually came. *Of course they would come*, Kirk thought. Someone had to check the roads even though it was Christmas Eve. People were still working. Maybe the snowplough guy had walked out to get help. He must have gone somewhere.

That thought made Kirk think again about the snowshoes in the hatch compartment. It was still worth a shot to hike out of here and find safety. If help didn't come, they couldn't stay here all night, especially if they ran out of gas. Then the cold would set in and they'd have no choice but to go.

This wasn't the Christmas he had planned. It was supposed to be really special. He wanted to make it memorable. It certainly was going to be now. He laughed.

"What's so funny?" Sonya asked.

He looked into her eyes, which seemed less frightened and more frustrated.

"Just thinking how crazy this all is," he said.

"More like a nightmare." She frowned.

He needed to keep her spirits up. He thought about what he had in his luggage, the whole reason they'd had to delay their trip to her parents'. Kirk had wanted to wait until Christmas morning, but maybe now would be a better time. He shifted in his seat.

"What are you doing?" Sonya asked, as he pulled the blanket off him.

"I need to get something out of my bag," he said, turning and leaning over the seat into the hatchback compartment.

"What is it? Get back under the covers with me."

He shoved the snowshoes to one side. "It's a present."

"A present? For me?" Her tone spiked. "But we promised we weren't going to buy gifts this year, not until after we graduated and started our jobs."

"I know," he said, unzipping his bag and reaching his hand in, rummaging around pants, shirts and socks till he found the box. He smiled as he pulled it out, not bothering to zip the bag back up. He sat back down beside her with the box in his hand. It was small and wrapped in shiny red foil paper with a white bow on top.

Even in the dimness of the car, only lit by the dashboard lights, he could see her brown eyes widen. Her mouth started to open, but then her lips came back together and spread in a smile.

"Go ahead," he said, holding out the box.

She took it delicately in her long thin fingers, which were shaking, if not from the cold, then from anticipation. She swallowed and then glanced into his eyes.

"Open it," he said, impatient. He hoped he wasn't making a mistake giving this to her now. But it felt like the timing couldn't be more perfect. Instead of sitting around the Christmas tree with her parents and younger brothers, it was just the two of them here on a cold lonely snowbound highway with the wind howling outside and the snow pelting against the windows. It was kind of romantic when he thought about it.

With delicate fingers, she pulled one end of the white ribbon and it unwound. She eased a finger under one flap of the wrapping paper, popping out the tape and carefully unfolding the wrap so as not to tear it, as if she wanted to keep the paper intact to savour and cherish it. She set the paper down and held a white cardboard box in her hand.

It seemed like her breathing stopped. She looked into his eyes and carefully pulled off the top half of the box, gazing inside at the smaller felt jewellery box inside. She took it out, holding it in her left hand while lifting the top with her right.

The diamond inside caught the light and reflected off the irises of her moist eyes. Her lips spread wide, showing shiny teeth as her mouth dropped open. A tear slipped from one corner of her left eye and a small gasp squeaked out of her throat. A shaking right hand brought her fingers to her lips.

"Oh," was all she managed to utter.

Kirk felt a sense of relief now the initial reaction had passed, but he still needed to hear it.

"Well?"

She looked at him, still smiling and holding the box in the palm of her hand. He realised she was waiting for him, and he felt a bit foolish for not understanding she needed to hear the words.

"Will you marry me?"

She squealed and threw her arms around him, almost knocking him back on the seat. She gripped him tight, squeezing the breath out of him. When she finally released him and leaned back, tears were flowing down her red cheeks.

"Yes!" she said. "Of course, yes."

They hugged and he once again felt the warmth of her body.

"I was going to wait until tomorrow morning," he said, "but this seems more appropriate."

"I'm glad you didn't wait." She beamed. "Now put it on me."

Kirk took the box from her and took the ring out, careful not to drop it. Sonya held out her left hand, fingers splayed and trembling. He held her hand to steady it and carefully slid the ring on, holding his breath, hoping he had gotten the ring sized right. It fit into place.

She held the hand up before her, admiring it.

"Oh, Kirk," she said. "I can't believe this."

"Well, we've talked about it for a year now."

Sonya giggled. "I know. But still, I figured after graduation at least. Once we started working and saved some money."

"I didn't want to wait," he said. He had originally thought about proposing to her on campus, had even conceived a grand plan of taking her for a ride on the Zamboni at the end of the tournament and asking her in the middle of the hockey rink. But then he decided to wait for Christmas, at her family home. Now this had turned out even better. What a story it would make when they reflected back.

She wrapped her arms around him and pulled him toward her, her lips locking on his, her tongue finding his. She kissed him long, until he could barely breathe, and when she released her mouth from his, her eyes glittered just like the diamond.

Her lips spread in a delicious smile.

"Now I have something to give you."

"You got me something?" He didn't realise what she meant.

She laughed. "No." She pulled off her sweater.

He was surprised and looked around the car, seeing the snow caked over all the windows, blocking any view. "Here?" he said, gazing down on her full breasts in her black brassiere that rose with the excitement of her breaths.

She didn't say a word, just nodded as she reached around behind her and unhooked her bra.

Kirk began pulling off his own shirt, pausing long enough to gaze at her beautiful breasts. He reached out, pulling her to him and locking his lips on to hers, darting his tongue into her mouth, feeling hers swirl around his. He reached his right hand up to feel the softness of her breast. He leaned back, pulling her down on top of him onto the seat. Her hands reached down and began fumbling at his pants button and zipper.

There wasn't a lot of room in the small back seat of the hatchback, and they nearly bumped heads as they tried removing each other's jeans. They laughed, briefly, and then brought their lips back together. He had managed to kick his boots off and was now naked except for his wool socks. Somehow on this cold blustery night, he felt he should keep his socks on, even though the inside of the car was warm. Or was that the passion burning inside him?

She sat up on him, and he stared at her beautiful naked form. God, he felt so lucky to have her. She reached down and guided him inside her and he felt the most warmth he had all this cold, cold night. Sonya ground her hips back and forth and he joined in her rhythm, using his hands on her flanks to guide her motion.

He savoured the thought that this was the woman he was going to be making love to for the rest of his life.

CHAPTER EIGHT

Dean Hagen felt cramped and hot in his rental coupe. He now sat shirtless behind the wheel, having discarded his vest, tie and shirt. With the window cranked three-quarters of the way down, the icy snow pelted his flesh, but still it wasn't enough to cool him down. With the engine off, the only sound was the wind whipping the snow around the contours of his vehicle.

Why hasn't anyone come? he wondered. It was a mistake to come back home this time of the year. Everything got screwed up at Christmastime. His old man had to go and slip on the ice and fracture his hip. His flight out of Alaska had been diverted to Newark and the extra long drive in this crappy car burned up most of the gas.

Dean had shut it off to conserve fuel, but also because it had been so damn hot in the car, even with the heat off. How was that possible? He should be freezing. It was a damn blizzard out there.

He leaned his face out the window, feeling the prickly snow and biting wind till his cheeks were numb. That was better, he thought, pulling his head back inside. He kicked his shoes off, straining to reach down and remove his socks. They got stuck when he tried to ease them over his heel and he bent farther, his chest up against the steering wheel. He finally got them off, pressing into the horn and sounding it with a loud beep.

Dean leaned back and laughed.

Nobody's going to hear that anyway. He pressed onto the horn and gave it a long blast.

"Anyone coming?" he yelled out the open window. "We need help here!" He chuckled. *No. No help here. Nobody coming. If it wasn't so damn hot, I'd freeze my nuts off.*

That's when he thought about removing his pants.

CHAPTER NINE

In the SUV, sideways on the turnpike a short distance behind the snowplough, Mason Drake was tired of arguing with his wife, Joy. The relentless bickering didn't help their situation one bit. But she insisted on reminding him that she'd told him not to try and pass the tractor-trailer, that the roads weren't safe. But dammit, that's why he had a four-wheel-drive vehicle, so he could manoeuver in these kinds of winter conditions and pass all the idiots going too slow. But even he knew he shouldn't have pushed it. But hell if he'd tell Joy that.

They'd only had one more exit to go, another couple miles and they would be off this blasted highway. The trucker was going too damn slow. He should have figured the guy was experienced and knew what he was doing, but the truck's licence plate read North Carolina, and Mason figured he knew better than some southerner how to drive on New England roads in the winter. Plus, Mason was desperate to get off this damn highway before the storm got much worse. Around the trucker and one more exit. Just one more damn exit.

Mason thought they had enough time to beat the storm home, but it struck quicker than expected. The two of them should have left the city earlier. If only he hadn't insisted on a few drinks after work with some of the guys. And of course he'd convinced Joy and some of her office gals to join them. A celebratory Christmas Eve drink before heading home. The storm had just been a flurry of flakes then. He'd assured Joy they would have time to have a few quick drinks and then hit the road.

But then Mason had gotten the text message from their sixteen-year-old son, Duncan. Higgins Department store had gotten in a new shipment of the video game he desperately wanted for Christmas, *Space Marines IV: The Ice Planet*. It was the hottest game going and most places had been sold out. He knew how much his son freaked out over the game and hated to disappoint him. Duncan had broken his leg during a ski team meet, and was going to be spending Christmas vacation sitting in a chair with a cast all the way up to his knee. This one particular gift would make the boy happy. Higgins was staying open till six tonight, and they could make it in time. It took some convincing for Joy to agree.

"The storm's getting worse, Mason," she had cautioned when they left the downtown bar.

"I'll just run in, grab it, and run out. You can keep the engine running." He motioned to the snow falling on them. "This is nothing. It's not going to get worse until much later tonight."

How wrong he turned out to be, but Joy reluctantly relented.

Of course, it took much longer at Higgins than he'd expected. Getting the game was no problem. The store had plenty when he went to the electronics department, and he felt a rush of relief once he finally held it in his hands. Just holding the box gave him some of the excitement Duncan was going to experience.

Joy had come into the store with him, not trusting that he wouldn't dally. But now that he had bought an extra gift for the boy, she realised they needed to get another one for their daughter, Daria.

"It's only fair," Joy reasoned.

She never got as much as her younger brother, because boys' things just seemed more expensive than her gifts. The Drakes ended up at the jewellery counter, where Joy picked out a snowflake pendant.

"After this storm, no one's going to want to look at snowflakes," Mason said, and then wished he had just kept his mouth shut, because it made Joy start to rethink her decision and he realised they were wasting more time.

After some contemplation and looking at several other necklaces and bracelets, Joy finally decided on the snowflake pendant. By the time they got to the checkout, the lines were long. And of course Joy insisted the items be gift-wrapped, so they wouldn't have to worry about it when they got home. That took more time, and they finally left the store just before closing time. But what should have been a forty-five-minute ride home had now turned into a nearly three-hour ordeal.

And they had only one exit to go.

Mason's salt-and-pepper beard was spotted with wet drops from the melted snow after his latest excursion outside the SUV. He had used his briefcase to clear the snow out from his exhaust pipe. The trucker cautioned them about it after their investigation of the snowplough.

That incident still perplexed Mason. What had happened to the damn snowplough driver? He must have walked out, probably to the next exit – the one Mason needed to take. Maybe they could walk out too? He looked at Joy. She wore a thin sweater dress under a light blazer and leather boots that went up over her calves. Not exactly snow-hiking attire. He himself wore a sports jacket under his wool coat. A little better, but still not suited to these extreme conditions.

They could have dressed better for the storm, but both had figured they'd only have to go from their respective office buildings to the vehicle. He'd never expected to have to venture outside for any duration. Just the trip to the snowplough ahead had chilled him to the bone. By the time he had finally warmed back up in the vehicle, he decided to go back out to clear the snow away from the back end. Now he just wanted to stay comfortable.

Joy muttered something.

"What?" he asked, irritated that she hadn't said it loud enough for him to hear.

She glared at him, as if contemplating whether it was worth it to repeat her musings. "A stupid video game," she said, and then rolled her eyes away from him.

Did she really want to get into this again? His bones still ached from the cold and he gripped the steering wheel tight, debating in his head whether it was worth a response.

"We can't change what we already did," he said, trying to tone down the frustration in his voice.

"The kids had plenty of stuff for Christmas. They didn't need anything extra."

It was all he could do not to snap at her. It was a pointless discussion, and he just wanted her to let it go. Mason was sure she'd had some drinks at her little office gathering before meeting him and his co-workers at the bar, so there was no doubt that played a part in her constant reminder of what got them into this situation.

"Enough," he said, hoping his tone made the message clear. He knew she was also worried about the kids at home and not being able to contact them, but they were teenagers and used to taking care of themselves. But still, it was Christmas Eve. Duncan and Daria must be wondering where their parents were.

CHAPTER TEN

Clark Brooks sat in the passenger seat of Graham Sawyer's sedan, thinking about how much he hated winter. The snow had caked up on the windows of the vehicle so the outside was barely discernible. Not that it mattered. It had been impossible to see more than a few feet through the swirling snow anyway. Clark didn't have to worry about snow in California. That was one of the reasons he ended up moving there.

He'd been fine celebrating Christmas alone with a brief visit from a handful of friends. That was easier than deciding which of his parents to spend most of the holiday with. They had divorced ten years ago after forty years of marriage, and Clark had only come home for Christmas that first year. He felt he was in a tug-of-war between the two of them for the amount of time they wanted to spend with him. His parents seemed to get along all those years, but now they couldn't stand to be in the same place together.

That's why Clark found it best to avoid the holiday, and stay home in Emeryville. That way they couldn't fight over him. And he could avoid the winter months. But it didn't matter anymore now that his dad had died this past summer. He was glad his father hadn't died in the winter. That season was dreary enough without thinking of standing on the frozen ground in a frigid cemetery saying goodbye to the old man. No, summer was better for funerals. Sunshine and warmth somehow made death feel so much better.

"I'm sorry," Clark said.

Graham turned toward him. "Sorry? For what?"

"Dragging you out into this mess." Clark rubbed the fog off the side window, but still couldn't see much. "I should have just taken the bus."

"Nonsense," Graham retorted. "They probably stopped running, and you would have been stuck in Boston on Christmas Eve."

Clark had to laugh. "As opposed to being stuck on the turnpike?"

Graham chuckled too. A boyish laugh. "What are best friends for?" It was more a statement than a question.

Clark and Graham had been friends since their days at Franklin Pierce Elementary School in Evergreen, and even though they were on opposite coasts now, the distance didn't diminish their bond.

"I took you away from your family."

"Yeah, I have to be honest, Natalie wasn't too thrilled with me going out to get you. But she and the girls will be fine. Besides, I needed to get out of the house. It's tough being the only guy in a household of five."

"Your wife never liked me anyway," Clark jested, knowing full well that Natalie adored him and the friendship he had with her husband.

"Nah, not too much."

Clark hoped Graham and Natalie lasted at least as long as his parents, but hell, even forty years wasn't enough. What the hell had happened to his parents? Clark had been away too long to see the cracks that had dismantled their union. Maybe it was best he hadn't, certainly not after what he had just been through in California. How ironic that he had chosen to become a divorce attorney. At least he didn't have to suffer representing one of his parents. That in itself was a good reason to be on the opposite coast.

During the course of his career, he saw the end result of a lot of marriages gone bad. But of course, nothing like this last one. Clark hadn't seen that one coming at all.

His client's name was Benson Read, an older gentleman in his late sixties. His wife, Aubrey, was more than thirty years younger. There were plenty of marriages like that in California, but Clark never understood any of them. Typically the husband had money – lots of it – and the woman was always a knockout. This was no exception.

The pattern Clark usually witnessed was that, when the man got beyond a certain age, the interest from the wife waned. Benson's wife filed for a divorce, and Clark represented the older man. It was an acrimonious affair. Benson wanted to hold on to things Aubrey demanded, things that Clark felt were futile. He went back and forth with Aubrey's lawyer, trying to reach some common ground.

But common sense was what they really needed. As Benson got more and more agitated with his soon-to-be third ex-wife, his behaviour and demands became erratic. At one point, Benson shouted to Clark that he wanted the immediate return of his garage-door opener that he claimed Aubrey was holding hostage. That didn't make any sense, since Aubrey was the one in the house at the moment. Benson was residing in a condo he owned at the beach (probably scouting for wife number four). But Benson owned a lot of sports cars he kept in the four-car garage at the house, and wanted access to them. Clark managed to get the remote from Aubrey – a minor victory.

That wasn't even the most ridiculous claim. Oh no. Clark was dumbfounded when Benson demanded that his wife reimburse him for the cost of her breast implants. He had paid for them, he claimed, so that he could enjoy them, not other guys. Clark tried to talk the old man out of that request, but Benson was relentless and made him write it up in the paperwork. Of course the judge denied the reimbursement.

About a week after the divorce was finalised, Clark received a call from Benson, asking him to stop by his house, that he needed some legal help. Clark was confused, since Aubrey got the house in the settlement, but he reluctantly agreed, wishing his dealings with Mr. Read were over. He figured he'd stop by the house, listen to the old man's request, and refer him to someone else.

After Clark arrived at the house, Benson let him in, his face ashen, his hands shaking, drops of sweat dotting his bald dome. Clark was led into the kitchen, where the old man had a half-finished glass of whiskey over ice on the counter. It wasn't even noon yet.

"What am I doing here?" Clark asked him, thinking maybe he needed some kind of help other than legal advice.

"I got what I wanted," was all Benson said.

"What are you talking about?" Clark asked, not wanting to get too close to him, regretting even coming over, not thinking to ask how the man got in. Aubrey must have changed the locks. Of course she would have. A strange pallor had come over the old man.

"Over there, on the kitchen table." Benson pointed with a shaky finger. "I think I'm going to need another lawyer."

Clark walked over to the dining room table and stopped short. On the table was a bloody carving knife. Beside it were what looked like two clear plastic balls, smeared and dripping red. It only took a second before he realised what they were: Aubrey's breast implants.

Clark stepped back in horror; his heart nearly stopped in his chest.

"What have you done, Benson?" His immediate thought was to get out of this house, not even taking the time to call 911 until he got outside.

"She's in the bedroom," Benson said. "She wasn't willing to give them up easily."

Clark looked at the man, mouth agape. Benson's eyes were glazed over. He took a sip of his drink. Clark knew he should leave immediately, but something kept him mired to his spot. He wondered about Aubrey and thought he should check, to see if she was really here. Maybe this wasn't what he thought it was.

"Where's the bedroom?"

Benson pointed down a hallway.

Clark felt his body shaking, legs wanting to give out as he walked down the carpeted corridor to an open doorway. He peered inside.

Aubrey lay on her back on top of the white comforter on the bed, naked from the waist up, arms splayed out to the edges of the mattress. Her eyes were closed, her chest cavity drenched in blood.

Bile rose in Clark's throat and he brought his hand up to suppress it. A sharp gasp startled him as Audrey's eyes shot open, her chest heaved and her head tried to lift up off the pillow before settling back down.

Oh my God, she's still alive!

Clark sprung into action, pulling out his phone and calling 911 while at the same time sprinting into the adjoining bathroom and grabbing a towel to try and staunch the bleeding. He straddled the delirious woman while he talked to the 911 operator, shouting what had happened and where they were.

Aubrey lived. Benson killed himself about a week later. Clark's boss made him take a leave of absence. *Why not?* Clark thought. It was Christmas time anyway.

It gave him a chill just thinking about it and his body shivered.

"Still cold?" Graham asked, turning up the fan on the heater.

Clark tried to smile. "Still can't get used to this climate," he said, not wanting to tell Graham what had really given him the chills.

"You spent most of your life here. The cold should still be in your blood."

Clark didn't want to be here. But now that he only had one parent, he could endure going home for Christmas. Besides, he eventually had to settle his father's estate, and the house that was left to him. Close it up and sell it most likely. Unless he wanted to keep the house and move back here, be closer to his ageing mother. She was alone, just like his father had been.

The two of them had spent all that time together, raising a family, only to end up alone at the end. What was the point? Couldn't they have stuck it out together a little while longer?

Clark didn't like the thought of dying alone. He had no one special in his life back in California. Relationships never seemed to last more than a year, if even that long, before withering away. But who could blame him, considering what he saw in his day-to-day business life. Relationships and marriages crumbled. Or worse, they ended up going down a dark hole like Benson Read and his wife.

And after what had happened back in California, he needed to get away. The head of the firm insisted he take some time off. A mental health vacation.

Clark looked out through what little view he had of the outside. Some vacation spot.

And that's when he saw the naked man run by.

CHAPTER ELEVEN

After their lovemaking, Kirk and Sonya lay in each other's arms, naked under the blanket in the back seat. Kirk wasn't completely naked. He still had his socks on. In the heat of passion, it was always the one item he never managed to remove, as if the act of pulling off those two pieces of clothing interrupted the rhythm of the moment. There was no subtle way to reach down and pull off socks.

Sonya had drifted off to sleep, after muttering something about how much she loved him. Kirk was tired as well, and could barely keep his eyes open. He kept thinking about the lives they were about to begin now that she had accepted his proposal. They both had jobs awaiting them in Boston after graduation, and they had already begun looking for a place in the city they could afford.

He wanted to be close to Boylston Street, near Fenway Park. There were a lot of bars and restaurants in that area, a place a lot of young professionals congregated. Kirk couldn't wait to go to Red Sox games at Fenway. Sonya looked forward to the Museum of Science. There were so many things they wanted to see and do in the city: the North End, Faneuil Hall, Quincy Market, the New England Aquarium, the Freedom Trail and the Theatre District. The Boston Pops and Swan Boats in the summer; the Bruins and Celtics in the Garden in the winter.

But first they needed to get out of this mess, and Kirk thought about what he should do. If he was going to be Sonya's husband, he needed to be her protector. It was his fault they were stuck where they were. He had to wait for the ring because he wanted to propose on Christmas Day. Now that was out of the way, he needed to find a way out.

Kirk thought again about the snowshoes in the back of the car. Sonya would never let him hike out alone, but maybe he could go while she slept. She would be mad when she awoke and found him gone, but would think him a hero if he came back with help.

He would need to bundle up real good. The damn ski vest would leave his arms unprotected, but he could add another sweater to help. The rest of his gear would suffice. He was sure he could make it to the next exit, and then it couldn't be far to find someone's house. Maybe even a twenty-four-hour service station. The question would be whether he could find phone service even there. It would be pointless to walk all that way in the raging storm only to find someone's house or a business without phone service. That wouldn't accomplish anything. Then he would be in a nice warm place, while Sonya was still stranded here.

At least it was still toasty in the car, and there was enough gas in the tank to keep it running for hours. Maybe it was best to just wait. Kirk ran all kinds of scenarios through his head, trying to find a logical resolution. *Come on, Kirk*, he said to himself. *You're supposed to be the smart college kid. Can't you come up with something?*

He felt helpless. The one thing he didn't want to feel. He wanted, no needed, to be in control. Sonya would expect that of him. She always looked to him for that kind of security, and he needed to provide it.

Kirk's head felt jumbled. So many thoughts bounced around inside, he couldn't think straight. It was hard to concentrate. Maybe if he slept a little, he would awaken with a clearer mind. Maybe he just needed a little snooze. It would be easy to fall asleep like this, with Sonya's naked body against his. This was how he wanted to fall asleep every night.

But before he drifted off, before his thoughts unscrambled, Kirk still couldn't help but think he was forgetting about something important.

CHAPTER TWELVE

Graham Sawyer stared at the bloodstains drying on the fingers of his leather dress gloves from when he had climbed into the cab of the snowplough. He thought about the red drops dripping off the heating vents, pooling on the rubber floor mat. What had happened to the driver and what could have caused so much blood? Did he have an accident, maybe cut himself? Or had someone else done that to him? He might have been attacked by some lunatic in the storm, possibly someone driven snow-blind. Snow-mad? Was there even such a thing? But why? And where was the body? It could have been dumped out in the snow by the side of the highway, buried now, no doubt.

Graham needed to get the blood off his gloves. He couldn't go home to his girls on Christmas Eve with bloody gloves. If he was even going to make it home tonight. He rolled down the driver's side window of his car and reached his left hand out, scooped up some snow from the side of the car and rubbed it on the fingers of his gloves, as if the wet sticky substance were soapsuds and he were washing his hands.

That was when the naked man ran by.

Graham caught a quick glimpse of the man and recognised him as the driver in the coupe stuck behind the tractor-trailer truck. The man hadn't gotten out of his car when Graham and the others had gone to investigate what was going on up ahead, but he remembered talking to him. The guy had been wearing a suit then. Now he wore nothing.

"Did you just see that?" Graham said, looking at Clark beside him, almost too stunned to speak.

"Yes," Clark said, staring in disbelief. "I'm glad you said something, because I thought I was imagining things."

"The guy must be crazy."

"He'll be dead if we don't stop him."

Graham zipped up his jacket as he and Clark got out of the car. The wind hit him the moment he stepped out, and he looked over the roof of his car at Clark, who was dipping his head and holding up one hand to shield his face. Clark yelled something as he came around to Graham's side.

"What?" Graham yelled back, though the words were shoved back into his mouth by the wind, almost gagging him.

"Do you see him?" Clark repeated.

Graham shook his head. It was hard to see anything in the mist created by the swirling snow. The man had been running straight down the middle of the highway in the opposite direction from the way they had come. Graham could barely see the outlines of snow-covered vehicles, including a large truck or something. He looked down at footprints the man had left behind, already being wiped away by the storm winds.

"This way!" Graham yelled, pointing south, the direction the man had been running. Pulling the collar of his coat up around his chin to provide some protection, Graham led the way, Clark sticking close by, as they waded through the drifts. His feet were already chilled; he couldn't imagine what the naked man felt like. Or was he so crazy he didn't feel anything at all? Graham wondered what had compelled the man to strip and run outside, but insanity was the only explanation. He had seemed normal when Graham had spoken to him earlier, a little rude, but otherwise sane.

The vehicles before them had their lights on, but snow covered the headlamps, creating an eerie muted glow. The car directly behind his was a hatchback, but Graham couldn't see anyone inside. The car was nearly buried, and he wondered if the occupants had abandoned it. But that wouldn't make much sense. There was nowhere to go.

So where was the naked man going?

Graham turned to look behind him, to make sure Clark was still there. His friend was so close, he was practically on top of him, but Graham had barely felt his presence. It was as if the wind and snow forced a barrier between them.

Clark's clothing was even less practical than his own, and Graham thought about sending him back to the car. He had come from California totally unprepared for this onslaught. But Graham himself hadn't expected to be out in the elements. He should have been wiser.

He turned back into the wind and proceeded, passing a minivan. A woman's distraught face looked out a snowy window by the driver's seat. Graham thought about stopping to check on her, but she was probably nice and warm, and he was freezing his ass off. If he stopped now, he wouldn't be able to keep going. His pant legs were soaked from the wet snow and frozen stiff, making each stride a struggle. As he passed the minivan, a couple of kids peered out from the middle seat of the van. He couldn't even tell their genders from behind the frosted glass, but he couldn't help wonder what they were doing out this night. They should be home awaiting Christmas morning, like his girls were.

After the minivan, there was a stretch of open highway, snowdrifts almost up to his waist. Graham didn't know how much farther they should go. There was no sign of the naked man. There was really no place to go unless he ran off into the woods that lined both sides of the highway. Graham wasn't sure how far back it was to the last exit.

He continued, looking back every few seconds to see Clark still behind. Each step Graham took sank into the snow. His toes were numb as well as his face. The cold bit into his body. This was hopeless.

A large RV loomed before them, dark. Maybe its occupants had bedded down for the night, waiting out the storm. That would be a nice place to be with all the comforts of home. Graham wished he were home. Wished he had never gone to pick Clark up at the airport. Damn, Natalie was right. She had told him to wear a heavier jacket, but he'd assured her he wouldn't be getting out of the car much. How wrong that turned out to be. He should have stayed home with his girls. It occurred to him that he'd forgotten to kiss his girls goodbye before he left for the airport, thinking he wouldn't be gone long. He told himself that was the first thing he was going to do when he got home tonight. Or whenever it ended up happening.

This is senseless, Graham thought, stopping after they passed the RV. Ahead was a darkened station wagon. He leaned up against it and peered inside. Its engine wasn't running like those of the other vehicles. The interior was dark and empty. Another driver must have decided to abandon his car and march out, he figured. He straightened and looked past the station wagon to the empty highway behind it. Nothing but white.

Something bumped him, and he turned to see Clark, who had stumbled into him.

"I – can't – go—" Clark struggled speaking. His face was red, his eyebrows and eyelashes crusted with snow.

His friend was suffering and Graham knew it was pointless worrying about the naked man now. If the elements were having this much effect on Clark, then there could be no hope for the other idiot.

"We'll go back!" Graham yelled into Clark's ear and saw some relief on his friend's face.

He grabbed his friend's arm, trying to turn him around to go in the other direction. That was when he heard a bell ringing.

Graham looked behind him and saw a shadowy figure lurching out of the distant mist. It staggered back and forth, buffeted by the wind, one arm raised and ringing a bell, the tones penetrating the howl of the wind to reach him.

It wasn't the naked man, for this figure wore a long coat and a visored cap. Though he could tell it was a man, Graham saw long hair beneath the cap, falling to the man's shoulders. The figure stopped and stood still. Maybe he had spotted them, Graham thought, or maybe he just couldn't go any farther. The man kept ringing the bell.

"Stay here!" Graham yelled into Clark's ear. His friend nodded. He leaned Clark up against the station wagon, afraid he wouldn't be able to stand on his own.

Once he was sure Clark was set, Graham headed toward the bell ringer, struggling through the drifts. Though the man was not that far away, it seemed to take forever to reach him. Graham wished the man had made at least more of an effort to meet him halfway. But the way the guy kept ringing the bell gave him the impression he might not have even seen Graham at all. It was as if he was ringing the bell for help to come to him.

When Graham reached the man, he grabbed him by the shoulders, staring into a face frozen by the icy wind, or maybe just fear itself. The man looked catatonic. He kept ringing his bell.

The man had a stubbled chin and pointy nose. His coat and hat were part of a Salvation Army uniform. His long hair was saturated with icy strands. He stared past Graham, as if not realising he stood right in front of him. Graham shook him by the shoulders and the man's eyes rolled to meet his.

"You can stop now!" Graham yelled. "You're okay."

The man was silent, eyes narrowing as if trying to comprehend what Graham was saying.

"What?" the man finally asked.

"I said you can stop!"

The man still looked confused. "Stop?"

"Yes!" Graham said. "You can stop ringing the damn bell!"

The man looked down at his extended right arm, as if not even realising he was holding the metal object.

"Oh," he finally said.

"Did you see anyone else back there?" Graham asked through chattering teeth, wondering if he had seen the naked man.

The Salvation Army man looked back into the white wasteland behind them. He shook his head. "Ain't nothing back there."

"Is that your car?" Graham asked, pointing back at the station wagon.

The man nodded.

"Let's get you back inside it." He grabbed hold of the man's left arm and started to lead him, but the man did not move.

"Ran out of gas," the man said. "No heat."

Graham nodded, trying to catch his breath. The man must have tried walking out.

"Did you see anything?" he asked the man, wondering where the exit behind them was. "How far did you get?"

The man's face stiffened. "We ain't where we think we are."

There was that look of fear in his eyes. Graham wondered if this man had been driven mad too.

"Come with us," he said, figuring he could bring him back to their car. He led the man to where Clark still leaned against the station wagon. His friend was covered in snow, almost blending in with the vehicle.

Clark grinned when he saw the two of them, as if grateful not to be alone.

Graham tried to lead the pair back the way they had come, not realising how far they had travelled from his car. Clark stumbled and fell down into the snow. He lay there, not making an effort to get up. Graham let go of the Salvation Army man's arm and bent down, grabbing a hold of Clark and trying to lift him. His friend didn't move, as if content to lie in the snow until it buried him.

Most of Graham's body was numb with cold, and he now worried none of them would be able to make it back to his car. He believed he could make it himself, but not if he had to drag these two. But he couldn't just leave them. He needed help.

Exasperated, and almost at the point of desperation, Graham thought of just saving himself.

And then he heard a bugle call.

CHAPTER THIRTEEN

Tucker Jenks lay in the sleeper cab of his tractor-trailer figuring it was going to be a long night. He'd seen a snowbound highway before, about ten years ago near Buffalo. A line of cars and no place to go. There was nothing to do tonight but wait for the state to get some ploughs to clear the road, and that wasn't likely to happen till the storm subsided.

It was a crappy way to spend the holiday. Tucker had planned to go to his sister's in Cranford, New Jersey, after dropping off the load of electronics at the store in Manchester. But he saw the weather radar map as the storm swept down from Canada and then curled up the East Coast through Pennsylvania, New York and New Jersey, bearing down on New England fast. That was when Tucker reversed direction and headed north, trying to outrun it. He had a trucker buddy in northern New Hampshire and had been able to contact him on his CB before service fizzled out. He had a warm bed waiting for him, if only he could get there.

Outside was a scream. Not really a scream, just the wind blowing with the force of a banshee. It reminded Tucker of a story his nana told him back in North Carolina, where he grew up. It was the tale of the Tar River Banshee, a legend passed down in fireside chats by his family. The story dated back to the Revolutionary War when a loyalist who owned a grist mill was drowned in the Tar River by British soldiers. Before the mill owner died, he warned them they would be haunted by the banshee who floated along the shore of the river.

The banshee was a mythical messenger of death, his nana told him, and since then the entity came every year to warn of someone's pending demise with her ominous wailing.

That's what Tucker heard outside his truck now, the banshee wailing, though he knew it was only the fierce wind driving down the highway between the tall pines. But still it gave him chills even though the truck cab offered him plenty of warmth as his engine idled.

Maybe it was because of what he and that other fella saw when they opened the cab of the snowplough up ahead. The younger guy didn't say a word to Tucker, but their eyes locked. They had both seen the blood on the dashboard, the seat, puddled on the floor mats by the pedals. Something nasty happened in that truck. That was an awful lot of blood to be just some minor mishap the ploughman suffered. That wouldn't have come from some cut on the hand.

And the weird thing, Tucker thought, was there was no sign of blood in the snow outside the plough. If the ploughman had been injured and left his truck to find help, why wasn't there any blood in the snow? If he had gone for help, he was probably buried out there under the snow, because Tucker couldn't imagine anyone getting far in this storm. Sure, he was from the south, but he had spent enough time trucking throughout the northeast in a lot of miserable winters. This wasn't a storm to deal with lightly. He wouldn't dare venture out. Wherever the snowplough man went, he probably hadn't got far.

Outside, the banshee wailed.

CHAPTER FOURTEEN

Clark felt blood flowing back into his toes as he warmed them inside the RV. They started to sting, as if going from frost to fire while he wiggled them, feeling like they might fall off. When he first heard the bugle call, he thought he had succumbed to delirium and the cavalry was coming, like in those westerns he used to watch as a kid with his grandfather. He even thought he saw a cavalry officer in uniform. It wasn't until Graham grabbed hold of him and dragged him toward the RV, its lights flashing madly, that Clark realised the bugle call was the vehicle's horn sounding.

An old man helped him, Graham and the uniformed man into the side door near the rear of the camper. Was the man in uniform a policeman, or soldier, Clark wondered, or just a figment of his frozen mind?

Clark had reached the point of wanting to succumb to the cold outside and the numbing pain biting deep into his bones like the jaws of some ferocious beast. Letting it overtake him would have been preferential to the struggle outside. Let the snow bury him and the highway crews could dig out his frozen body in the morning.

He wouldn't have blamed Graham if his friend had left him out there and saved himself. Clark wasn't properly dressed for this weather and wouldn't have lasted. He imagined the naked man hadn't lasted even that long. What could have possessed the man to remove his clothes and run madly into the night? The storm must have driven him insane. Or was it something else?

Graham and the old couple in the RV were talking about it now. Clark reclined on a cushioned bench on one wall. Across from him, at a seat before a small dining table, the uniformed man sat hunched over, elbows on the table holding him up, water dripping onto the Formica surface from the strands of his long hair dangling past his pointy chin.

A tall white-haired woman brought a steaming mug of something to the table and placed it before the uniformed man, whose hands immediately cupped it. He had removed his soaked cap and set it at the edge of the table. Clark saw the Salvation Army logo on the front of the cap and realised the man wasn't a policeman or soldier and certainly hadn't come to rescue them. It appeared they had rescued him.

The old woman brought another mug to Clark and she had to guide his hand to hold it.

"It's hot cocoa," she said with a smile.

Clark held it, too exhausted to raise it to his lips for the moment, but satisfied to feel its warmth radiate from his hands through the rest of his body. Across the way, the thin man at the table dug a shaky hand underneath his long coat and pulled out a tin flask. Fingers struggled to unscrew the cap. When he succeeded, he poured liquid from it into his mug.

"The man seemed normal when I talked to him in his car earlier tonight," Graham said to the old man, also white of hair. The two sat in the front seats of the RV. "I wouldn't have imagined him running naked into the snow a few hours later."

The old man cleared his throat. "They say hypothermia can make one feel as if they're hot instead of cold."

Graham shook his head. "Have we been out here that long that hypothermia could set in already?"

The old man shrugged.

"We tried to find him," Graham continued, "but had no luck. That's when we found this one." He nodded at the man at the table, who just stared back with glassy eyes, as if they had fogged over in the cold and hadn't defrosted yet. He looked catatonic.

Graham turned to face Clark. "How you doing, buddy?" his friend asked.

Clark held his mug up in a gesture and tried to smile, but his face was still numb and he couldn't tell if his expression even moved.

The old couple introduced themselves as Werner and Francine Volkmann. They had been travelling around the country in their RV, visiting relatives with plans to spend Christmas with grandchildren in New Hampshire. They had run behind schedule and got caught in the storm.

Francine had taken Clark's and Graham's wet coats and hung them in the bathroom. His pants, which had frozen stiff and felt like cardboard, thawed and were now drenched from the knees down. He was uncomfortable, but the warmth in the heated RV soothed him. He couldn't believe how close he'd come to just giving it all up out there in the storm. What had gotten into his head? Easy living in California must have softened him too much that a bitter winter storm could drive him to his knees. It was snow and cold, nothing more. He could have died out there, and for what? His mother would not have been able to handle his death. Clark disappointed himself.

He looked across at the Salvation Army man, who still had not spoken a word since they'd got inside the vehicle. Francine had tried to take his wet coat, but he refused to give it up. He sat motionless, clinging to his mug.

Graham let Francine take back the front passenger seat, and he sat across the table from the Salvation Army man. The man glared at Graham.

"What's your name?" Graham asked.

The man looked like he wasn't going to answer, instead bringing the mug up to his lips and slurping the cocoa. The Adam's apple in his scrawny neck bobbed as he swallowed the hot liquid.

"Felker," he mumbled after setting the mug back down. "Lewis Felker." His eyes stayed locked on Graham.

"You said something out there. About not being where we think we are. What did you mean by that?"

The man stared, eyes unblinking. "Nothing," he finally muttered, glancing down at his mug.

Graham shook his head. "Didn't sound like nothing to me."

Clark wasn't sure what his friend was trying to get at. It was obvious the poor man wanted to be left alone. He looked like he'd been through a lot. They all had.

Felker drew in a deep breath, as if breathing for the first time. His whole body shuddered, maybe from the wet coat, maybe from something else. He leaned forward over the table. "There was no exit back that way." His voice was almost a whisper.

Graham leaned toward the man. "What do you mean 'no exit'?"

"I walked quite a ways, trying to get to the last exit I had passed before getting stuck. It ain't there." He took out his flask and poured more liquid into his mug.

Maybe the man was drunk, Clark thought. Or maybe he was delirious from his time out in the cold. Clark looked at the faces of the others, and saw confusion and uncertainty.

Volkmann cleared his throat. "It's blowing so hard out there, you can't see anything anyway."

Felker scowled at the old man. "I'm telling you, the exit ain't there. There's nothing there. Just snow."

"Nothing?" Graham sounded sceptical.

"Nothing but snow," Felker said, eyes dropping down, hands gripping his mug tight.

Clark started to feel chilled again.

CHAPTER FIFTEEN

It had been a while since Shelby had seen the people outside her vehicle. Her nerves were shaking, but she had to hold it together for the kids. She'd managed to get Macey to stop crying and had let her come up to the front passenger seat of the minivan. Her daughter felt more comforted next to her mother.

If she only knew how Shelby really felt, her insides churning, nerves frayed. Every few minutes she kept trying the radio, hoping to hear something. What? Christmas carols? No, something about the highway and when rescue might come. Someone had to come.

The storm hadn't let up. Her wipers couldn't keep up with the amount of snow dumped onto her windshield. The thick layer was darkening the inside of the vehicle. It felt like they were being buried alive, as if the minivan had become a coffin and someone was shovelling the snow over it. It actually made it hard to breathe.

"We should have stayed at Dad's," Luke said from the back seat.

Shelby tried to keep calm. "But we always have Christmas at our house." Why couldn't the boy understand?

"Our house is boring."

Shelby took a deep breath. *Ignore him*, she told herself. *He's frustrated and bored, and maybe even a little scared, though he wouldn't show it. Maybe that's why he wants his dad, the strong one.* She had to demonstrate she could be strong too and handle this situation.

Her kids were going to be with her on Christmas morning, no matter what. Luke could pout all he wanted. She'd gone out into the storm to get them, and she was damn well going to bring them home. She gritted her teeth to hold in a gasp, wanting to cry.

Keep it together, damn you. Don't let him win. He's probably passed out by now anyway, him and that young girlfriend of his. Let that little hussy put up with his alcohol-fuelled rages. Shelby had put up with enough. She thought about the time Macey had written a letter to Santa Claus, saying all she wanted for Christmas was for her parents to get along. She would forfeit any gifts for just that one.

Shelby had cried over that letter. She knew then that the last straw had come, and she needed to get out of the marriage to save the kids.

But who was going to save the kids now? Her?

When she saw the people outside the van, she had no idea what they were doing. At first she had hoped it was someone coming to rescue them, but they walked right by her vehicle. And since then there had been nothing. She didn't even see any signs of the people in the hatchback stuck in front of her.

Had they gone somewhere too?

Shelby's heart began pounding. What if everyone else had found their way to safety? Panic set in. Maybe that's why she saw people outside. They all found a way out. Maybe all the other cars on the turnpike were empty, and she was the last one. Her breathing deepened. Somehow, the others had gotten out, and her vehicle had been overlooked. She and the kids had been forgotten, left behind. She gasped. No one noticed them. How could they not have seen them in the van? It was a big vehicle. They should have seen her. *I don't want to be alone*, she cried inside.

She pounded the horn on her steering wheel, the beeping wailing out into the dark night.

CHAPTER SIXTEEN

Joy Drake looked at her husband in the seat beside her in the SUV, wondering if he was the man who could save her from their situation, even though his aggressive driving was responsible for getting them into this mess. That got under her skin, because he never seemed to be a cautious driver. But that was one of the things that attracted her to him more than twenty years ago. Mason had an edge to him. Of course it had softened now they were both closing in on fifty, that was to be expected. But he never backed down from anything.

That came in handy with his job as a parole officer. She knew he had to deal with a lot of tough characters, and he had to make sure he was the one in charge. They had to know he was the boss and respect that.

She sure did. And Mason would get her out of this. Joy needed him to rescue her, especially following the guilt she'd felt earlier today at her office Christmas party.

Though it wasn't really her fault. She was always a bit flirty at work. She just saw it as harmless fun. That's what people did in an office setting. Sexual tension and innuendos ran rampant at the office. That was typical in any business she had worked in. It was just a way of coping with the stress and routine of the job.

Add alcohol to the mix and things sometimes got a little out of control.

Jerome was a few years younger than her and extremely handsome with a sweet physique, his dress slacks stretched taut across his firm-looking buttocks. He worked out at a local gym and was very active, and it showed. All the girls in the office were drawn to him, and he knew it and fed off the attention. But still, it was all very harmless, a smile here, a joke there, a squeeze of the arm in the break room. Sometimes when Joy was having intercourse with Mason, which was a rarity these days, she would fantasize that she was having sex with Jerome. She closed her eyes, picturing his younger, muscular frame and abs on top of her, driving down hard into her, instead of her husband's paunchy belly rubbing against her.

And when she was in the office, looking at him, she'd think of those moments, knowing it was all fantasy. Except today had been different. At some point during the office party, she had found herself alone with him in his office. He had a small token he wanted to give her, a little gift as a gesture for her friendship at work. Jerome handed her the small wrapped box.

Joy felt a little embarrassed getting something from him. It had been totally unnecessary. He shrugged it off as nothing. She unwrapped the package and saw the scented candle. She sniffed its cinnamon spice odour and thanked him, giving him a hug. She meant to just brush his cheek lightly with her lips, but his head moved and his mouth was on hers.

That's when the hand slid up the side of her sweater till it found her left breast and he squeezed it, holding on firmly. She didn't brush it away, instead letting it linger and enjoying the sensation running through her body. Her lips returned his kiss, but she kept her tongue inside.

Then she abruptly nudged him aside with a smile. "None of that," she joked. His hand released her breast but the sensation still lingered. "That's not proper office etiquette." She winked and left his office. Part of her had felt like a teenager getting felt up for the first time. But mostly Joy felt guilty, knowing how improper her behaviour had been, and worried all the flirtation had sent the wrong message and led poor Jerome on. She also knew though how enjoyable and naughty that brief embrace was. And it kind of scared her.

Not scared like she was now. This was a different kind of fear.

Looking at her husband, she realised what a horrible mistake she made at the party, and how awkward it would be when she went back to work after the holidays. She dreaded that and cursed herself for how foolish and childish she acted. Mason had been her husband, father of her children and the man she'd loved for a long time. She understood that, maybe not always appreciating it. But she needed him now more than ever. He would be the one to save her from everything.

CHAPTER SEVENTEEN

Graham Sawyer didn't like the thought of going back out into the storm.

He had been admiring the comforts of the Volkmanns' RV when he thought about the others trapped in their vehicles, especially the children he had seen looking out the window at him from the minivan. What if his own daughters and wife were trapped out here? That family might be safe in their van, but they must be scared and feeling helpless. The same with that young kid he had walked with to the snowplough.

"We should bring the others in here," he said to Werner Volkmann. "It's warm and safe." He hoped he wasn't overstepping his bounds with the old man.

"Of course," Werner said, popping up from his captain's chair, which swivelled around to face the interior of the cabin. "We have plenty of propane to keep the heaters running all night."

"And we have food," Francine Volkmann stated. "We can have a Christmas Eve feast." She smiled.

Graham moved to the bathroom in the rear of the cabin to grab his boots, still soaked from his earlier excursion outside.

"Wait," Werner said, following him. "Those are drenched. You put those back on and go out there, your toes will freeze off. What's your shoe size?"

"Nine and a half."

"My boots are a ten, and they are nice and dry." The old man opened a narrow closet and pulled out a pair of black winter boots. He handed them to Graham, along with a winter coat and ski pants. "These should fit you too. You need to be better dressed for this." He also took out a pair of wool socks and gave them to him.

Graham felt much better about the prospect of going outside with this new apparel. He thanked the old man and got dressed. Werner even had a dry winter ski cap.

"Francine and I were planning to do some cross-country skiing, so we're well equipped."

Clark got up from the bench seat. "I'll go with you," he said.

Graham looked at his dear friend, who indeed looked rested from his near collapse outside. But still, he didn't think Clark would be up to it.

"You had quite an ordeal last time. Just stay here and relax."

"I'm fine now," Clark said. "And you shouldn't go out there alone."

"A buddy system would be better," Werner said.

Graham looked at Clark, and then the rest. His only other options were an old man, an old woman and Felker, the weird scrawny Salvation Army guy, who had dispensed with his coffee mug and now drank straight from his flask. Not much of a choice. His gaze fell to Clark again, looking him up and down. He'd rather have his friend with him, but....

"You don't have the right clothing," Graham said.

"I have my winter parka and ski pants," Francine said, looking at Clark. "And I'm big enough that they should fit you."

Clark chuckled at that.

"Are you sure you're up for this?" Graham asked, already noticing his friend's spirit seemed better.

"I want to do this."

"Okay. Suit up. But we stay together."

"I won't let you out of my sight," Clark said.

Sweat built up inside Graham's clothing from the insulation of the gear and the warmth inside the RV as he waited for Clark to dress. But he knew that would change as soon as they stepped outside into the winter maelstrom. Once Clark zipped up his powder-blue parka and squeezed a pink snow cap onto his head, they were ready to go. Graham laughed at how Clark looked in Francine's winter gear.

"I wouldn't go out there if I were you," Lewis Felker said, his eyes beady, his thin cracked lips barely parting.

Graham stared at the man, who sat at the table and still had not removed his wet wool coat. He didn't know if it was even worth answering the guy, but he did. "Someone needs to help those people."

"If they're still there." He brought the flask to his lips and tipped it back.

Graham looked away, into Clark's cautious eyes. He nodded at his friend and then pushed open the side door, the icy wind immediately clawing at him. The snow was up over his knees as he stepped onto the road. He could barely keep his eyes open, wishing he had goggles. Bending his head down, he barreled forward through the drifts, pushing a path through the snow with his legs because it was impossible trying to lift each leg and plant a foot ahead. Graham kept looking over his shoulder, both to give his eyes a break from the nipping wind and to keep an eye on Clark to make sure he didn't lag behind.

His friend was there, struggling as well but keeping up. Clark waved a hand to signal he was fine. Graham wanted to make sure he stayed close. The mist created by the swirling snow made it nearly impossible to see in front of him. There could be no cars at all on the highway and he wouldn't be surprised. In fact, he could barely tell he was on a highway. He might just as well have been walking through a snowy meadow. Graham imagined how easily one could get lost out here.

If I walk a straight line from the RV, I'm bound to come upon the other vehicles.

He looked behind him, beyond where Clark was struggling to keep up. Graham could barely see the RV already, as if a white curtain had dropped down behind them. There was only a faint boxy outline in the background. It didn't help that the vehicle was also white.

What colour was the minivan with the kids? He tried to remember. There had been so much snow on it when he passed it, that he hadn't noticed. It had just looked white to him. Plus he had been paying more attention to trying to find the naked man, who must be long dead and buried beneath a drift somewhere. It would probably be days before the ploughs unearthed his frozen corpse. *What a way to go.*

Graham's thoughts were jarred by a sound.

At first he thought it was someone crying out. He stopped in his tracks, trying to listen over the howl of the wind.

He recognised it, the blare of a car horn just ahead.

Clark bumped into him, startling him. He looked over his shoulder at his friend, who had been walking with his head down and hadn't even seen Graham.

"This way," Graham shouted, knowing Clark probably couldn't hear him. He motioned with his gloved hand and ploughed ahead. In a few feet, the minivan came into view. The wipers were going on the rear window, slow, struggling to brush off the sticky snow.

A smiling boy's face peered out the window. He waved at them.

Graham waved his hand with little effort to return the gesture and bulled ahead. When he reached the van, he paused, putting his right hand on its back corner, almost as if to make sure he had really found it.

Thank goodness, he thought. This had been harder than he imagined. With his hand never leaving the side of the vehicle, he trailed along till he got to the driver's side door. It had crusted over with ice and he banged on it, both in an effort to break off some of the ice as well as to alert the woman behind the wheel.

The driver's side window slid down with a groan and Graham looked into the teary face of the woman behind the wheel. She still had her hand on the steering wheel horn. He reached in and gently pulled her hand off it.

"It's okay," he said. "You'll be all right."

The woman's shoulders hunched as she erupted in tears.

Graham patiently waited for her to finish, rubbing her shoulder with a wet gloved hand.

"Are you here to rescue us?" she sputtered between sobs.

"Sort of," was all Graham could think to say. It was not exactly rescue, just an opportunity to be in a better environment. "We're gathering in an RV just a little ways back."

The woman's face gave him a confused look. Graham felt he disappointed her, telling her she was just going from sitting in one vehicle to sitting in another. But after the incident with the naked man, and whatever mysterious circumstances had befallen the ploughman, he felt they'd all be safer together.

"Bundle up," he said, "it's just a short walk."

The woman finally seemed to understand, and turned to relay the info to her boy and girl. It looked to Graham like the boy was excited, pulling on his boots and coat. The girl in the front passenger seat didn't move. She was already bundled up, and Graham guessed she hadn't gotten out of her jacket the whole time, even though it appeared pretty toasty in the van. The warmth pouring out the side window felt good on his face.

The side door of the van slid open and the boy popped out, slamming it shut and running off into the snow.

'Luke!" the woman screamed, craning her neck out the window.

The boy didn't stop.

"I've got him," Clark yelled and bounded after the boy.

"Come on," Graham said, opening the driver's door.

The woman stepped out into the snow, and then looked back at her daughter.

"Let's go, Macey," the woman said.

The girl just looked at the two of them, but didn't move, instead scrunching down in her seat.

"Macey, please," her mother pleaded.

The girl looked about the same age as Graham's middle daughter and he recognised the fear and uncertainty in her eyes.

"They have nice hot cocoa and snacks in the RV," he said to the girl, keeping his voice gentle though he still had to elevate its volume to be heard above the wind. "And it's very comfy in there. They even have a TV."

This brought a half smile to the girl's face and she crawled across the seat to the open door.

"It'll be easier if I carry her," he said to the mother.

She nodded and then looked at her daughter. "Macey, is it all right if this nice man carries you?"

The girl looked at her mother, and then glanced at Graham. Maybe it was something in his eyes and smile that he had nurtured from the years of raising three daughters, but the nervousness dissipated in the girl's face and she nodded. Graham scooped her up.

The woman shut off her lights and engine and they turned to begin the march back to the RV.

CHAPTER EIGHTEEN

When Lewis Felker watched Graham and Clark go out the RV door, he didn't expect to see them return. He tried to warn them, but they shrugged him off, so he didn't care what happened to the pretty boys. To hell with them. They had a snowball's chance in hell of making it back.

What concerned Felker more, as he tipped back his flask to drain the last drops of whiskey in it, was that he was out of booze. His jittery eyes scanned the interior of the RV. The Volkmanns stared back at him, probably just as uncomfortable with him as he was being with them. He used the back of his hand to wipe a drop of whiskey from the corner of his mouth, licking it off his skin in the process.

"You're lucky they found you out there," Francine said, smiling at him.

Felker shrugged. "I guess," he muttered, his voice a bit ragged. "Don't matter none."

The old couple exchanged glances.

"Would you like some more hot cocoa?" Francine asked.

Felker looked down at the empty mug on the table before him, and then to the flask beside it. He brought his gaze up to meet hers. "Anything a bit stronger?"

Werner got up from his captain's seat. "I'm sure I have something lying around."

Felker watched the old man go to a cupboard and rummage around one of the shelves, reaching one hand in to the back. Felker licked his lips as he watched Werner pull out a bottle.

"Will this do?" he asked, showing him the label. It was bourbon.

"Grateful," Felker said, nodding.

Werner unscrewed the cap and poured the liquor into the mug. The old man watched him as he poured, as if waiting for Felker to say when it was enough. But Felker didn't say a word. When the liquid reached the edge of the rim, the old man stopped, screwed the cap on and returned the bottle to the cupboard.

He wished the old man had left the bottle on the table.

Ignoring the couple, he brought the mug up to his lips and sipped a healthy portion. It burned going down and that was good. He squeezed his eyes shut. Felker wanted to keep them closed and enjoy the lightheaded feeling the liquor gave him. Maybe it would help him forget this night.

Lewis Felker had spent most of Christmas Eve standing outside Higgins Department Store, ringing his bell by the Salvation Army bucket, and not believing they wanted him out in a blizzard. But it was the last night of the holiday shopping season, and the captain at the centre told him as long as shoppers were going to be out, the Army was too. This was usually one of the biggest nights for donations, the captain said, and everyone would be out in force to collect whatever they could.

And his boss was right about one thing: the storm didn't stop the shoppers from coming out in droves, the greedy bastards. They had no problem throwing money away on crap inside, coming out with bags crammed with goods, but few even bothered to pitch a couple measly coins into his bucket. Most of them averted their eyes, as if making contact with him would have made them feel guilty, so it was best to pretend they didn't see him. That made him ring his bell even louder, knowing how annoying the sound was to the passersby. Hell, the constant clanging got on his nerves even after just the first few minutes.

The snow had piled up around his feet as he stood on the store's sidewalk, shuffling from foot to foot trying to keep warm. The store's stock boys did their best to keep the walkway shovelled, but the snow came down fast. At first Felker was cautious about taking swigs from his flask, not wanting anyone to spot him and report him to the local branch. But as the cold mounted through the night, he said to hell with it and drank as freely as he wanted. Let someone squeal on him, he thought. It was Christmas Eve, for Christ's sake. Let him enjoy it however he wanted. He was the one stuck out there.

By the time the store closed, he'd packed up his bucket in the station wagon, noticing how light the load was. He grabbed a few of the paper bills from the bucket and made it over to the liquor store before it closed, where he bought the cheapest bottle of whiskey he could find.

He prayed his vehicle would make it, knowing how worn the treads were on all four of his tyres, but he couldn't afford new ones at the moment. As it turned out, the best tyres in the world wouldn't have gotten him through on the turnpike, and judging from the other vehicles that had become stuck on the highway in front of him, no one else's would have either.

By the time his car ran out of gas and the cold began penetrating its interior, he had nearly polished off the bottle of cheap whiskey he had just purchased. The amount of warmth generated by it couldn't keep up with the amount dissipating from the vehicle, and Felker realised he couldn't stay there for long. He turned the ignition and lights off, useless as they were anyway.

He remembered passing an exit and tried to remember how far back it was. It wasn't like he had much of a choice. Or maybe it was just the alcohol that made him feel brazen. He refilled his flask with the remains of the whiskey bottle and then buttoned up his coat, pulled on his gloves and opened the car door, stepping out into the storm.

The wind bit hard. Felker pulled the collar of his coat up to offer what little protection he could to his chin and cheeks. He grabbed the brim of his cap and tugged it down to secure it a little more and began walking. Of course, what he was doing could hardly be called walking. It was more like stumbling or staggering through the knee-high drifts. It was going to be challenging, but once again he thought he had no other choice. He could stay in the car and freeze, hoping for help, or try and make it out on his own.

You're crazy, he thought. *You shouldn't be out in this. You'll never make it far.* He tapped the right breast of his coat, to make sure he could feel the hard tin of the flask beneath. *This will help. Maybe not much, but every little bit counts.*

He thought he should turn back, head toward the other cars he saw stuck ahead of him on the highway. But were they any better off than he? Sure, they still probably had their engines running, and that would offer much-needed warmth. But for how long? And Felker knew that last exit was not too far. If he could make that....

He stopped in his tracks.

He wasn't sure how long he had been walking. It seemed like he had covered quite a bit of ground, even as plodding as his progress had been. Maybe it was the ferocity of the swirling snow that created a white fog that left a curtain across the highway. Or maybe he had been struck snow-blind.

There was nothing in front of him but white.

It was like staring at an empty canvas some artist had yet to begin. There was no longer the outline of any trees lining the two sides of the highway. Highway? There wasn't even any sign that he was on a road, nevertheless the turnpike. No guardrails, no median. Nothing but white.

I can't see! Felker thought, panic ratcheting up inside. *Or maybe I've just reached the end of the world. Or maybe I'm already dead and hell has frozen over.*

His heart thumped inside his chest as if wanting to get out. And his blood, slowed by the cold, oozed through his veins.

Felker fumbled with the top buttons of his coat, his fingers tinged with numbness. He could barely get them to work, but when he managed to unbutton the top of the coat, he reached in and pulled out his flask. He screwed off the cap and let it fall because it was secured to the neck with a chain. He brought the flask to his lips and tilted his head back, letting the whiskey flow over his tongue and down his throat. He thought about the metal freezing to his lips and getting stuck. If so, he'd just keep drinking till it was empty and get ready to die.

But he brought the flask away okay and screwed the cap back on. His insides felt warmer as he put the flask back inside his coat. He shoved his gloved hands into his deep coat pockets to try and keep them warm. His right hand felt something hard. It was his Salvation Army bell. His numb fingers curled around it for some sense of security, not sure why. Felker stared out into the white, not caring that he couldn't feel his toes. The whiskey hadn't reached that far down yet.

If this was the canvas of some madman, the artist had begun to work his brush, because an outline appeared in the distance, a figure taking shape. It was far back; Felker could almost say it was on the horizon, if there had been one. He had no depth perception in the white, so he couldn't tell exactly how far away it stood. Or how close.

It was a man, he was almost sure. How tall he could not say. The man wore a black coat and had a red shirt underneath with dark pants. From the distance it looked like his hair was ashen, unless it was just covered in snow. That was when he realised something odd about the figure. Something about the black coat the man was wearing.

It was black.

Felker looked down at his own coat and saw it spotted with white sticky clumps of snow. Glancing back up (and hoping the figure was just a hallucination and wouldn't be there, but of course it was) he saw the white-haired man's coat had no snow on it, as if he was impervious to the storm.

Felker also noticed the man held something in his right hand. It looked like a curved piece of metal. He didn't know how he could even see so clearly through the misty haze and swirling snow, but the object stood out. He knew what it was, had even seen one once in an antique shop on Route 4. It was a large pair of metal ice tongs, the kind delivery men used to bring big blocks of ice to people's houses back before the days of refrigeration. He remembered his grandmother telling him stories of the ice trucks coming to her house. The iceman would use the tongs to pinch the ice block with its metal tips and then carry it on his back up to her house and deposit it in her icebox.

That was what the figure was holding, in his gloved right hand slung down by his side. But there was something else about the tongs, Felker noticed. Something that stood out bright among all the white ahead. Something that froze the blood in his veins, so that no amount of whiskey would help.

Blood dripped from the tips of the tongs into the snow at the man's feet.

Felker turned around and stumbled back through the snow the way he came, pulling the bell from his pocket and ringing it frantically.

CHAPTER NINETEEN

Clark Brooks helped Graham get the woman – Shelby was her name – and her children settled in the RV while Francine brewed up some more hot cocoa for the new guests. The woman sat on the bench, between her son and daughter, while Werner Volkmann hung up their wet coats in the bathroom shower stall and tucked their boots away into a corner.

It was getting crowded in the vehicle, yet they still had some more people to try to bring in. There was a young couple, the trucker and the middle-aged couple. That should account for everyone that Graham had told Clark about. It was going to be tough to fit everyone in here comfortably, but it might be better than waiting the storm out by themselves.

Clark glanced at the RV's table, where Lewis Felker sat by himself. He looked a little frightening, so maybe that's why no one wanted to sit with him. Or maybe he just looked frightened. He had seemed surprised to see Clark and Graham return. *Maybe he thought we weren't coming back.* He'd warned them about going out there. Had Graham said something to Felker about the snowplough man disappearing?

Clark looked at Shelby and her children. Even with her dishevelled hair and windburned cheeks, she was very attractive. He wondered where the kids' father was. Why wasn't he out with his family on Christmas Eve? How did they get stuck out here? The kids should be home in bed waiting for Santa Claus. More than likely the dad was no longer in the picture.

"Are you ready to go back out?" Graham asked him.

Clark was just beginning to feel warm again, but smiled at his friend.

"Let's get it over with." He looked at Shelby and her kids again. He felt guilty about leaving them so soon, especially with Felker and the Volkmanns as their only companions.

"Thank you both," Shelby said, a smile creeping onto her exasperated face.

"We'll be back soon," Graham said, and Clark wished he had thought to say it.

Outside, the wind seemed a little less ferocious, Clark thought. Maybe the storm was easing up. But just as he thought that, a gust kicked up, practically lifting him off his feet. He followed Graham, who bowed his head and bulled ahead. They followed the path they had previously broken when they chased the doomed naked man. It made the trek just a bit easier.

Once alongside the minivan, they both braced themselves against it to catch their breath. Clark wiped snot from his nose onto the sleeve of Francine's parka. He hoped she'd understand. Graham didn't need to say a word, just made eye contact, nodded and they marched forward.

Up ahead, there were faint red lights, barely discernible in the snow. Clark squinted and saw the hazy light was beneath some snow. He saw the outline of a low shape. It took a moment to make out the rear end of a vehicle. The snow had piled up behind it over the bumper, nearly burying the car. Clark heard the faint sound of its idling engine.

Graham reached it and brushed snow from the driver's side window, peering inside as Clark came up behind him. Graham looked up.

"No one inside," he yelled, barely heard above the wind.

Clark didn't understand. Had they left the vehicle to go for help? That would have been crazy. He brushed the window to the back seat and brought his face to the glass. In the dim light the dashboard cast in the interior, he saw the outline of figures lying in the back seat beneath a blanket. They looked asleep.

"Here!" he yelled to Graham, pulling open the door, grateful it was unlocked. "Hey!" he hollered to the occupants inside. It was a young man and woman, huddled beneath the blanket.

They didn't move.

Clark reached in and gently shook the man's shoulder. The man did not stir. Clark looked over at Graham, who stood behind his shoulder, curious. Clarke removed the glove on his right hand and pulled the blanket away a bit. It surprised him when he saw naked flesh.

The young woman lay mostly on top of the man, her head nestled in the crook of his shoulder and neck, her brown hair draped across her bare back. The man's left arm had been cradling the woman, the hand grazing the small of her back where Clark could see the design of a tattoo.

Clark swallowed hard, gazing down at the bodies. He could no longer feel the cold or even the wind at his back, as if his whole body had gone numb. He reached down to the woman's lower back, to where the man's hand lay, and felt his wrist. There was no pulse.

"Shit," Graham whispered behind him, and it seemed loud.

Clark turned to him and shook his head. He then tried brushing the woman's hair away from her neck and felt the flesh beneath where her artery would be. There was nothing. He looked at her left hand, resting on the man's chest. There was a diamond ring on one finger. Clark stared at the dead couple, thinking how young they looked, and how this one intimate act was the last thing they had experienced. His insides ached.

"The snow covered up the car's exhaust," Graham said, somehow no longer needing to yell. It was as if the howl of the wind died down just for this one solemn moment. "The trucker warned us to keep our exhaust pipes clear of snow. The kid must have forgotten."

Clark glanced into the back of the hatch. It was crammed with suitcases, two pairs of snowshoes, a plastic bag filled with wrapped presents. Someone's Christmas just got shitty. He pulled the blanket up over the couple's shoulders. They probably never realised anything, he thought, before closing the door.

"Shut the car off," he said to Graham. When his friend had accomplished that, he grabbed him by the arm and leaned in. "Say nothing about this to the others."

Graham nodded, understanding.

"They don't need to know about this." He decided to take the lead and motioned for Graham to follow him. He knew it was urgent to check on the others before something else happened.

CHAPTER TWENTY

Tucker Jenks lay in the sleeper berth of his tractor-trailer truck cab, eating corn chips. He had just finished a joint and he had the munchies. He liked the noise the crunching of the chips made. It helped drown out the howl of the banshee from outside. He parted the curtain that separated his bunk from the driving compartment and looked at the windshield. A layer of snow blocked any view.

Better off that way, Tucker thought. Nothing to see out there. He knew what was up ahead. A state highway snowplough stuck in the middle of the turnpike, empty, driver missing, puddle of blood on the floor mats.

And the banshee still howled. That meant she was heralding more death before this storm was finished. He let the curtain drop and lay back on his pillow. Judging from the amount of snow this storm was dumping, Tucker didn't expect any help to arrive till morning. Once the snow stopped, the digging out could begin. He was content to wait. Nothing else he could do anyway.

Lying back there reminded Tucker of going to the drive-in movies with his nana and sister, sitting in the back seat with a big bowl of popcorn and a steamed hot dog smothered in catsup, mustard and relish. They often went to see scary double features. His nana always knew the right moment when to tell Tucker and his sister to close their eyes.

That's all he felt like doing right now. Closing his eyes. This was one time he didn't want to look through the windshield to see what was playing outside. He wished his radio worked so he could at least listen to some music. That way it wouldn't be so dang quiet, with nothing but the wind wailing in the night. He wanted to hear anything else but that.

And he did.

A thumping sound.

Was someone knocking on his door? He lay still, unsure if he indeed heard something. It came again. *Thump, thump.*

Someone was outside. Had help arrived already? Tucker didn't feel right about it, thinking maybe if he ignored the sound, it would move on. He turned the overhead light off in the compartment and lay still in the dark.

Thump, thump. Louder.

Nobody's home, Tucker said to himself. *Go away.*

The sound persisted. He set his bag of chips down and sat up, leaning over to the window of the sleeper berth. It was frosted and iced over, making it nearly impossible to see out, but he thought he could make out a shadowy shape by his driver's side door.

Damn, he thought. Why couldn't he be left alone? He struggled to get his girth into the front of the truck cab and sidled over into the driver's seat. He was about to open the door, but then thought better and just rolled down the window, leaning his head out.

There were two men standing outside his door. Their winter caps and jackets were pasted with wet snow. He recognised the taller one as the fella who checked out the snowplough with him earlier in the evening. That seemed forever ago.

"What's up?" Tucker yelled down.

"How you holding up?" the taller man asked.

"I'm good," Tucker replied, not sure why they felt they needed to check on him.

The tall man pointed south, toward the back of the truck. "There's an RV a little ways back. We're gathering everyone there to hole up till help comes. It's warm and roomy, and there's food and hot drinks."

Tucker had to chuckle, thinking how his large body would make the RV seem not that roomy. Besides, he had all the comfort he needed right here in his truck cab.

"Thanks for the offer," he replied. "But I'm all set here. Got everything I need."

"Are you sure?" the other man asked, the shorter one who hadn't said anything up to this point.

"I'm doing fine." Sure, it was maybe a bit lonely, but that was all right with him. "But there's a couple in that SUV up ahead you can check with. They may think different."

"Okay," the taller man shouted back. "We'll be back there if you change your mind."

Tucker waved them off and watched them walk on ahead.

He wondered if they could hear the banshee too.

CHAPTER TWENTY-ONE

Mason Drake saw something out the side window of his SUV, which, since it was parked cockeyed on the highway, looked south behind him, toward where the tractor-trailer's hulk still loomed beneath the white mist. Shadowy figures were coming his way.

Rescue? he pondered.

"Someone's coming," he said to Joy.

"What? Help?" his wife queried, craning her neck.

Mason stared at the lurching figures.

"I'm not sure." He grabbed his gloves and hat and put them on.

"What are you doing?"

"I'm going to see who it is."

She reached out and grabbed his arm. "And leave me here? Alone?" He saw fright in her eyes and something else…maybe a little anger.

"I'm just going a few feet outside. You'll be fine." He didn't comprehend her concern. She had no reason to feel that way. He, however, still had thoughts of the missing ploughman in his head, and whatever the trucker and that other guy saw in the man's cab. They hadn't said anything, but he had seen glances exchanged. Their faces held a similar expression to Joy's right now. "Keep the doors locked."

"What—"

He exited the vehicle before she finished what she was saying. He didn't want an argument. The cold snapped him alert, and he already regretted coming outside. The figures didn't seem to have gotten much closer. The snow was piled thick in the road. It looked like two men approaching, the shapes thick and bulky. Mason wanted to move toward them, intercept them before they reached his vehicle. He wasn't sure why. Maybe it was some way of protecting Joy.

Mason swallowed hard and rubbed his gloved hands together.

The figures reached him. One of the snowy faces looked familiar.

"Hello," the man said. It was the one who had checked out the plough.

Mason just nodded.

"We're gathering everybody in an RV back a ways." The man pointed back the way he came. "Food, heat and light. All the comforts of home."

The man tried to smile, but in the frigid cold and wind, it looked to Mason more like a grimace.

It wasn't help, but it offered something. Misery loves company, right?

"That sounds great," he yelled back, also trying to smile. "Let me get my wife." He turned back to his vehicle, opening the door and leaning in.

"Is it rescue?" Joy asked, her face hopeful.

"Not exactly." He explained the situation to her, not sure she felt it was any better.

"How far back is this RV?" she asked.

Mason shrugged. "I'm not sure."

She looked down at the clothes she was wearing, and her suede skirt and boots. "I'm not exactly dressed for walking through the snow."

He gazed at her, exasperated. "Would you rather just sit in here?"

That did it. He saw the look on her face change.

"No," she said. "I feel like if I sit here any longer I'll scream. At least I can move around in an RV."

Mason wasn't sure how many people were gathering in the RV, so he didn't know how much moving she'd be able to do, but he didn't want to broach that topic. He watched her zip up her coat and pull on leather gloves. He backed away from the door as she started to clamber over the centre console. She was almost at the door when she stopped suddenly.

"Wait a minute," she said, turning and reaching into the back seat, grabbing the bag of Christmas presents they had gotten at Higgins Department Store.

"We don't need those," he exclaimed.

She glared at him. "We went through a lot of trouble to get these gifts tonight. I'm not taking any chances if we can't get back to our vehicle right away after getting rescued. I don't want to disappoint our kids any more than we probably already have tonight."

"Fine," he relented, not wanting to waste any more breath on the subject. It was hard enough to breathe out there with the wind sucking the air out of him.

Joy stumbled out of the vehicle, nearly falling to the ground, but he caught her and steadied her. The snow was up over the top of her suede boots, and he could tell as she looked down that she was pissed.

"Let's go," he said, letting her move ahead of him as they fell in behind the two men.

He prayed that they were making the right decision.

Mason brought up the rear in their little parade, marching through the thick snow as they made their way around the jackknifed tractor-trailer, its running lights still on, casting a glow on the snow. Up ahead, one of the two guys had taken a hold of Joy's arm, assisting her through the snow.

I should be up there, helping her, Mason thought. He didn't need anyone else taking care of her. He was fully capable. But he was having a hard time himself, wearing only dress shoes. He was no more equipped for this than she was.

Mason hadn't gotten far when a screech stopped him in his tracks. It could have been the wind ripping through the night, transforming from a howl to a higher pitched wailing, but it sounded much more ominous. He turned and looked behind him.

A figure stood in the snow just before the tractor-trailer. Its rotund shape, especially around the middle, made him think it was the truck driver. The other guys must have forgotten to check on him. The figure was covered in snow. How long had he been standing outside the truck? It was like he was painted in white. Even the hat he wore was frosted with snow.

Mason waved, trying to signal him to come over.

The figure didn't move.

What the hell's wrong with him?

Mason started to move back the way he had come, to see if the man needed help. Something grabbed his shoulder. He whirled around.

The man he spoke to earlier was beside him, face leaning in.

"What are you doing?" the man yelled.

"The guy over there," Mason yelled back, pointing toward the truck. "I think he needs help."

The guy peered over Mason's shoulder, rubbing snow off his face.

"What guy?"

Mason looked back. There was nobody standing in the snow.

CHAPTER TWENTY-TWO

The ten of them now gathered in the warmth of the recreation vehicle.

"What was your worst winter memory?" Mr. Volkmann asked while his inquisitive eyes surveyed the weary faces of the travellers. The old man had grey hair slicked back over the top of his head, revealing a widow's peak so sharp it looked like it could cut glass. He looked from face to face, both young and old, waiting for a response. None was forthcoming, so the old man licked his dry lips and smiled.

"Let me tell you mine."

As a young boy, began his tale, he had grown up in a mountain village in Germany. Christmas was always a time of great anticipation, awaiting a visit from St. Nikolaus. But of course, every girl and boy in the village knew they had to be on their very best behaviour, or else they would get a different kind of visit. For St. Nikolaus was not the only entity paying children a visit that time of year. Bad children, the very worst of them, got a visit from an entirely different kind of otherworldly being. Those children were warned that if they did not behave, they would be visited by Krampus.

Krampus was the dark servant of St. Nikolaus, part beast, part human, with horns, a black face, long slithery tongue and a hairy wolflike body upon two cloven hoofs. He carried a birch switch with which he would spank unruly children to discipline them for their naughty behaviour. The really bad children, the old man said, would be thrown into a wooden basket strapped to Krampus's back and taken away to his lair, often never to be seen again.

The old man looked around at the audience crammed into his RV as the wind screeched outside with the fury of a locomotive and the icy snow pelted against the windshield sounding like the scratching of the claws of the mythical creature of which he spoke. The huddled group looked on, some with feigned interest, others only putting up with the distraction. But the two children in the group were mesmerised, eyes wide with wonder as the old man spun his tale.

"We would put our shoes by the front door," he continued, "and in the morning they would be filled with treats and gifts." He looked at the young boy and girl. "*If* we were good."

One St. Nikolaus night, as a young boy, he was walking home after suppertime, returning from an errand to bring a loaf of home-baked bread to his oma. His parents had sent him on the errand and, because he wanted to be a good boy, he obliged. On the way home, after the sun dipped beneath tall evergreen trees on the horizon, he followed the snowy path as thick flakes fell from the darkened clouds above. His hands thrust deep in his pockets for warmth, he quickened his pace, anxious to get home and huddle before the fire to warm his bones until it was time to retire to his bedroom.

He stopped in his tracks, looking behind him where a sound had disturbed the silent night. *Footsteps?* Maybe. Something crunched the snow. Was there someone following him home? It was certainly too early for St. Nikolaus. He wouldn't come till he was fast asleep. Behind him, the wooded path was empty as far as the moonlit night would let him see. There was nothing there, he told himself, but when he turned back to continue his trek, he quickened his pace.

The next sound he heard came from the trees on his left. Was the sound he heard before now flanking him? Maybe a wild animal descended on the village that night, down from the forest to forage for food? He scanned the trees but saw no movement in the darkness between the thick trunks. He looked ahead, to the lights from his neighbourhood. He hadn't long to go, but it still seemed far away. He started to run.

Something struck his face, knocking him to the ground. His nose throbbed and he removed a mitten from his right hand and felt it. Wetness came away in his fingers and he saw red. In the moonlight he saw drops of blood drip onto the white snow. He heard laughter.

From behind a tree on the ridge above the path stepped a figure. He recognised the older boy from the neighbourhood, Gustov. The laughing boy scooped up more snow, moulding it before hurling another snowball at him, striking him in his chest with a thud.

He tried not to cry, wanting to be brave.

"Krampus will get you for this!" he yelled, tears spilling out between words despite his effort to suppress them.

Gustov laughed harder. "There's no such thing as Krampus, you big baby."

The laughter rang in his ears, and he got to his feet and began to run toward his house and away from the laughter that echoed in the cold night. Once inside the safety of his home, he said nothing to his parents about his encounter in the woods, not wanting them to know he had disobeyed their instructions not to take the wooded shortcut home. He told them he had tripped, which resulted in his bloody nose. His mother cleaned him up and gave him some hot cocoa before sending him to bed.

Not until he was under the covers did it occur to him that lying to his parents might be enough to warrant a visit from Krampus. With that thought on his mind, he was unable to sleep, instead lying on his back in his bunk and listening to every movement in the house. Most he recognised as his parents, performing whatever functions they needed before finally retiring to their bedroom for the night.

Then the house became quiet, and that was when he listened with more intensity to every creak and groan of the wooden structure. At some point he must have finally drifted off to sleep, because when he did notice a sound, it was because it had awakened him.

Footsteps.

At first he thought they were on the stairs leading to his bedroom. He gripped the covers and pulled them up to his chin. But as his ears followed the sound, his eyes rolled up to look at the rafters above. It was coming from the roof.

St. Nikolaus? he thought. *Or something else?*

Each soft step marched a cadence across the roof, and he imagined a shadowy figure creeping along the peak. *I've been mostly good*, he kept telling himself. *I haven't been bad.* When the sound got to the edge of the roof above his bedroom window, it stopped.

The boy was frozen. This was supposed to be an exciting night, not one draped in fear. Snow slid off the roof with a scraping sound, followed by silence. He waited, listening. The next sound he heard came from a distance; a creaking sound, like the opening of a door, or a window. He dared to glance at his own window, shut and secure.

But he still didn't feel safe, so he pushed the covers off and swung his legs over to the floor. The wooden boards were cold on his bare feet, sending a shiver up his legs and spine. Maybe it wasn't just the cold floor. Maybe it was also the fear that coursed through his body. He went to the window. The frosted glass obscured any view, so he unlatched the window and pushed it open. Flakes of snow drifted down onto the street below. He leaned out the window, turning to look up toward the edge of the roof. Snow fell onto his face. Above the empty peak of the house was the white of the snowflakes fluttering from the sky.

A sound drew his gaze to a house across the way. It was Gustov's house. His stomach tightened as he watched a shadowy figure crawling out a second-floor window and dropping to the ground. It stepped into the moonlight, and he saw the horns on its long head, between pointy ears. A basket clung to the thing's back. Something moved in the basket, a head pushing up on its cover that was lashed shut. Eyes peered out from beneath that cover – Gustov's eyes filled with terror.

He gasped, and the beast turned toward the sound. From across the way, he could see red glowing eyes staring back at him, before the beast took off into the snowy night.

Everyone seemed captivated by the old man's far-fetched fable, but maybe that was because most of them were finally somewhat comfortable for the first time during their ordeal on the highway.

Shelby Wallace saw completely opposite reactions to the story from her kids. Her younger, Luke, was grinning madly, utterly enthralled by the horrifying image of Krampus carting off the misbehaving boy to whatever punishment the mythical creature would dole out. On the other hand, Macey looked downright frightened, glancing back at her mother with wide eyes, looking for some assurance that it was only a story. Even though she was two years older, she appeared more gullible, believing in the existence of such a creature as Krampus.

Shelby reached out a reassuring hand to caress her daughter's shoulder.

"Don't worry," she said. "It's just a fairy tale." She glanced up at Mr. Volkmann, not wanting to be ungracious, but concerned that they had been through enough tonight without having to worry about the children being scared on Christmas Eve.

"Of course you don't have to worry," the old man said with a hearty laugh and a slap of his knee. "You two children look much too well-behaved to have any reason to fear the arrival of Krampus. He's only looking for the bad ones." He grinned, looking around the vehicle at the others.

"And the rest of us aren't children anymore," his wife, Francine, said, as if to keep the adults at ease. "But speaking of children, I bet I know a pair who'd like a special treat." She stood up and approached one of the cupboards and retrieved a small paper bag from it. "I have some homemade gingerbread cookies." She held out the open bag before the kids, and Luke and Macey each took one of the treats and began munching on them. She set the bag on the table, but none of the adults indulged.

It was cramped in the RV, but Shelby still felt better, comforted by the presence of the others. She sat on the cushioned bench seat, her kids on either side of her. Clark Brooks sat on the bench with them. She thought he was very handsome, with nice dark hair, even though it was matted and unkempt from the winter cap he had been wearing earlier. The Volkmanns had taken everyone's winter coats, hats and gloves, and put them in the bathroom to dry out. All except Louis Felker of course, who refused to part with his coat.

Felker sat on one side of the small dining table, beside Graham Sawyer, while Mr. and Mrs. Drake sat on the other side. Graham was handsome too, she thought, but the lighter haired man wore a wedding band, and Clark did not. She felt like a silly schoolgirl, thrown into this situation with handsome men to rescue her. Felker's beady eyes glanced over at her, and the odd man's brutish face unsettled her, and she put her arms around both children's shoulders to draw them closer for comfort.

Mrs. Volkmann returned to the front passenger seat beside her husband. Their seats swivelled around to face the interior of the cabin.

As Shelby looked around, something occurred to her.

"Is everyone here?" she asked no one in particular. Silence greeted her question.

Mason Drake finally broke it. "They said the truck driver didn't want to come. He'd rather stay in his rig."

"Yes," Graham agreed.

"Oh," Shelby said, thinking for a moment. She remembered sitting behind the hatchback for several hours tonight, and seeing the couple inside. It was hard to tell from just silhouettes, but they seemed younger than the Drakes.

She looked at the middle-aged couple. "Were you in the hatchback?" she asked them.

"No," Joy Drake answered. "We have an SUV. We got stuck just behind the snowplough, up ahead of the tractor-trailer."

Shelby assimilated this information, glancing down for a moment, then back up.

"Then what about the couple in the hatchback, right in front of me?"

Again there was only silence. She saw Graham and Clark exchange mysterious glances.

"We checked on them," Graham said. "They were quite comfortable where they were when we left them." His smile looked forced.

"I see," Shelby said, but she didn't really. Graham's response was a bit off, but she couldn't quite understand why. "I hope they'll be okay."

"We can check on them again later," Clark offered.

Shelby felt a little more comforted with that response. It sounded genuine. She really shouldn't worry, she told herself. She had enough on her shoulders just taking care of Macey and Luke without worrying about complete strangers.

But weren't they all really strangers, thrust together by this unfortunate series of events? And now they had to somehow rely on each other while they waited for...what? Some kind of rescue? It had to be. Someone had to come. The highway would have to be cleared eventually. The storm couldn't last forever.

Could it?

Mr. Volkmann clapped his hands, which broke the quiet moment.

"Now, who else would like to share their worst winter memory?" he asked, his eyes scanning the room before falling on Shelby. "You, young lady?" The old man grinned.

Even though the RV was warm, the smile Mr. Volkmann gave her chilled her insides, and she tightened her grip around Macey's shoulder in protective mode. This nice couple had taken her in, so she thought there was no need to be worried. The question he asked didn't have to linger in her mind long before a memory was conjured up, and it did not have anything to do with her ex-husband tossing their Christmas tree out in a fit of frustration. No, another image came up, one much more frightful.

The eyes of everyone were upon her, waiting for her to respond. She shook her head. "I don't really have anything," she said, pushing the memory far back into her thoughts. Not anything she wanted to tell in front of her children anyway.

As if Francine could hear her thoughts, the old woman spoke. "If you'd like, you can let the children lie down in our bedroom. I'm sure they must be exhausted."

"It is getting late," Mr. Volkmann chimed in.

"That's a great idea," Shelby said.

"Aw Mom," Luke protested. "I'm not tired."

"It's been a long night," Shelby said, pulling up her sleeve to check her watch. "It must be – oh my God." She looked up at the others. "It's after midnight."

"It's Christmas!" Luke squealed.

Everyone else voiced exclamations of wonder at how much of the night had gone by since they'd been trapped on the highway. Some of the comments displayed amazement, others frustration. Mason Drake sounded downright angry.

Werner Volkmann got up from his driver's seat. "Well, this calls for some kind of Christmas toast at the very least."

"Yes," Francine said, also rising. "I think there's still some warm cocoa in the pot." She squeezed her way to the kitchen area, filled mugs and handed them out to everyone.

Mr. Volkmann raised his mug. "To a very unusual Christmas gathering. May we all have a safe journey home when this storm ends."

Shelby certainly could drink to that. But would this nightmare ever end? She was beginning to wonder. She brought the mug to her lips, and the chocolate drink was lukewarm, but smooth and soothing.

"Now, how about I get that bed ready?" Francine said with a smile.

"That would be nice," Shelby answered.

"Do we have to, Mom?" Luke whined.

"It's late and there's no reason to stay up. We'll just be sitting here waiting out the storm. The time will go faster if you sleep."

"But it's Christmas already."

Mr. Volkmann knelt down in front of the boy. "Now be a good lad," he said, face to face. "You don't want Krampus to come looking for you."

Luke glanced up at his mother, and though Shelby didn't appreciate the old man putting these thoughts in her children's heads, she saw a look of real concern on her son's face. Mr. Volkmann looked up at her and winked. There seemed something sinister in that too.

"You heard the man," she said to her son.

"Will you lay with us?" Macey asked with pleading eyes.

"Of course, baby."

"This Christmas stinks," Luke said as his mother started to follow Francine toward the back of the RV.

"Wait," Joy Drake said, jumping up from her seat at the table.

Shelby turned to look. The woman grabbed a bag she had on the seat beside her.

"Maybe, since it's Christmas already, your kids would like to open a present. I just happen to have a couple here for a boy and a girl."

"What?" exclaimed her bewildered husband.

"Oh, no," Shelby said. "That's not necessary." She saw both her kids' faces light up, then become disappointed.

"Nonsense," Joy said. "It's Christmas after all, the season of giving. I insist."

Before Shelby could say another word and before Joy's husband could utter a protest, wrapped packages were thrust into her children's hands and their faces were once again alight. The glittering wrapping was torn to shreds in seconds.

"Wow," Luke exclaimed. "*Space Marines!*"

Shelby looked as Macey opened the small jewellery box and held up the snowflake pendant in delicate fingers. It was the first smile Shelby had seen on her daughter's face all evening. The girl was too amazed to even utter a word.

"What do you say to the nice lady?" Shelby prodded, a hand on each kid's shoulders and giving in to the fact the gifts were in their hands, despite the look of frustration on Mr. Drake's face.

"Thank you," both kids exclaimed in unison.

"Now how about that bed?" an exhausted Shelby said to Francine.

Mrs. Volkmann led them down the hall to the back of the RV, opening a door that led to a small room with a full-sized bed. Shelby let out a breath of exasperation at the sight of how inviting it looked. She turned to the old woman, almost as if to protest their taking the couple's sleeping quarters, but then thought otherwise.

I deserve this, she told herself. *And so do my kids.* She didn't want to give it up to anyone. She removed her boots and crawled into the bed along with Macey and Luke, who were still clutching their first Christmas gifts.

"We'll try to keep it quiet out there," Francine said, before throwing a quilt over the three of them. "You just relax."

When the woman shut the door behind her, relax was what Shelby tried to do. Her arms around her son and daughter, her head pressed into the softness of the pillow, she closed her eyes and tried to shut out everything about the storm outside.

But what she couldn't shut out was the memory of her worst winter.

CHAPTER TWENTY-THREE

Tobin Hill in her hometown of Evergreen, New Hampshire, was a popular sledding spot in the winter. A towrope pulled people up to the top, where a small shack had offerings of hot drinks and greasy snacks.

Shelby was home from college during the winter break with her boyfriend of two years, Kirby Decker, a tall lanky fellow with a toothy smile and sandy hair. They'd met as freshmen at the University of New Hampshire and realised they only lived a few towns away from each other.

Kirby might not have been the hottest guy Shelby had ever gone out with, but he was certainly the sweetest. And his smile always warmed her heart, especially on a night like the one on Tobin Hill.

They had made several toboggan runs already down the groomed west slope, the towrope bringing them back up each time for another ride.

"One more," Kirby kept saying, laughing, grabbing her mitten-covered hand. She could feel him squeeze her fingers through the knitted material, not enough to hurt, just enough to show he wanted to hold on to her.

"I'm exhausted," she uttered at the top of the hill as darkness fell on a still night. "I can't even catch my breath."

He pulled her tight. "I'll breathe for you," he said and kissed her mouth hard.

What did she expect for an English major? "You're so corny," she said, pushing him away in jest.

"Corny and horny," he exclaimed with a laugh.

"There's no hope for you." She laughed back. It felt good to laugh with him.

"One more time," he said, tugging on the toboggan rope and gesturing down the hill.

"Last time," she said. "I mean it this time."

He pulled the sled to the edge of the hill and got in front. Shelby climbed on behind him, wrapping her arms around his thin frame.

"Hang on!" he cried, pushing off with one hand while gripping the rope with the other.

Like a roller coaster breaching the first big hill, the toboggan teetered at the top before tipping forward where gravity reached up and pulled the sled down. It raced down the steep decline, and Shelby buried her face in Kirby's back to avoid the rush of wind that swirled around them. It was exhilarating as they raced down the hill, and Shelby lifted her head over his shoulder to whisper in his ear.

Kirby turned his head. "What?" he yelled back.

"I love you," she repeated, a little louder.

His eyes met hers and locked on to them, his grin displaying his big front teeth.

Shelby saw the flash of green ahead and looked up just in time to see them heading toward the pine tree.

There was no time to scream. There was no time for anything.

She didn't remember feeling the impact. All she remembered was lying in the snow on her stomach, face buried in the powder. The first thing that Shelby sensed was the fluffiness of the snow. They weren't on the packed trail anymore. They had gone off. Then she remembered the tree.

Shelby lifted her head, brushing snow from her face, crystals sticking to her skin. She looked around. Where was Kirby? She saw the tree and broken branches scattered about. She saw the toboggan. It was split down the middle, shattered bits of wood around it. Several feet away she saw black ski pants.

Kirby!

She thought she yelled his name, but realised she had yet to find her voice. She also couldn't find her feet, her head swirling in a daze, so she crawled through the snow to get to him. When she reached where he lay facedown in the snow, she shook him.

"Kirby!" she finally managed, though not as loud as she'd liked. She wanted to scream his name. She latched onto his jacket and rolled him over.

A ribbon of blood ran from the top of his head down over his bent nose. His mouth was open, displaying broken shards of red teeth. His eyes were open too, but they couldn't see anything, and never would again. And then she did scream.

CHAPTER TWENTY-FOUR

Lewis Felker drummed his fingers on the table inside the RV. He looked down at his empty cocoa mug, before shifting his eyes over toward the stove. It wasn't that he wanted more of the hot liquid. No, not that at all. He was plenty warm, especially since he still wore his damp wool Salvation Army coat. Several times the old lady had wanted to take it from him and hang it up. But Felker didn't want to take it off. Sure he was warm, toasty in fact, but he wouldn't relinquish his coat.

There was something not quite right outside, and despite the fact that things seemed safe and secure inside this RV, he wanted his coat and boots on in case he needed to make a run for it. His gloves were tucked inside his coat pockets, and his cap lay on the table before him. He had everything he needed right there, except one thing.

His flask was empty. That's why he looked at the chocolate remnants swirling around at the bottom of his mug. He didn't miss the cocoa; he missed what he had emptied into it. As he stared over toward the stove and the cupboards above it, he wondered. *These old people must have more liquor in here than the bottle of bourbon the old man pulled out earlier. Who goes travelling without a bit of booze in tow?* He thought about asking the old couple. No harm in that. But if he did, he might end up having to share it with everyone else. It could be a long night, so he didn't like that prospect. But it was so crowded in the RV that he didn't think he'd get a chance to poke around.

I'll bide my time, he thought, *and wait for a distraction*.

He gazed across the table at the Drakes on the other side. Their faces were familiar and it only took a moment for Felker to remember them from the department store earlier that night. They had come out of the store and passed him on the sidewalk as he rang his bell by the Salvation Army kettle. The way the storm was building, not many people were stopping, so he wasn't surprised when they passed him by. But then the woman stopped and turned around, getting out her wallet, and came over and dropped some bills into the pot.

Felker smiled, thanked her and wished her a merry Christmas. When he glanced up at her husband, he noticed the annoyed look on the man's face. As they walked away, he heard Mr. Drake mutter under his breath. "Do they have to keep ringing the damn thing? It's not like we don't know they're there."

Did the guy think he liked standing out here freezing his nuts off ringing this bell? He was the one who had to listen to it all night. That along with the damn Christmas carols blaring over the department store's loudspeaker on a never-ending loop. Try listening to that all day, for Christ's sake.

He was doing this to be charitable, to help out those unfortunates. Felker had imagined flipping the guy off behind his back, and now here he was, sitting across the table from him and his wife, sharing the shelter.

The old lady got up from her seat and moved to the bench seat in the vacant spot created when Shelby had taken her kids to the bedroom. "I'll share my worst winter memory, if no one else wants to," Francine said, "now that the children have gone to bed."

She began her tale about the winter when she was ten years old, living in Berlin, New Hampshire. That winter was fierce, the region trounced by multiple nor'easters that swept arctic air down from Canada and pummelled the state with heavy snowfalls. The town ploughs worked around the clock trying to keep the streets clear so people could maintain their daily routines. But once one storm was finished and cleaned up, another was on its way. The snowbanks piled up along the streets, eight feet high in some spots.

At first the kids enjoyed the snow. Francine told them how most of the streets were shut down, so she and her friends would go sledding down Mt. Forist Avenue during February school vacation week. The street sloped down toward Main Street and they didn't have to worry about cars coming up the hill.

But soon the fun ended, she told the others, her face growing grim. A city plough made a grisly discovery on Unity Street, just down the road from the paper mill. As the truck's blade cut through the banks along the road, widening it, a body was uncovered. It belonged to a man who worked second shift at the mill, and usually walked home on Western Avenue after work. At first there were concerns the man had been hit by a plough. But they soon found out otherwise. The man's throat had been punctured on both sides of his neck, a frozen puddle of blood beneath him.

And he was only the beginning.

Not long after, the body of a waitress was found on the pedestrian bridge over the Dead River near the railroad tracks by First Avenue. The body lay in a pool of blood, the same round puncture wounds on both sides of her throat.

"People were afraid to go outside," Francine said. "Not that people wanted to go out anyway. Berlin was a very frigid town in the winter, but that year there was no end to the deep freeze and the snow kept coming!" She threw up her hands in dramatic exclamation.

Francine told them how schools remained closed even after vacation ended. Shops downtown shut down as most people either couldn't get out of their houses, or were too afraid to. The paper mill and the factories kept running; people still needed to work. But businesses struggled.

"I remember staring out the window into the whiteness of my front yard," Francine said. "It was beautiful, the pure untouched snow. No footprints or boot marks to mar it. No snowman or snow fort built by my brothers. And though I wanted to go out and play, it was just too cold." She said the only thing good about being stuck inside was not having to smell the pungent odour of the paper mill.

Francine said as the weather got more brutal, even the killings seemed to have stopped, as if it were too cold for murder.

But then the temperature finally climbed above freezing, and she remembered begging her mother to let her go outside. Her mother said she could, just to check the mail as she had seen the postman walking down the street by their house just a few minutes earlier. Francine said her mother bundled her up in her winter coat, hat, mittens and boots and sent her out to fetch the mail and come right back.

Francine thrashed through the snow down the front walk, to the edge of the road before the mailbox. She needed to stand on her tiptoes to reach the box. She pulled the lid down and took off her pink right-hand mitten to reach in and grab the envelopes stuffed in the mailbox. As she pulled her hand out, one letter slipped from her cold fingers and fluttered to the ground. She bent to retrieve it when she noticed, a few feet away, a red line in the snow. Her eyes followed the line up the street to its source.

The body of the mailman lay sprawled facedown on the side of the road, mailbag discarded beside him, a red puddle seeping out from beneath his head and forming a stream flowing down the street through the snow toward her.

She glanced up, forgetting about the envelope on the ground, to see a man walking away from the body. He carried an object in his hands. It looked like the large metal ice tongs used by the guy who delivered ice blocks to their house in the summer. Blood dripped from the pointed tips of the tongs.

The man had straw-like scraggly hair flowing over the collar of his black coat. He turned and looked over his shoulder at her, round bloodshot eyes above a pale creased face. The thin cracked lips of his mouth did not move. He did not smile, did not talk, did not even break stride, only stared back before turning away and continuing up the road.

Felker no longer felt warm inside as Francine told her story. It was as if some cold beast ripped open his flesh and crawled inside him, curling up along his spine. He swallowed hard, wishing he hadn't finished his flask. She had described the image of the man he had seen out in the snow earlier. How was that possible?

"Did the man get away?" Felker asked in a shaky voice, his fingers drumming on the tabletop again. But did her answer matter? She said this happened when she was ten years old, and she had to be close to eighty, if not older. That would be over seventy years ago. It couldn't be the same man. But he asked anyway.

"Based on my description, the authorities figured out who the culprit was," Francine continued. "His name was Everett Wick, and he worked for the Jericho Ice Company, delivering blocks of ice to residents throughout the town. He lived in a cabin with his mother on a private road in the woods out off Route 110 near Jericho Lake." She paused and licked her lips. "The papers ended up nicknaming him 'the Iceman'."

Felker got the impression she enjoyed telling this tale. The others in the RV listened with intensity, no one interrupting.

"The state and local police converged on his cabin. What they found inside was the remains of Wick's mother. They say she was cut into pieces with a saw and stored in his icebox. Rumour has it he and his mother had been snowbound for a while in the cabin, and that poor Everett Wick had gone stir-crazy and killed his mother and then all the others." The old woman leaned forward from her seat. "They say some of the remains in the icebox looked like they had been gnawed on." She leaned back and there was maybe just a touch of a smirk.

Mason Drake cleared his throat. "And did they find this Wick guy too?"

Francine nodded. "Bloodhounds found him out back and chased him through the woods and out onto the frozen Jericho Lake. He had his ice tongs strapped to his belt and was carrying an ice saw. Before they got to him, he had cut a hole around himself in the ice, and let himself drop through."

"So – he's dead," Felker spurted out, his voice strained.

Francine shrugged. "One would suppose."

"Of course," Graham said. "Froze like a popsicle, I'm sure."

"Could be," Francine said with that sly grin. "But they never found his body. They even dragged the lake in the spring when the ice thawed." She paused. "No remains were ever recovered."

CHAPTER TWENTY-FIVE

Clark heard the back bedroom door of the RV open and looked up to see Shelby emerge. Her hair was mussed, her cheeks flushed and the slightest hint of bags had begun to form under her eyes, but he still found her rumpled state attractive. She looked like a real woman, not pretentiously made up like a lot of the women he met in California. He slid over on the bench seat a bit to make room for her and she plopped herself down between him and Francine, but inched a little closer toward him. Clark liked that and smiled at her.

"The kids are asleep," she said to everyone, but looking at him. "I tried, but the wind kept me awake."

"The storm doesn't seem to be letting up any," Clark said.

"I lay there listening to that morbid story." She now looked at Francine, and the old woman just smiled. "It gave me the willies."

"We're just sharing our worst winter memories," Francine said. "Would you like to tell us yours?"

Clark watched the lines on Shelby's face. He could see the tension in them and knew she remembered something horrible.

"No thanks," Shelby said.

"We may be here awhile," Graham said from his seat at the table. He glanced toward the front of the RV to where Mr. Volkmann sat in the captain's seat. "How's your fuel supply?"

"Gas and propane tanks are pretty much full. We could last out here for days."

Joy Drake perked up from her sleepy state beside her husband. "Oh Christ, I hope we're not here that long. I'd go stir-crazy."

"Of course it won't be that long," her husband responded. "Highway crews will most likely be out here by daylight, if not sooner." He looked hopeful, or was it a façade?

Graham stirred in his seat. "Well, it's good we can keep warm for the immediate future. But we're still in a pretty dangerous situation. I just want to make sure everyone understands that."

Clark sensed Graham was going to say something about the young couple's bodies they had found in the hatchback. Clark didn't think it was a good idea to let everyone know about what had happened to the couple. Seeing Shelby's fragile state, he didn't want to worry her any further. She had enough on her plate trying to keep her kids secure. He looked at Graham and shook his head ever so slightly, hoping no one else would notice. He mouthed the word 'no' and his friend got the hint. Felker eyed him suspiciously. Had the man seen his signal?

"How about if I tell about my worst winter memory?" Clark said, trying to shift the topic. He looked at Shelby beside him. "And I promise it won't be as gruesome as Mrs. Volkmann's tale."

She half smirked in response. "I hope not."

Clark dug into his memory bank, rummaging through the details. Not gruesome, he remembered. But not entirely without some unease.

Clark was ten that winter, living in Evergreen with his parents, his younger sisters and his grandfather. Grampa Brooks had given him an early Christmas present, a snow globe he bought at a gift shop in North Conway. Inside the glass ball was a winter scene: three snowmen on a snowbank before a copse of balsams. The snowman in the middle was taller than the other two, a black top hat perched on its round white head. Two black coal eyes loomed over a crooked carrot nose. Its jagged mouth looked like something more appropriate for a jack-o'-lantern than a snowman. A red-and-white striped scarf wrapped around its neck and hung down over its middle. Branches formed its arms, twigs at the end like long narrow fingers.

The other two snowmen on either side were shorter, one of them a bit more rotund and wearing a Santa cap. The carrot it had for a nose was short and stubby. Its mouth was round, as if frozen in the middle of a laugh. The third snowman wore a black pork pie hat with a wide brim, its carrot nose long and narrow. They both also had tree branch arms, bent like elbows with twiggy fingers.

Clark shook the snow globe and set it down on the desk in his bedroom, watching the snowflakes inside the watery glass orb flutter with fury over the three snowmen, as if they were trapped in a storm.

"I love my snowball, Grampa," Clark told the old man with excitement.

Grampa Brooks didn't correct him, letting Clark call the ornament by its misnomer.

"That's not the only surprise I have for you today," his grandfather said.

"What else?" Clark asked, trying to contain his enthusiasm.

"We're going to pick out a Christmas tree today."

"Oh boy," Clark said. "Down at the church parking lot?"

His grandfather harrumphed. "That's not how to pick out a Christmas tree," he said. "We're going out into the woods to cut down a fresh one. That's what we did when I was your age."

So the old man loaded up his pickup truck with snowshoes, a saw, some rope and a wooden toboggan.

Clark's father was hesitant about the excursion into the woods. "I wish you'd just let me get one downtown, Pop," he said as the two of them climbed into the pickup.

"Nonsense," Grampa said. "Waste of money. The forest is full of trees. The boy needs to learn that you don't have to buy everything."

"Just be careful," his father relented. "You're not a young man anymore."

"Poppycock," his grandfather responded. "I could outlast you on a hike through the woods." And he was probably right. His grandfather was a sturdy old man, still hiking, fishing, hunting and camping, even at his age, while Clark's father was not much of an outdoorsman, content with indoor activities.

"There's snow in the forecast later today," his father said. "Don't take too long out there."

"Of course it's going to snow," Grampa said. "It's winter. It's supposed to snow." As the old man started the engine of the pickup, Clark's father came over to the passenger's side door. Clark rolled down his window.

"Look out for your grampa," his father told him. Clark wasn't sure what that meant or what his dad expected from him.

In the woods, Clark saw plenty of trees that would look good in the corner of their living room, but his grandfather dismissed them all as either not tall enough, not full enough, not the right shape or having some weird gap in their branches. Snow began to fall as Clark followed the trail his grandfather blazed, the old man pulling the toboggan behind him.

Clark's legs were tired from the arduous hike through the snow and he wanted to ask his grandfather if he could ride on the toboggan, but he thought about his father's concern for the old man and didn't want to be a burden. He wanted to be tough, like his grandfather. So he plodded along, one snowshoe step at a time as the old man led them deeper into the woods, down one slope and up another, the trees growing larger around them, shadows darkening the landscape and the snow thickening in the air.

His grandfather came to a sudden stop.

"What is it, Grampa?"

The old man stood still, as if frozen, and Clark's breath shortened. Then his grandfather raised his gloved hand, pointing, and spoke.

"There it is."

Clark looked ahead and spotted the lone balsam, entrenched in a clearing of pure white snow. It was a perfect triangle, with thick green branches powdered in white flakes. It reminded Clark of the trees inside his snowball at home, though he knew those were made of plastic.

Grampa dragged the toboggan over to the tree and grabbed his saw.

"Hold the tree steady, boy, while I cut it."

Clark reached in between the branches, grabbing onto the trunk of the tree with a gloved hand while his grandfather hunkered down in the snow at the base. Clark gripped the tree tight, listening as the saw blade chewed through the trunk. Once the tree was removed from its base, the two of them lowered it onto the toboggan. Grampa tied the rope around the branches and secured the tree to the sled.

"Okay," his grandfather said with a clap of his hands. "Let's go."

Clark walked beside his grandfather, who pulled the toboggan along behind him as they retraced their path.

"Wait till Mom and Dad see our tree," Clark said with glee.

Grampa responded only with puffs of exhalations as they trudged up a hill. Snow fell heavier, the flakes thick. Hadn't his father said something about a storm approaching? Clark stopped to look up, opening his mouth to catch one fat flake before it hit the ground, melting the instant it touched his extended tongue.

"Do you think the tree will fit in our living room?" Clark asked. "It's pretty tall."

Again his grandfather didn't respond, only breathing heavily as they ascended the hill. He didn't understand why the old man had grown silent. Had he said something wrong? Clark decided to keep quiet, not wanting to annoy his grandfather.

Just before reaching the crest of the hill, his grandfather stopped in his tracks, head tilting back.

Clark glanced from him to the sky above. Was the old man analysing the clouds, concerned about the storm? Clark grew worried too.

Grampa's face twisted, his jaw grimacing, as if something had frightened him. He dropped the rope to the toboggan and grabbed at the front of his jacket, as if trying to tear through the fabric.

"Grampa?"

The old man keeled over onto his side in the snow.

"Grampa!"

Clark rushed to where he had fallen, kneeling down beside him. His grandfather's eyelids fluttered, his right hand flapping around in the snow like a trout pulled from an ice fishing hole. Drool dribbled out of one corner of his crooked mouth. Tears welled up in Clark's eyes as he set his hands on his grandfather's shoulder, shaking it gently.

"What's wrong, Grampa!" The tears flowed down over his cold cheeks. He couldn't tell if the old man knew he was there.

All Clark could think was that he needed help. But they were in the woods. Where could he find help out here? A thought burrowed into his brain. *No one knows where we are.* His father's words came back to him: *Look out for your grampa.*

What to do? What to do?

Clark looked at the toboggan and the tree strapped to it. He went to it and began untying the rope. It was fortunate his grandfather's fingers hadn't been able to tie very tight knots. Still, it seemed to take forever before he got the last knot undone and shoved the tree off the sled. He pulled the toboggan over beside his grandfather and with great effort, rolled the old man onto it.

Grampa's eyes were now closed, but his chest still rose and fell. Clark tied the rope across his grandfather's chest, waist and legs. He stood up, grabbing the rope, and began to pull. The toboggan wouldn't budge. It didn't help that he was trying to pull it up a hill. That and the fact his grandfather weighed a bit more than that stupid tree.

Clark dug his heels into the snow and pulled again, straining with all his young might. The toboggan moved a few inches. He adjusted his feet and pulled back on the rope again. A few more inches. It went like this for the ten feet or so to the top of the hill. Clark tried to keep his tears submerged, but the slow pace frustrated and terrified him.

He finally reached the peak of the hill. Once they were over the crest, gravity took over and the toboggan picked up speed. It was going too fast and he had to jump out of the way as the sled careened by him down the hill, Grampa strapped in tight. Clark ran down the hill trying to catch up, stumbling and tumbling into the snow a couple times.

When he reached the stopped sled, Clark glanced at the path ahead, the one they had blazed on their way into the woods. It was mostly level, with just a few slight dips and rises. The hardest part should be over. But would he make it out in time? He looked down at his grandfather, who looked peaceful, as if he were taking one of his usual naps on the couch.

Clark stood, grabbing tight to the reins of the toboggan, bore down and began pulling. The snow fell heavier, and he worried it would bury the path they had made. He had to hurry. One foot in front of the other, he kept his head down and stayed the course, the weight seeming lighter.

He paused at the top of a slight incline, trying to catch his breath, looking around at the desolateness of the woods. His eyes caught something.

Through the snow-covered trees about a hundred yards behind him, there was movement. He brought a gloved hand to his forehead to keep the snow out as his eyes strained. There! He saw a figure standing between a pair of trees. It looked like a man. What was he doing out here? A walk in the woods? Didn't seem likely. Had he been looking for a tree too? He didn't appear dressed for a winter excursion. He wore a black coat, unbuttoned, exposing a red shirt tucked into black pants. He wasn't wearing a hat, his long white hair kicking up with a gust of wind.

Clark waved. "Hello!" he yelled at the man.

The man didn't move. No response at all.

Something's not right, Clark thought. Something was odd about this man.

The urgency to get his grandfather out of the woods increased, Clark grabbed the rope and began pulling the toboggan again. *Got to get out*, he repeated to himself. *Need to get Grampa somewhere safe.* Desperation spurred him on and he didn't want to look back. When he did, the figure wasn't there.

Clark was glad the tears had stopped. They had felt like cold streams down his face. Fear stifled them. He barely felt his feet in his boots, numb from either cold or fright. In fact his whole body felt disconnected, as if his thoughts were moving and his body just kept pace with them. He stopped, his breathing hard. He bent over and rested his hands on his knees, chest hurting. *Just a few seconds*, he told himself, *and then I'll keep going. But I need a moment. Just one moment.*

Clark heard a crow caw and looked up. He spotted the black bird in the sky to his right, swooping down to rest on a naked branch of a maple tree about fifty yards away. His eyes scanned down the thick trunk of the tree to the ground. Standing beside the tree was the man in the black coat and red shirt.

The sudden appearance startled Clark and a knot tightened in his chest. He stared at the man. The man stared back. He didn't understand the sensation that came over him, but he felt he knew what the man wanted, what he had come for.

Clark picked up the rope, not taking his eyes off the figure, and began pulling the sled, turning away. After several feet he looked back over his shoulder. The man was still there.

"You can't have him!" Clark yelled. "I won't let you take him!"

The man didn't move.

Clark turned away, legs pumping faster, the toboggan seeming lighter still as he focused on the path ahead, the one they had cut through the woods, which seemed like ages ago. *Keep moving. Can't stop. Keep moving.*

Clark came over another rise into a clearing and looked ahead. There was his grandfather's pickup parked on the side of the road. *But I don't know how to drive*, he thought, not even sure he'd be able to lift his grandfather into the vehicle.

He looked at the way he had come and the woods behind him. There was no sign of the man in the black coat. But Clark felt he was still out there somewhere, in the snow and the woods – waiting.

Clark looked back at the pickup and up and down the road. There was a house not too far away. That's where Clark went to get help.

Later that afternoon, while his grandfather lay in intensive care at the hospital the ambulance brought him to, Clark lay on his bed upstairs in his room staring at the snow globe Grampa gave him. He shook it and then held it in his palm, watching the snowflakes drift down over the trio of snowmen. The tall one in the top hat with the crooked nose and twisted grin stared out at him. It reminded him of the figure he saw in the woods. Did he really see that? *It was just your imagination*, he told himself. *He wasn't really there. He didn't want to take your grandfather. Then why isn't Grampa here? Why isn't he all right?*

Clark threw the snow globe across the room. It hit the wall and bounced off, dropping onto the carpeted floor with a thud. He had wanted it to shatter, but the glass was sturdier than he thought. Then he regretted it. It was a gift from Grampa and he jumped off the bed to retrieve it. There was a small crack at the top, but not enough to spring a leak. He set it on his desk, snow still swirling, and left his room, wanting to go outside, his nerves too churned up to sit still.

Once outdoors, he decided to build a snowman in his front yard. He needed to make one that had a happier face than the tall one in his snow globe. With the fresh snow that had been falling throughout the day, he managed to roll a large ball for the base of his snowman. In no time he placed a smaller ball on it for the middle, before working on getting a good-sized head. He had to dig under the snow near the road to find some rocks, gathering these up in his gloves. There were two small chunks of tar that he pushed into the snowman's head for eyes. The rocks he arranged in a curve to form a smile.

Clark heard the front door open and saw his mother emerge.

"I brought you a carrot for your snowman," she said, handing it to him. She hadn't put her coat on before coming out and was shivering, wearing only a stained apron over her blouse and slacks. She must have been in the kitchen cooking.

"Thanks," he muttered, taking the carrot from her. He stuck it in between the space below the eyes and above the mouth and stood back. The carrot was long and straight, with a sharp point.

"Doesn't that look nice," his mother said.

He nodded, agreeing, glad the carrot wasn't crooked like the one on the snowman in the globe. "Any word?"

"Your father called from the hospital. No news yet."

No news is good news, isn't that what they say?

"I can find an old hat for your snowman if you want."

"No thanks," he said quickly. He didn't want that. That reminded him too much of— "No."

"Okay," his mother replied. "I'm going back inside. It's freezing out here. Don't stay out too long. You'll catch a cold."

She left and he was glad to be alone again. Besides, he hadn't finished. He walked around to the trees on the side of his yard and found some dead branches on the ground. He picked up a couple and brought them over to the snowman, sticking them into the sides for arms. Now his snowman was complete. The branch for the right arm was bent in the middle and rose up, twigs at the end forming a misshapen hand. It made it look like the snowman was waving hello. Clark liked his happy snowman. But as he looked at it, he started to think that maybe the snowman was waving goodbye.

He went in the house, having had enough of snow for one day.

Clark, his sisters and his mother ate alone, waiting for word from the hospital. He had no appetite, but took mouthfuls of beef stew, slurping it down, not really tasting the meat. Not long after dinner, his father came through the door, his face grim.

Clark stormed out of the house after his father delivered the news, not believing that Grampa had died. He had saved him, pulled him through the woods in the storm, giving everything he had, keeping him away from the dark figure in the trees, bringing him to safety. What was all that for if he just died anyway? It wasn't fair. It wasn't right. He didn't deserve this.

Clark had rushed out without his coat and now found himself shivering. He wrapped his arms around himself, rubbing them to keep him warm. He wanted to go back inside to the heat of his home, but didn't want to see the others just yet. Didn't want to see his father and wonder if he'd let him down.

He walked over to his snowman. Something had changed. Maybe the snow had softened, because the right branch had slipped down, the arm no longer raised and waving, but sticking out…as if reaching. For what? Him?

Clark took a step back.

Some of the rocks that formed the mouth had fallen out, leaving now a gap-toothed grin instead of a smile.

And the carrot nose had broken, bent in the middle.

Clark stepped forward, swung his right hand, and knocked the head off onto the ground.

He looked at the headless snowman, whose arms seemed to wave in a panic.

Down on the ground, the grinning face with the crooked nose and deep black eyes stared up as if mocking him.

CHAPTER TWENTY-SIX

Tucker Jenks stirred from a state of semi-consciousness in the sleeper cab of his tractor-trailer. He wouldn't quite call it sleep, more a dazed condition. Who could sleep with the wind howling like that? If that was the wind. Its cry seemed more preternatural than natural in origin. He listened, the back of his head sunk into his pillow. *Why won't it stop calling me? Just leave me alone till this damn storm ends.*

He thought about how convenient this delivery run had been when he'd originally got the route. Zip up to New Hampshire with a load of toys and electronics for the department store and then he could make it to his sister's home in Cranford, New Jersey, in time for Christmas Eve cocktails. Now the storm had driven him farther north and he wouldn't even be able to make his friend's house. Once the roads got cleared tomorrow, he could try and turn around and head back to New Jersey. But that's not even where he wanted to be anymore. North Carolina was where he wanted to be. *The hell with this northern climate. They can keep it.*

A knocking sound came from outside.

Had those guys returned? He told them he was staying put. He didn't need to cram into some RV with everyone else. He had all the comforts he needed right here. Maybe they were worried about him. They didn't have to be. He wasn't worried about any of them.

Knock, knock.

Tucker lifted his head off the pillow.

Maybe the guys got in trouble out there, he thought. Could be they got lost, turned around in the storm and maybe never found their way back to the RV. Now they were out there knocking on the door of his cab, trying to get his help. They would be freezing. Tucker tried to think about how long it had been since they were here. How much time had passed? Out in this weather they would be near hypothermia, no matter how much they were bundled up.

Tucker sat up. He started to put his boots on when he heard the knock again.

It came from behind him.

It came from inside the trailer of his truck.

What the hell? Someone (or *something*) had gotten in there. How could that be? He had locked the truck, hadn't he? Of course he had. Or maybe not. Maybe after making his delivery at the department store, in his rush to get back on the road before the storm got worse, he had forgotten to lock the trailer door. Maybe those guys had sought refuge in the trailer, lost in the blinding whiteness of the snow.

There's only one way to find out, he said to himself, grabbing his boots and shoving his feet into them. *Go look. They must need help.* Something inside him thought this wasn't a good idea. The banshee was still howling outside, calling for someone's death. *Don't make it yours. Let some other idiot die out there. You're safe right now. Stay safe.*

Knock, knock.

Tucker looked at the back wall of his sleeper cab and started wondering about who, or what, might be on the other side in the trailer.

"Damn!" he uttered. *Be a fool,* he thought as he put his coat, gloves and hat on. *Be a stupid fool.*

Once outside, he instantly regretted it, the cold clawing at his face with icy nails, the wind sucking the breath from his throat, crystallised snow stinging his eyes. Stepping down, he sank into the snow up to his crotch. It took extreme effort for his legs and thighs to plough a path through the snow, stopping at the juncture where his cab connected to the trailer, which angled off at forty-five degrees.

Tucker kept his left hand on the side of the trailer as he pushed through the snow, afraid if he let go, he'd wander off and get lost. The connection made him feel secure, grounded to something real in the surreal atmosphere of this blinding whirlwind of weather.

How could there be so much snow? Damn! He longed for North Carolina and Nana's house, where the rare snowfall occurred every so often, but never like this. *No need to worry about shit like this,* he thought.

Though wasn't it Nana who told you the stories about the banshee that haunted the woods along the river? But those were just stories.

The wind howled.

Nana told those stories to a curious boy to give him chills on a lonely night in the Black Mountain woods. They weren't real, and North Carolina was a long way from here.

But couldn't the banshee follow you?

Look at where you are now, on a lonely road in the woods, with a river running nearby. Maybe the banshee followed you here, chasing after you like some vengeful spirit. But why would the banshee want him? Why would she need to warn him? He had done nothing.

Tucker reached the back end of the trailer truck. The door was closed. He looked in the snow but saw no disturbances. If someone had opened it up to climb in, they had left no tracks.

No tracks, so go back.

Looking back, down the highway, he could see the shapes of the vehicles stuck on the turnpike behind him. They were nothing more than rounded humps in the snow. He couldn't see any sign of an RV.

How far back was it? He wondered if he should make his way there. Maybe the security of other people would be better. And he could forget about the noise inside the trailer.

But of course he wouldn't.

Because you're stupid. Didn't Nana say that to him when he did something senseless. *Don't be a stupid boy,* she'd say. *Where's your brains at?*

He grabbed the metal handle of the trailer door latch. It was frozen tight and he jerked it a couple times, trying to unlatch it. *See, of course no one could have gotten in here. Leave it well enough alone and get your ass out of there.*

Tucker tried one more time and the latch released. He rolled the door open, the rattling of the wheels on the track barely heard amid the screams of the storm. He climbed up into the trailer, exerting great effort, his legs feeling stiff from the cold of the night, his soaked pants hardening like cardboard.

At the far end of the trailer, buried in shadows, was a large box.

Hmmm…. He remembered emptying the contents of the trailer at the department store. There had been nothing left over, just some empty pallets stacked up on the side. This trailer should be empty. There shouldn't be anything here.

"What the hell?"

The square cardboard box was about four feet tall and the same wide. He couldn't have forgotten it, no way.

Then where did this come from? *Don't be a stupid boy,* Nana said. *Of course you forgot it. Why else would it be here in your truck? You're going to be in trouble for forgetting to make a delivery.*

No. He emptied the truck. Of course he did. *Where's your brains at?* Nana asked.

What if it was something important, something the store needed very badly? But it was too late now. The store would be closed; it was already Christmas morning.

Christmas!

Maybe this was a present. Maybe it was something the truck company left for him, like a Christmas bonus.

Don't be stupid.

It's Christmas morning. Go ahead and open your box.

Forgetting the storm behind him and the snow cascading down from the night sky beyond the open trailer door, Tucker shuffled farther into darkness toward the box.

Standing before it, looking down, he noticed the top of the box wasn't taped or stapled closed.

That's not right, he thought. *That's against regulations. All cargo should be secured.* Who had left this box open?

Tucker reached a gloved hand toward the top of the box.

He felt an excitement in his chest, a sensation of exhilaration, like a boy on Christmas morning. Isn't that what he was now? A boy? A stupid boy?

The wind screamed behind him, startling him, and he turned.

The open end of the trailer seemed far behind him. Too far, as if the trailer had elongated and stretched itself out. If the door started to close on its own, there was no way he'd be able to run fast enough to reach it and he'd be trapped inside here. With the box.

Don't be stupid.

What was the scream out there? Was it her? The banshee?

The snow outside the door whipped around in circles, dancing on the wind, the thick flakes shuffling to and fro. The flakes shined, like constellations in the night sky. He could almost make a shape out of them, like seeing images in a cloud.

A face appeared. No, not appeared. Forming. Somehow the flitting flakes were constructing a shape in the air, something moving and writhing, pulled and tugged by the different directions of a fickle wind. The snow mesmerised him, transfixing his gaze. He raised a hand, as if reaching for it.

He started to forget about the box behind him. His present. He just wanted to stare at the snow and how it was forming a....

A figure.

There was a face in the snow. It looked like a beautiful face, a woman's face with dazzling eyes and a leering smile. Tendrils of snow formed a flowing white gown made of silk, trailing behind the figure as it floated in the air just beyond the entrance of the trailer door. It was calling to him, or was that the wind? A soothing cry, almost like a song. He wanted to just stand there and enjoy the vision and its wailing tune.

He smiled. Though he couldn't even feel his lips move because of how numb his face had become in the freezing cold, he was pretty certain he was smiling.

The face in the snow changed. The flakes thickened as the figure bobbed in the snow, and the face seemed to pull apart and reshape itself. It was no longer the beautiful banshee. It was...what? *What are you becoming?*

Then he saw it. His nana's face, with the look of anger she got when he had done something wrong, something stupid.

And she screamed.

Maybe it was just the wind, whipped up in a furious frenzy. But the face leered forward, a mouth opening, and screamed: *Run!*

Tucker broke from the gaze that gripped him and turned to look behind him.

One flap of the cardboard box lip was open.

Metal rattled behind him as the trailer door began to slide down.

Tucker turned to run, but his legs wouldn't move. The wet pants had frozen stiff, as if his lower half had become encased in cement. The top half of his body lunged forward while the bottom half remained still. He tipped over, falling on his face on the floor of the trailer. He could hear the cracking of his pants as his legs shifted, his knees finally able to bend and his legs pushing his heavy body up.

He ran for the door that descended slowly on its frozen tracks.

Not going to make it, he thought. His body just couldn't move fast enough. Too much fast food on the road had made him out of shape. It was going to cost him. The door kept coming down, shutting out the night and the swirling snow that dominated it.

I'm going to be too late.

As his momentum picked up, and he got closer to the edge of the trailer, he saw the gap narrowing as the door neared the bottom.

Tucker dove forward, hurtling his body into a headfirst slide.

He slid out the opening and dropped into the snow outside as he heard the trailer door slam down with a *thunk*, like the snapping of jaws.

Tucker lay in the snow, looking up at the back of the trailer, unable to move. The latch locked itself when the door shut.

Just lie here, he thought, staring at the door. It suddenly felt warm with his body sunk down deep into the snow. *Lie here and be comfortable, the snow drifting down over you, covering you like a warm blanket. Let it bury you. They can find you in the morning when help comes. They'll find you with a smile on your face, but it will be too late for you.*

The banshee screamed again.

Tucker's eyes popped open. He hadn't realised they'd been closed. He struggled to his feet, knowing he needed to get back inside the cab of his truck and get warm. He used his right hand to feel the side of the trailer as he retraced the path back the way he had come. It took longer, his legs stiff and numb, barely able to move. He kept listening, worried he would hear the trailer door opening again. The only sound was the wind and he was grateful.

He reached the cab of his truck and stepped up onto the runner, trying to grab the door handle but his frozen fingers had trouble co-operating. He was worried he had gotten this close but wouldn't be able to get the door open and end up freezing to death out here, but then his fingers wrapped around the handle and he pulled. The door opened.

Before he clambered inside, he heard the banshee scream one more time.

Tucker turned to look behind him, toward the woods on the opposite side of the highway. On a small hill before the edge of the woods, he saw three figures. They looked like snowmen, the one in the middle taller than the two beside it. The middle one had a top hat perched on its head. A scarf wrapped around its neck fluttered in the wind. A stick arm poking out of its right side also bobbed in the wind.

It looked like it was waving at him.

CHAPTER TWENTY-SEVEN

Mason Drake was fuming inside, irritation gnawing at his innards over the fact Joy had given that woman's kids the Christmas gifts they had bought earlier tonight. He knew he couldn't protest without looking like a dick, so he bit his tongue and kept his annoyance buried. Maybe his wife could read his eyes, or his body language. If so, that was good. He wanted her to know he was pissed she had done that. The whole reason they had ended up stuck in this storm was because they took the time to get those gifts at the department store.

Now she had given them away, so it was all for nothing. And here they were, crammed into this vehicle with a bunch of strangers, listening to their tales of winter woes. He hoped no one else had one like that Clark guy. Mason didn't believe for a second most of the guy's far-fetched story. It seemed more suited for an October night around a campfire than Christmas Eve. Hell, even he could top that if they wanted to hear about a crappy winter.

"Who would like to go next?" Francine asked, as if reading his thoughts.

Mason looked around at the others, hesitating to see who else might have something to share. The stringy-haired Salvation Army guy, Felker, looked uncomfortable, fidgeting in his seat across from him. He had locked eyes with Mason a couple of times since they'd got inside the RV and looked agitated. Mason smelled booze on the guy. He had a good sense for that, spending all those years checking on his parolees. They could never pull one over on him. He knew this guy wasn't going to speak up.

Clark's friend, Graham, who sat beside Felker, held a smile that Mason thought looked like a cover-up. Hiding something, Mason suspected. He seemed to be in too good a spirit for the mess they were in. Over on the couch, beside Clark, the kids' mother appeared restless. Mason could tell she liked that Clark guy, had noticed her inching a bit closer to him. But her face looked grim right now, and Mason felt she had a story in her past she didn't feel like sharing.

"Anyone?" Werner asked from the front of the RV.

"I've got one," Mason said, realising no one else was going to make an offering. He sensed Joy's eyes upon him but did not acknowledge her attention. She knew what story he was going to tell, had heard it before many years ago. "My worst winter memory happened when I was a teenager."

Mason had been returning from skiing one winter night with two of his buddies, Selden Crockett and Trent Cronin. It was after midnight. The trio had spent a long night on the slopes taking runs up until the final lift. Selden had brought a wineskin filled with cinnamon schnapps. It had been a great night on the mountain, crushing black diamonds and impressing some of the snow bunnies. They even went off trail a couple of times, making sure the ski patrol didn't notice, and cut some virgin paths through the woods. Selden usually took the lead on those. He was the crazy one.

It was exhilarating but exhausting and Mason was dozing in the front passenger seat on the way back, with Trent driving. Selden was still jacked up a bit, sitting in the back seat but leaning up over the front between the two of them, reliving some of the highlights of the night with a laugh.

Mason remembered wishing he'd just shut up. Sometimes Selden could be a bit much, especially when everyone else was winding down. He just didn't seem to have a cool-down button.

The car was barreling down Route 115 and Mason never noticed Trent was drifting. He was probably just as tired as Mason, and maybe Mason should have been a better copilot considering how late it was. The curve in the road came up suddenly, and when Trent realised the tyres were crossing the fog line, he overcorrected. They hit black ice and the car went sideways.

Mason had always heard about how car accidents happened in slow motion, but it wasn't the case for him. He looked at Trent's face concentrating on getting the car under control, but out the driver's side window the frozen lake loomed large and before he knew it the car was flipping.

Mason reached out, trying to brace himself, at the same time wondering if he had his seat belt on. The crack of the ice as the roof of the car hit it was sharp, like a thunderclap, and the next thing Mason knew, icy water was pouring around him. How he got himself upright and oriented he wasn't sure. He didn't even know how he got out the door. He just remembered standing waist-deep in frigid water, but the adrenaline pumping through his body kept him warm. He didn't feel the cold.

The wheels on the car were still spinning, just above the hole in the ice the vehicle had plunged through. The bank of the lake was just a few feet away, and Mason made for it without even thinking of the others. *Damn you, Trent*, he thought as he reached the shore. *What the fuck have you done?*

Once on shore, he realised Trent was beside him. He hadn't even noticed him getting out of the car or running through the water. It was all just crazy. Looking at his friend, he had the sudden urge to break out laughing. Maybe because that was what Trent was doing, as if the whole thing was one big riot. But as he started to join Trent in the hilarity of the fucked-up situation they just escaped, he realised Selden wasn't with them.

They both looked back at the car and starting screaming his name.

But Selden wasn't there.

That's when things began to finally slow down. The rest of the night became a haze. Someone in a nearby house had heard the crash and called for help. Police, fire and ambulances arrived. Under protest, Mason and Trent were put into an ambulance and taken to the hospital. If he had hypothermia, he wasn't feeling it. He wasn't feeling anything, just numbness.

His parents picked him up at the hospital and when he got back home, he drove to the scene of the accident. A small crowd was still gathered across the road from the hole in the ice. The car had been towed away, but rescue divers were still in the water.

Even at his young age, Mason knew it wasn't a rescue anymore. It was a recovery.

Some kids from high school were among the dwindling crowd, but no one approached him. That was good. He wanted to stand this vigil on his own. And he wouldn't leave. He ended up not having long to wait.

They brought Selden's body out of the water, his sandy hair slicked back, his face pale, frozen arms outreached as if waiting for an embrace. They laid his body on the side of the road, and the stiffness of it struck Mason as fake, like a mannequin.

Put your arms down, he thought as he looked at what was left of his friend. *You look like an idiot, put your arms down*. Selden's hands were clenched into fists.

Mason wanted to yell, scream, run from the scene.

But something kept him there, waiting until they took his friend away.

Mason didn't think any part of this horrid event could be any worse. But the next day, he heard that the divers found Selden's body way out toward the middle of the pond. The authorities figured he swam out of the car and became disoriented underwater, unable to find the hole in the ice the car had broken. They said he must have felt around the ice, looking for the hole, but kept swimming farther away from it.

Was that why the arms on his frozen body were raised, his hands balled into fists? Was he trying to break his way through the ice?

CHAPTER TWENTY-EIGHT

Joy caressed her husband's arm, surprised he had shared that story and wanting to comfort him, knowing how difficult a tale it was for him to tell. She knew the story still bothered him, even waking him from an occasional nightmare, especially on those cold winter nights when a fierce wind blew.

Seeing his distressed expression when he finished his story made her regret even more what had happened with Jerome at her office party. Joy looked at her husband's soft eyes and thought she didn't deserve him. She needed to be better.

He didn't look toward her as she admired the lines on his face, the strength of his bearded jaw. He was a strong man whose heart was still softened by that horrible memory.

Joy knew exactly how he felt. She was someone who could relate to that and he knew it. Maybe that was what had brought them so close in the first place when they'd met so long ago. They didn't share right away, but when the time was right, it turned out they were both haunted by similar tragic stories. It became a bond, something they both had endured alone, but the relationship they forged allowed them to share that pain.

She wouldn't share that story tonight. No, not with these people. That was one difference between her and Mason. She still kept her story between the two of them.

The fact that her story involved a night of skiing was beyond ironic. It was one more thing to connect them. Her friend was named Quinn Bowie. Not a boyfriend, just probably the closest male friend she'd ever had. They always joked about hooking up some day as the two of them traipsed through the tribulations of young adult life, giving each other helpful advice with endless attempts at securing a meaningful relationship, and being there for comfort when those failed miserably.

But they remained just friends, and it was probably better that way, not to move beyond that boundary and risk losing what they had. Because what they had was perfect, but it didn't prevent her from wondering.

That night on the mountain was just another example of how much she enjoyed their time together. If only a suitor could provide that much contentment. Quinn was the one who taught her how to ski. He convinced her to eschew taking lessons and let him bring her up to one of the ski areas in the state. He was patient and considerate, never getting frustrated with her as she took tumble after tumble before finally getting the hang of it. And once she did, they spent many nights, often on the spur of the moment, heading to the slopes when neither of them had other social engagements.

Quinn was an accomplished skier, and she learned a lot just trying to keep up with him. He liked to go fast, but never left her behind, making sure he reined it in enough for her to keep up, even when it meant sticking to the intermediate trails instead of the black diamond ones he preferred.

It was the last run that awful night, when Quinn convinced her to try one of the more experienced trails. She sat beside him in the chairlift with butterflies in her stomach. But somehow, he soothed her, removing most but not all of her fears. He made her feel safe. On that ride up the ski lift, she started to wonder if maybe they shouldn't try to be more than just friends.

They were off the ski lift in a flash and Joy was amazed she was able to keep up with him as they swooshed down the slopes. It was a good thing it was so late that there was hardly anyone else on this trail. It made it easier for her not having to worry about running into another skier. She knew Quinn could go much faster, but was glad he made sure not to get too far ahead, looking back over his shoulder every now and then to make sure she was okay.

It was one of those glances back at her when Quinn must have hit some bump or icy spot in the snow, and soon his body was flailing. He tried to regain his balance, but at that speed it was no use and he pitched forward, slamming into the ground and barreling over several times.

When he finally came to a stop, near the edge of the trail, Joy headed for where he lay, surprised she was able to keep her composure enough to concentrate on what she was doing. She wasn't too concerned at first. Quinn was a great skier, so she was sure he knew how to take a tumble.

It couldn't be the first time he had fallen. She almost expected him to pop up laughing before she even reached him.

He did manage to push himself up on all fours by the time she came to a stop by his side. Joy didn't get a chance to even ask him if he was all right. She heard a gurgling sound, and as he lifted his head, she screamed.

Quinn's ski pole had snapped in half during his fall, and the jagged end had been thrust into his throat. Blood was pouring out the wound, even as Quinn brought his gloved hands up around it, trying to stem the flow. In the light cast down from the lampposts on the trail, she could see a stream of blood flow down the slope from where he kneeled. In the dimness of the night, the blood looked black, as if Quinn's shadow was melting.

Joy often thought about what she could have done different. Maybe if she had tried to find something to wrap around the ski pole in his neck to staunch the flow of blood, he wouldn't have bled to death on the mountain slope in front of her. But all she did was scream for help. By the time it came, it was too late.

So the fact that she and her husband had suffered separate tragic losses as a result of a night of skiing was an odd occurrence to bond over. But it somehow brought them together, and right now, as this horrible storm raged outside, trapping them in this vehicle, there was no one she would feel safer with than Mason.

But she would not share her story with the rest.

CHAPTER TWENTY-NINE

Lewis Felker played with the brim of his Salvation Army cap, which rested on the table in front of him. He listened to these people's stories, thinking they knew nothing of horror. Some old man dies of a heart attack in the woods. Big deal. And what was that hogwash about a dark figure following them through the forest? What was that pretty boy trying to insinuate? That someone had come to collect his grandfather?

Felker shivered.

He thought about the figure he had seen in the snow tonight and its apparent resemblance to the Iceman who slaughtered all those people years ago. Could this Clark guy have seen the same man Felker had when he was a boy? Or was it all a strange coincidence? There were too many bizarre things going on tonight, and it made him want another drink.

If they wanted him to share his story, that's what it was going to cost them.

Felker cleared his throat, and everyone's heads turned toward him.

"I have something to tell," he said in a raspy voice. "But I'm a little parched right now. Something to soothe the gullet would be helpful." He shifted his eyes back and forth between the Volkmanns.

"Why of course," Werner said, getting up from his captain's seat and sauntering over to one of the cupboards above the refrigerator. He took down the bottle of bourbon, unscrewed the cap and poured a healthy amount into Felker's empty cocoa mug.

The old man smiled down at him as Felker licked the top of his chapped lip. He brought the mug to his mouth and took a swallow. It ignited his mouth and was hot going down his throat. It was his turn to smile.

"Anyone else like some?" Werner asked, glancing around.

"Sure," Mason said, offering his empty mug, which Werner gladly filled.

That was what Felker was afraid of, and he glared across the table at Mason. He didn't want others horning in on what little booze probably remained in the RV. Especially this guy who didn't even want to drop a few bucks into his Salvation Army pot but had no problem spoiling his kids with last-minute Christmas gifts. Besides, Felker might need a few strong belts to get through his story.

"I had a horrid winter one year," he began, "back when I was a much younger man."

It was nighttime that long winter ago, when Lewis Felker and his friend Brodie Kane went snowmobiling on a trail off Route 107. The two had met in rehab, both trying to kick alcohol addiction. It didn't work for either of them and once they finished their preliminary stint at the facility in Manchester, they hung out together, usually at dive bars.

Felker's brother-in-law owned a snowmobile that Lewis used to borrow some winters, back before he went into rehab. One night, he convinced his relative that his stint in rehab had changed him, and the guy reluctantly let him borrow the snowmobile again. It was a mistake.

The moon was full and reflected off the smooth snow of the trail the night Felker took Brodie out for a ride. They drank the whole drive to the trailhead, where they unloaded the snowmobile and Brodie jumped onto the seat behind him. Trees lined both sides of the trail that cut through the woods. Felker had the snowmobile cranked as it sped across the snow, its headlight beam piercing the darkness to guide the way down the narrow path. He could hear Brodie laughing behind him as they picked up speed.

Up ahead the trail curved to the left, but Felker knew a path shot off from the trail into a farm field. It was a shortcut he had taken before, and it allowed him to really rev the machine up across the open field and then pick up the trail again on the other side.

He slowed the sled down slightly, not wanting to miss the cutoff.

"Hang on!" he yelled over his shoulder to Brodie, who continued laughing.

The opening was there, and as Felker steered the machine into it, he could see the open field about fifty yards ahead. He let out a laugh as he gunned the throttle and the snowmobile shot forward. He knew he could catch some air coming out into the field if he got his speed up enough. He wanted to scare the shit out of Brodie.

As the machine raced toward the opening, Felker grinned madly.

The moonlight glinted off something ahead.

Felker's face froze in mid-grin. It was barbed wire.

He had no time to slow down, no time to hit the brakes. He only had time to shout "Duck!", and then he dropped his head down beneath the protective shield on the front of the snowmobile. The machine tore through the barbed wire fence and it did get airborne, rotating a quarter turn to the right side, and his body went flying.

Felker landed in the snow, about thirty feet into the field. The snowmobile continued on past him another fifty feet before landing upside down in the snow, the engine sputtering out.

I don't feel anything, Felker thought. *No pain, I'm not hurt.* He was afraid to move at first, lying on his back in the snow, looking up at the stars in the night sky and the bright moon that had probably saved his life. *I'm okay*, he thought. *I'm really okay.*

Someone was screaming.

That's not me, is it? Felker thought. *I'm not screaming, am I?*

No. The screaming was coming back toward the edge of the woods. Something told him Brodie hadn't ducked.

Felker got to his feet somehow, reassuring himself that nothing was wrong with him, no broken bones. He ran back toward the way they had come, toward the tangle of torn barbed-wire fence and the sound of the screaming.

When he got to Brodie's prone body, lying on his back at the edge of the woods, he stared down, cursing the full moon that now cast a spotlight on his friend in the snow. Either the cold air or the vision of horror before him snatched the breath from his throat.

Brodie's arms were spread-eagled and his body was surrounded by splashes of red soaking into the whiteness of the snow. But the brightest red was on the face of his friend, or rather where his face used to be.

The barbed wire must have caught Brodie right under the chin, and the speed they were travelling had peeled the skin completely off his face, leaving a mask of pulsing red muscles and tendons surrounding the hole in the middle that was the source of the screaming.

Felker took another swallow from his mug and the others in the RV stared at him aghast, faces pale. No one uttered a word.

"He lived," Felker continued when he set his mug back down. "They even managed to reattach his face, though now he has an ugly scar running down around the edge of his face like a chinstrap." He tipped the mug back, draining the rest of the bourbon, before setting it back hard on the table. "That was my worst winter," he said. "Till this one, that is."

CHAPTER THIRTY

Shelby looked on in horror when Lewis Felker finished his winter tale. Clark could see the lines of anguish etched in her tired face. He reached over and patted her leg in an instinctive act of comfort.

"What's wrong with all of you?" she said to everyone, though her eyes never turned from Felker. "What horrible stories. Why would you tell them?"

Clark hoped she didn't include his tale along with the others. His might have had a tragic outcome, but it certainly didn't contain the lurid elements the others embodied.

"It's just a way of passing the time," Werner Volkmann said.

"Yes," his wife concurred. "To show that we've all had worse winter experiences than the one we're having. It's a way of finding hope in a dreadful situation. To know we've all endured much worse."

Clark didn't think Francine's explanation did much to soothe Shelby's current state. He kept his hand on the top of her thigh, sensing she didn't mind and enjoyed its comfort. She even shot a half smirk his way, as if to say it was appreciated.

"Maybe you'd care to share a story," Francine said.

Clark watched Shelby's face shift from an expression of bewilderment to one of resentment. She had a story, he could tell. But it seemed something buried too far down for her to want to unearth. He was sure it was distressing.

"You don't have to," he said, patting her leg again.

She turned to him now with a full smile and eyes that seemed to get reassurance from his. But still the smile seemed sad.

"I'm not going to," she said, as much to him as to the others. "Some memories are best kept to myself. Right now I think I'll check on the kids."

She rose and Clark felt disappointed she was leaving his side, but she surprised him when she turned and asked him to accompany her. He felt awkward and wasn't sure how to respond. Still, he followed her to the back room, noticing the smirk from Graham and a disturbing leer from Lewis Felker.

Once in the back bedroom, Shelby softly closed the door behind them, her face now only a dark silhouette before him.

"I wanted to tell you something," she whispered, after a quick glance back at her sleeping children on the bed. "I went to high school with you."

"Really?" he said in disbelief.

She laughed. "I was only a freshman, and you were a senior, so you wouldn't have known me. Plus I was kind of homely back then, skinny and a mouth full of braces."

"That's so funny."

"I kind of had a crush on you," she continued. "I remember you being on the hockey team, and I worried your handsome face would get smashed in or you'd lose a few teeth."

He chuckled at that. "I was a bit reckless on the ice sometimes."

Shelby smiled. "I just wanted a moment alone to tell you that, if I had to be trapped in a god-awful mess like this, I'm really glad it's you that's here."

And then before he had a chance to respond, she leaned up and planted a soft gentle kiss on his cheek. Clark was so taken by surprise, he didn't know what to say.

"We'll get through this," he said, taking her hand. "And when it's all over, we'll be able to look back at it as a special night." He hoped he didn't sound too corny.

"I'll let you get back to the others," she said. "Think I'll lie with the kids for a bit."

When he left the room and retook his position on the bench seat, he felt a touch of sadness she was not in the room. He enjoyed the comfort of her next to him and the glances they exchanged. It confused him to have feelings like this surface in such a bizarre predicament. He wasn't sure how to proceed with it. Unfortunately, there wasn't much he could do. They were snowbound in a confined space under extreme circumstances. It left him with a feeling of helplessness. He wanted to be strong and take some kind of leadership role. He just didn't know what to do.

"Anyone else have anything?" Francine asked. "How about you, Mrs. Drake?"

Joy had been resting her head against her husband's shoulder, and now looked up as if jostled out of sleep. "Oh no," she said, peering up at her husband. "I don't think so." Mason patted her hand and she dropped her head back onto his shoulder.

"Mr. Sawyer?"

Clark looked at his friend. Sure Graham had a story, and it was probably more tragic than anyone else's here, but would he tell it?

Graham grinned back at Mrs. Volkmann. "Gee, I don't know."

The old woman peered closer. "You must have something. Everyone in New England has experienced some horrible winter. You can't be an exception."

Graham was silent, seeming to study the woman, but maybe just reaching back into his memories, way back. Like with Shelby, Clark could see the pain on his friend's face. Even though Clark knew the story, he didn't ever recall his friend telling it to anyone. He doubted he would in this circumstance, but maybe it would help him purge the pain associated with it.

"Most of my winter memories are pleasant," Graham said.

Clark knew he was lying.

"All of them?" Francine asked.

"I really like the season. It's one of the reasons I stayed in New Hampshire. It's just a beautiful part of the country." He looked around the table at the others as if wanting to disperse any disbelief. "Seriously. My wife, Natalie, and I have three daughters and we made sure they all learned to ski and ice-skate so we could enjoy the season. And last Christmas, we bought snowshoes for all of us, so we could take winter hikes on some of the wooded trails."

"And nothing bad has ever happened to you?" Werner asked this in what sounded like a tone of disbelief.

Graham shrugged. "Not really."

Don't tell them, Clark thought. *Don't give them the satisfaction. Don't let them push you.*

Graham looked down at his clasped hands in contemplation and then raised his head. "There was one thing that comes to mind. It happened when I was a kid."

Clark braced himself for the story that was about to come, but it wasn't what he had been expecting.

"In middle school there was this bully by the name of Leroy Sledge. You remember him, Clark, right?"

He nodded, too surprised to vocalise an answer, wondering why Graham had chosen to tell this story.

"He thought he was a big shot," Graham continued, "just because his family was rich. They were the founders of the Sledge & Ferrin Game Company in Manchester. He used to brag about it all the time. He looked down on the other kids. Plus, he was bigger than our classmates, I think because he stayed back in school a couple years. He may have been well-bred, but he wasn't very bright. But he always talked about how he was going to inherit the company when he grew up, and we'd all end up working for him some day, just like a lot of our parents. He was a snot. We all tried to just stay out of his way, especially out on the playground at lunch or recess. But avoiding him was not always possible. Right, Clark?"

Indeed, Clark knew the day Graham was going to talk about. It was lunchtime and everyone was out in the playground. Clark and Graham and a bunch of their friends were playing king of the hill on top of this huge pile of snow from where the ploughs had cleared the hot top in front of the school. As usual, Clark and Graham had managed to keep their perch on top of the hill, tossing back down any of their friends who tried to usurp their claim.

They worked together as a team, but there could be only one true king, so when the bell rang to signal the end of recess, Clark gave Graham a shove and watched him tumble down the side of the mound, laughing when his friend landed at the bottom. Clark pumped his fist in the air, claiming his throne.

He descended the hill to prepare to head back inside the school, approaching where Graham lay, extending his hand to help his friend up.

"Screw you," Graham said, his pride hurt.

"It's called king of the hill, not kings," was all the answer Clark could offer before shaking his head and walking away. He knew his friend wouldn't be mad long and soon they'd be yucking it up in math class, if that was possible.

He turned to look back at his friend, just in time to see that Graham had risen and was winding up to launch a snowball at him. Clark saw the snowball hurling toward him and ducked. A look of fright came over Graham's face that Clark didn't understand until he turned around and realised the snowball that missed him had struck Leroy Sledge in the side of the face.

Leroy's face was red, not just from the impact of the snowball, but because of the anger that flared up inside him. He charged toward Graham like a locomotive and Clark yelled for his friend to run. Graham took off, with Leroy close on his heels.

Rubber snow boots were not very conducive to running, but Graham gave it his best effort, though there really wasn't any place to go. Clark followed after the duo, not sure what he could do except make sure someone was there to witness whatever came next. Graham raced around the playground, zigzagging, hoping to throw the enraged Leroy off his track, but the bully kept pace. Clark followed them down toward the ball field beside the school.

The three of them weaved in and out of the crowd of students filing into the building, some shouting encouraging words to Graham, others egging Leroy on. Nothing like a good schoolyard fight. Graham was a good athlete, and would eventually end up playing basketball and baseball in high school, but that day on the playground he just plum ran out of gas.

Down in the ball field he stopped, turning to face his pursuer.

"I give up," Graham said, raising his hands in a surrender pose.

Leroy bore down and charged into him, like a football lineman sacking a quarterback, throwing his shoulder into Graham's midsection and driving him into the snow. It was a good thing there was plenty of it on the ground, because it blunted the force of the impact when Graham landed with Leroy's stocky frame on top of him. Graham must have gotten the wind knocked out of him, because Clark did not hear him cry out.

By the time Clark got to them, still not sure what he could do about anything, Leroy had flipped Graham over onto his stomach and had grabbed a fistful of the back of his friend's hair. Leroy proceeded to give Graham a whitewash, shoving his face into the snow and rubbing it back and forth with a fury.

"Enough!" someone yelled behind Clark, an adult, one of the male teachers who had been assigned playground duty.

Leroy gave one final shove of Graham's face into the snow, and then rose off him. He shot Clark a deathly glare as he walked by, as if to say: 'You're next.' Clark trembled in his boots, relieved to have escaped some retribution, even if just for the moment.

Clark went over to where Graham lay, his friend struggling up to his knees. Graham's eyes were wet with tears, snow still clinging to his face, blood streaming from his nose. In the snow before him was the impression of his face, red smeared in the slushy mess.

Looking back, it all seemed silly, and now Graham laughed at the experience in the RV with the others as he finished the story. What bothered Clark was that it wasn't the story he should have told.

"That's it?" Felker asked, with a hint of disgust, looking down his pointy nose at Graham beside him with repugnance.

Clark thought about how the man's friend had his face ripped off and understood his disappointment, but if he only knew the story Graham withheld, he'd think different.

"Did the bully get punished?" Joy asked.

"I seem to remember he got suspended from school," Graham said, looking to Clark for confirmation.

"Sounds right," Clark said. "But then he was always getting kicked out of school, especially in high school. Got in a lot of fights. Think he eventually got expelled from school for drugs and stuff."

"Guess his rich family couldn't save him," Joy said.

"What did you say his name was?" Mason asked, his face intrigued.

"Leroy Sledge."

"The game family?"

"Right. Sledge & Ferrin Games. They make all kinds of board games, puzzles and stuff."

Mason sat back in his seat, his face bewildered.

"Everyone knows those games. They make everything. Huge company."

"I know," Mason said. "It's just…weird coincidence."

"What?"

"I know Leroy Sledge."

"You do?"

"I did. I was his parole officer."

CHAPTER THIRTY-ONE

Graham stared across the table at Mason Drake, stunned by the revelation, feeling like something nasty was crawling around in his stomach. This was beyond bizarre. Normally, he'd dismiss this as some freak coincidence, but coupled with what he'd seen in the snowplough and Felker's statement about the highway being gone, he felt on the verge of some unexplainable phenomenon, as if reality had tilted onto its side.

Play it cool, he told himself. *Don't overreact. We're safe in here, that's all that matters.* He just hoped that was true.

"That is very odd," was the response he flatly delivered. The fact that Leroy Sledge ended up having a parole officer was certainly no surprise. Graham guessed the family money had not been enough to keep him out of prison. Leroy was nothing but trouble in high school and never finished. That was the last Graham had heard of the boy. He figured the kid would end up on his feet eventually, given the family he came from.

"Sledge, huh?" Felker said beside him.

Graham turned.

"I know that name too."

Whatever was crawling inside Graham's belly sent reverberations along his sensory nerves, causing a prickling sensation all over his skin. What was going on here? He quickly shot a glance at Clark, who met his gaze with an equal amount of bewilderment. His friend said nothing however, apparently just as stunned. Graham looked back at Felker.

"How the hell do you know him?" he asked.

"I think it's the same guy," Felker said with a shrug. "Sounds like the name. I work at the Salvation Army homeless shelter. Guy named Sledge lived there for a bit a year ago. I caught him picking a guy's pocket while the man was sleeping and had him kicked out. We take people in all kinds of helpless situations, but we don't tolerate thieves."

Graham stared at Felker, thinking this man looked like he could live at a homeless shelter, and maybe he had at one time given the background to the story he told. Quite possibly that's how he'd started working for the Salvation Army.

"I'm speechless," Graham said, looking at Clark. "Can you believe this?"

Clark shook his head. "It's unreal. But it has to be a coincidence. Nothing more."

"Sure," Graham said, nodding, though he didn't believe it for a minute. And locking eyes with Felker, he could tell the man didn't think so either.

"I heard it said once," Werner piped in, "that there's no such thing as a coincidence."

"That's right," his wife agreed. "Everything happens for a reason."

"Then what's the reason for us being stuck here?" Mason said, though his tone belied a note of disbelief.

"I'm not sure we ought to find out," Felker said.

"This night is getting a bit too creepy," Joy said, hugging her husband's arm tighter. "Can we think of something else to talk about?"

A door opened and Shelby came out of the back bedroom. Graham was glad for the interruption.

"Kids are still asleep," she said, "thank goodness." She regained her spot on the couch next to Clark. "The walls in the place are pretty thin, and I could still hear everything you were talking about." This was directed to the whole group.

"We're not trying to frighten anyone," Graham said. He noticed the eye contact she and Clark were making, and it made him happy for his friend. Maybe once they got out of this mess, some good would come out of Clark's visit home. That would be nice considering the way his trip started.

"I wanted to sleep," Shelby said, "but I think I'm too nervous."

"And what are you nervous about, dear?" Francine asked.

Shelby hugged herself. "I'm not sure. Just wondering when we're going to get out of here."

"We'll get out eventually," Clark said, trying to reassure her.

"But what's taking so long? Why hasn't anyone tried to come by? In either direction? Isn't that odd?"

"They must have shut down the highway."

"But wouldn't they think people would still be on it? It doesn't make sense."

Graham knew she was right, but understood Clark's attempts to reassure her. It wouldn't do any good for any of them to panic. "I'm sure there are lots of rescue personnel out taking care of lots of emergencies. They just haven't gotten to us yet. I bet the power is out everywhere. We know the cell towers are all down, so communication is an issue. There are probably accidents, not to mention the elderly to look after. The authorities must be busy as hell."

"Someone should have been by," Joy said, letting go of her husband's arm and pushing aside the curtain to look out the window. "I mean, there is literally no one out there."

"We're okay as long as we just sit tight right here," Graham said, wishing Shelby had fallen asleep in the bedroom with her kids.

"But what about the people in the car in front of me?" Shelby asked. "Shouldn't we see if they are okay?"

"And the truck driver," Mason added.

"We're the ones who wanted to seek refuge here," Graham said, trying to calm the others. "And the Volkmanns were nice enough to offer. The trucker chose to ride it out on his own, and that's fine."

"And the people in the hatchback?" Shelby questioned.

Graham looked at Clark for help, seeing the concern on his friend's face. "We don't need to worry about them."

"Why not?"

Graham hesitated, trying to think of an appropriate answer, and he could tell from Shelby's look that she saw something in his pause that caused her to know something was wrong.

"What is it?" she demanded, leaning forward.

Graham didn't want to look at Clark, because he knew his friend's look would try to prevent him from saying what came out next.

"They're dead."

Shelby gasped, bringing a hand up to her mouth in shock.

"Hey!" Joy yelled, still looking out the window, and Graham was grateful for the interruption. "There's a light out there!"

Everyone clambered over to the windows to look. Graham nearly pressed up against Felker's shoulder, absorbing a noxious stench from the man, whose sweat had festered inside the heavy wool of his Salvation Army coat. Graham pushed aside the curtain and peered out.

He saw nothing except darkness and the falling snow.

"Where?" he asked, keeping his face to the window.

"Through the woods," Joy said. "There's a light in the distance."

The trees along the edge of the highway were thick, branches dipping from the heavy burden of snow. There were only shadows between the trees as Graham's eyes scanned the horizon. Then he saw it. Deep in the woods, a faint light glowed.

"I see it." He turned to look back at Clark, who was still on the bench seat comforting a visibly distraught Shelby. "Take a look at this," he said, gesturing.

Clark released Shelby's hand, offering her some comforting words and then patting her arm. He came to the other side of the RV, leaning over Graham's shoulder.

"There," Graham said, pointing to the spot in the woods.

"I don't— Oh, wait, yes, there it is."

His friend stared in silence, eyes squinting.

"What do you make of it?"

Clark shrugged. "It looks like a light from a house."

"Of course," Joy said, still looking out on her side of the table. "It has to be."

"How far?" Graham asked.

"Hard to tell," Clark said. "Maybe half a mile, or more."

"But if it has electricity…."

"Could be candlelight."

"But it might not be. If they have power. We could try to reach it."

"Maybe they have a generator," Mason offered.

True, Graham thought. Lots of people had generators these days, especially since the ice storm of 1998 that left parts of the state without power for weeks.

"Even if they have power," Clark said, "and I'm not saying they do, it doesn't mean they have phone service."

"So what are you saying?" Graham asked.

"Say we try to hike out there to the house, through the snow and those woods, and we get there, and even if they have a generator giving them some limited power, there's no guarantee they have any phone service or way to communicate." Clark looked down at him. "We'd be no better off than here."

"But there's some hope," Joy pleaded. "It's something."

"Might be a trap," Felker said, staring out the window.

"What the hell are you talking about?" Joy said, her voice tinged with anger.

"Things aren't always what they seem to be."

Graham ignored Felker. "Might be worth a shot. If line crews are out trying to restore service, that house is bound to get it eventually. And that's more than we'd have sitting here." He looked back out the window. The snow still fell steady and thick, but it wasn't swirling around as much, which meant the winds had died down. That was good. "The storm looks like it's slowing down. It looks better out there than it did when we went out earlier." He looked back to Clark. "We could get some rope, tie everyone together."

Clark glanced toward Shelby, and then back at Graham. "You think those kids will be able to trudge through this snow? Some of those drifts are taller than them." He paused and Graham could tell his friend was thinking. "If we try, it should just be a couple of us."

Graham thought for a moment. He was remembering something. Something from earlier tonight. "Hey! Wait a minute. I just remembered. That young couple's car. There were two pairs of snowshoes in the hatchback."

"Then it would be just the two of us."

Graham looked around at the others and saw signs of hope amid the expressions of exhaustion.

"Let's give it a go."

As they suited up once again in the snow outfits belonging to the Volkmanns, Graham couldn't help but be glad Clark was the one who was about the same size as Francine and had to wear her powder-blue outfit. The woman's jacket and snow pants detracted from the heroic task Clark was about to undertake with him, and it brought a smile to Graham's lips. It helped assuage the nerves that tightened inside him as they prepared to head back out into the maelstrom.

Shelby stood before Clark, assisting him in getting his gear on, wrapping a scarf around his neck and tying it.

"What happened to them?" she asked him, and Graham knew who she meant.

"Carbon monoxide poisoning is my best guess. The exhaust on their car was blocked with snow."

Shelby nodded, as if satisfied by the explanation. "And the trucker?"

"He's okay as far as we know. We asked him to join us, but he said he wanted to stay with his truck."

"All right," she said, somewhat satisfied. "And the snowplough driver?"

Clark glanced over at Graham.

"We don't know," Graham shrugged, pulling Werner's knitted snow cap down over his ears. "He's missing. He may have tried to walk out after getting stuck. I have no idea." *Of course you do. That's why you didn't mention anything about the blood covering the seat, the floor mats, and dripping out of the vents. No, don't tell her that part, because she would get hysterical and right now it's necessary to remain calm.* Besides, Graham didn't want to think about the blood, didn't want to think about Felker saying the highway behind them was no longer there. Felker was mad anyway, he thought, and reeked of alcohol. The man was most likely delirious. But that didn't explain the blood in the plough truck. None on the ground outside it, just inside the truck cab where the driver sat. What the hell had happened to him?

Graham didn't want to think about it. He just wanted to get on with their task. The light in the woods offered them some hope, and anything would be better than sitting around in this rig with this motley lot. Having an objective made him feel useful. He just hoped Clark was up to it. He had almost lost his friend the first time they ventured out in the snow. The guy just wasn't used to this weather, having spent too many years living on the West Coast. Even though he'd redeemed himself when they'd gone out the second time to gather the survivors, Graham still had reservations about him. But Clark had always been a tough, athletic guy, so he knew his friend had it in him. He would have to, because they were both going to need each other out there, even though the blizzard seemed to have subsided. It was still going to be a harrowing expedition.

He watched as Shelby stood on her tiptoes and planted a kiss on Clark's cheek, the little bit of his face that was exposed between the snow cap pulled down to his eyebrows and the scarf pulled up over his chin.

"Be careful," she said to him, and then turned to Graham. "You too."

"Thank you," Graham said. Werner Volkmann handed him a flashlight. They went to the door, turning back to look at the others. Hopeful expressions gripped most of their destitute faces. Only the Volkmanns smiled.

"Godspeed," Francine said.

Once outside the safety of the RV, Graham felt alone, despite the fact Clark stood beside him. He thought of Natalie and his girls at home, worrying out of their minds about his whereabouts. They probably had no way to contact the police, no way to contact anyone. Just sitting at home, maybe with no power, wondering where he was. That was why it was important to get to that house in the woods and try to reach someone – anyone. They needed help, because it was Christmas morning, and no one knew where they were.

The wind had died down, but the snow fell steady with fat flakes that would soon bury them. Drifts piled up around the RV and Graham led the way as they waded through them, sometimes pushing the peaks of the snow aside with his arms. It was easier breathing outside this time around, without the ferocity of the wind sucking the breath out of their lungs. He glanced back at Clark, who gave him a thumbs-up with a gloved hand.

Graham nodded and looked ahead, seeing the snow-covered outline of Shelby's minivan. It seemed long ago that they had come to her rescue, coaxing her and the kids out. Well, not so much little Luke, who was the only one of their lot who looked at their snowbound status as an adventure. Maybe that's the attitude he needed to take, Graham thought. Give this excursion some context. He was doing a heroic task, something they would probably write about in the paper, maybe even on the television news. How proud his wife and daughters would be, knowing he'd stepped up to the challenge and took charge.

Beyond the minivan, he spotted the hatchback. It was just a lump of snow in the middle of the highway, a mogul he might have skied over to catch some air to show off in front of his family. He would have smiled at the thought if not for the realisation that it was now a tomb for its unfortunate occupants. The truck driver had told them all to keep their exhaust pipes clear of snow. Why hadn't the kids paid attention? Young fools. Such a shame. He remembered looking at the young woman's naked body, the curves of her flesh. It made him hunger for his own wife's body, back home in their bed, waiting for him. *I'm coming, Natalie*, he thought. *I'm trying to get home.*

They reached the hatchback, Clark coming up aside him as they both began brushing the pile of snow off the glass of the back window. Graham tried to find the release for the hatch, but couldn't locate anything.

"Try finding the release inside," Clark hollered, though it wasn't as necessary without the intense wind.

Graham stumbled as he tried to walk around to the driver's side of the car, while Clark continued brushing snow off the back. He grabbed the door handle and pulled it open, having to tug hard to push the snow that had built up against the door. The dome light came on, exposing the interior of the vehicle. He didn't want to look at the back seat and see the bodies of the young couple. When he had forced enough of a gap, Graham leaned in through the opening, looking for the hatch release.

"I found it!" he said, pulling on it.

There was a whoosh of air as Clark lifted the hatch and climbed into the back.

Graham was about to back out of the car when he looked at Clark, who had one pair of the snowshoes in his arms. A strange expression had come over his friend's face, a look of consternation as Clark glanced down into the back seat.

"What's the matter?" Graham asked.

At first Clark didn't respond, but reached down and peeled back the blanket that covered the young couple's bodies.

"How long have we been here?" Clark asked, his face drawn and pale.

Graham peered over into the back seat, to see beneath the blanket the skeletal remains of the young couple.

INTERLUDE
SILENT NIGHT

The transient huddled beneath the stone arched bridge knowing no matter how much junk he shot up, there would be no comfort from the cold dank night, no sleep before the break of dawn. He had followed the path to the bridge guided by the trail of the beast whose tracks lay before him. The man (if he could still be considered a man) was weary but wired at the same time. His insides felt like a tug-of-war was trying to rip his body apart.

There was no way to tell when the beast had last come this way. The transient huddled against the cold stone surface as sleet fell beyond both sides of the bridge. He watched the icy pellets, mesmerised by the increase in their rhythm as they began in a slow drizzle before intensifying into a deluge.

But he was dry for now beneath the bridge. And he was away from the others, especially the one who cast him out. How many days had he wandered? Time had no meaning. Just the fix, which was all that had mattered. Because he knew what it would take to face the beast. He couldn't do it on his own. That was a sign of his cowardice. But he had found some courage in the needle and he tasted grit in his mouth.

A cry in the night signalled his destiny. It was coming. Far off in the distance, and it was heading this way, just as he knew it would, just like it always did. Now he would be ready for it. He rose from his spot, discarding his satchel with his meagre belongings. This was what his life added up to, a sad sack indeed. He wouldn't need it any longer. Not where he was going.

And where was that? Someplace better than this. Anywhere but this.

The beast roared.

He stood in its tracks, ready to take it on. Time to get it off his back. *I am not afraid*, he told himself, *for I have the power within me*.

The beast bore down, charging toward him. It blared its roar.

Did it see him? Did it know he was waiting for it? Did it even care?

The transient held his ground, determined to take on the beast full force.

But his body began to tremble. He thought he had taken enough to not make him feel, but there was never enough. There was always a need for another. And another.

And now he wasn't sure if he was ready for the beast. Maybe he wasn't strong enough. The beast roared again, sparks spewing from its mouth as it screamed, its cyclopean eye bearing down on him. Too late to move, he thought. His legs strained to hold him in place. But they wouldn't work to run. He was at the end of the line and the beast looked hungry.

It screamed, sparks blew out as it exhaled its foetid breath.

He cried out at the last second, knowing he was no match for the beast, before the hulking creature bore down on him and swallowed him whole.

PART TWO
NOT A CREATURE WAS STIRRING

CHAPTER ONE

Clark didn't want to look back at the highway as they left it, but he couldn't help glancing behind him. Somehow they had gotten lost in this storm and he wasn't quite sure where they'd ended up, but something had gone seriously wrong. Looking at their vehicles, now just so many mounds of snow-covered heaps, he felt a cold that had peeled away the layers of his skin beneath the protective clothing and settled inside him shivering.

Where are we? he wondered. *And how did we get here?*

After seeing the skeletal remains of the young couple, Graham and he didn't say a word to each other. What could they say? The shock had driven them mute. All they could do was focus on the task and push forward, whatever the consequences of the madness they stumbled into.

Maybe that was it. Maybe the snowbound state had driven them mad with cabin fever. Just like the Iceman trapped inside his cabin with his mother's corpse. He and Graham had suffered some shared delusion, like highway hypnosis. Is that what had driven that man to strip off his clothes and run naked down the turnpike? It was as good a reason as any.

So was the light from the house in the woods real? Or were he and Graham marching through the snow on some fools' errand? He looked at the hulk of the RV and wondered if he'd ever see any of them again. He thought of Shelby. God, he wanted to run back there to her, make sure she and the kids were all right. He missed her already, and he barely knew her.

But if any of them had any hopes of getting out of whatever mess they had become immersed in, then he and Graham needed to do this. The others were counting on him. Shelby was counting on him. He wouldn't let her down.

The snowshoes were a blessing, helping them clamber across the drifts covering the highway. Once on the other side, the ground sloped up to the woods, and Clark took the flashlight from Graham and started up the embankment. The wind had started to pick up again (*figures*) and he tried to shield his eyes from the snow whipping into his face. The blowing wind stirred up a white mist that blanketed everything like a thick fog. The flashlight was useless trying to cut through it.

The embankment was steep, the footing tenuous, and Clark yelled back to Graham to be careful, almost slipping a couple of times himself. He still hadn't gotten used to the awkwardness of the snowshoes, feeling like he was walking in swim flippers. He stumbled, but remained upright. The snow was thick and soft and the snowshoes sank in several inches, making it hard to lift each foot up and move it forward to the next step.

Clark kept his eyes ahead, searching for the beacon of light through the woods. The mist and swirling snow obscured the way. He hoped once they reached the woods, the canopy of tree cover would offer some protection from the storm. The trees seemed to move closer together. He worried he would lose sight of the light. He could barely see it now, as if it were retreating from him. It still looked a long way off.

He turned to look back and saw Graham had fallen behind a bit and veered off course. Clark couldn't slow down for him though, fearing he wouldn't be able to continue if he did.

Why wasn't Graham following in his tracks? His friend was about forty yards behind him and twenty yards to the right, where the ground sloped down before eventually levelling off by a frozen river that ran beneath the highway. It was as if Graham were following a different beacon.

Clark waved his flashlight over his head. It would be no use calling out, he figured, the wind would swallow his words.

Graham signalled back, acknowledging him, but kept on his course.

Damn, Clark thought. Maybe he saw an easier path through the woods.

Clark didn't want to backtrack, too anxious to reach the tree line and whatever shelter it would provide. Once among the trees he could cut across to where Graham was heading.

The wind grew fiercer, shoving snow back into Clark's face, stinging his eyes. He just had a short ways to go, but the storm seemed to fight him every step of the way. If it kept up like this, and he couldn't find the house, there'd be no hope for him.

Or the others.

Remember, you're doing this for everyone. And Shelby. And her kids.

He struggled to lift his feet as the snow clung to the top of his snowshoes, weighing them down. It felt like his feet were encased in concrete blocks. The edge of the woods was just a few feet away. His eyes zeroed in on one pine tree, setting it as his goal. *Just reach that one, and then worry about what comes next.*

He trudged ahead, his chest pounding, sucking in air through the knitted scarf that covered his mouth. Snot leaked out his nostrils, soaking into the fabric.

A few more feet.

If it took this much effort just to get to the woods, how the hell was he going to make it the rest of the way to the house? If he could even find it. Where was the light? He searched, squinting to protect his eyes from the onslaught of the snow and the stinging wind.

The pine tree was before him and he stumbled into it, reaching both hands around the stiff bark, holding tight to it as if the wind was trying to rip him from his spot. He rested, closing his eyes and trying to relax his breath. Ice crystals stuck to the end of his eyelashes, but he dared not let his hands free to wipe them away. He just wanted to hold the tree for a moment, just one little moment.

When his heart had resumed a normal beat, he opened his eyes and turned to the right to see where Graham ended up.

He could not see him.

Graham was gone.

No way he could have reached the woods yet, Clark thought. He had been farther away from it than Clark. Had he fallen?

Clark worked his way along the edge of the woods to his right, in the direction he last saw Graham, moving from tree to tree, using each of them to brace himself against. Despite the lousy visibility he scanned the snow surface with the flashlight beam between the highway and the woods. There was no trace of either of their tracks. The wind had wiped them away.

"Graham!" Clark yelled, knowing full well his friend wouldn't be able to hear him. He didn't know what else to do. "*Graham!*"

No response.

Clark edged farther along to the right, but detected no sign of him, or his tracks.

It was as if he'd vanished in the storm.

He looked back through the woods. The faint light and outline of a house was still visible. Had Graham somehow gotten farther ahead? Clark didn't see how that was possible. But he'd already seen something impossible today. If he had any chance at all, he would have to continue to try for the house and hope Graham got there too. But he hated the thought of his friend lost out in the snow somewhere.

He felt helpless, but delaying wouldn't do any of them any good.

Clark pushed on through the woods toward the light from the house.

CHAPTER TWO

Graham had handed the flashlight off to Clark and let him lead the way, too stunned by the scene in the back seat of the hatchback to function properly, his thoughts swirling in circles like the snow. This had all come on the heels of the weird coincidence in the trailer with both Mason Drake and Lewis Felker having encounters with Leroy Sledge. God, when was the last time he had even thought about that schoolyard bully? The kid had dropped out sometime during high school, and Graham had never given him a thought until mentioning him tonight.

Or rather, this morning. Because indeed it was morning now, though it was still dark. Sunrise seemed so terribly far away. Graham wished he'd never brought up Leroy Sledge. It was the only story he could think of telling, because he didn't want to tell the real tale of his worst winter. Even though Clark knew it, that was a story he wanted to keep to himself.

But a storm like this always brought that memory back. He had been ten when it happened. His younger brother Spencer was eight. The two of them had been building a snow fort at the end of their front yard where the banks were piled high at the edge of the road after the town ploughs cleared the streets.

They built a sort of parapet at the top where they could look down on any imaginary infidels approaching the fort. The two of them made an arsenal of snowballs to thwart an attack from invaders. But what they needed was a tunnel, so the two of them began to dig. Graham started at the top, and he instructed Spencer to begin digging out from the side below. If things worked according to plan, the two ends of their tunnels would intersect.

They shovelled out the snow with just their mitten-covered hands, Graham piling it up on top of the fort, while he imagined Spencer shoving the snow behind him as his smaller body burrowed beneath him. Every now and then he would call out to Spencer, trying to ascertain from his muffled voice where he was beneath him so he could work toward that direction.

When Graham heard Spencer's voice nearby, he began kicking at the bottom of his hole, thinking his brother's tunnel must be right beneath him. With one big stomp of his black rubber boot, the bottom of his tunnel gave way and Graham felt himself fall, crashing down into a cavity beneath, the snow from above collapsing on top of him.

He found himself wedged in snow, pushing chunks away from his face so he had space to breathe. "Spencer!" he hollered, not sure where his brother might be. "Spencer, I can't move." No response. "Hello?"

Had the younger boy gotten out and gone for help? Graham hoped so. Their mother had gone on some errands, so who knew how long it would be before she came home. Hopefully, Spencer had run to the nearest neighbour's house.

"Spencer?" What if he hadn't gotten out?

He listened quietly but heard only the crunching sound of the snow as he tried to shift his position. It was nearly impossible to move. "Are you here?" Graham breathed heavily, lucky he could breathe at all. He felt his own warm breath bounce back at him from within the pocket of space in the snow surrounding his face.

A whimpering sound seemed far away.

"Spencer!" Graham tried to move his arms, constrained by the tunnel wall. It had to be him, but where was he? It was hard to tell the exact direction of the sound. "Hold on, Spencer, I'm coming." He tugged an arm free, digging with his mitten just below him.

Or was it below? After falling, it was hard to tell what was up or down. Was his brother beneath him, or beside him, maybe just on the other side of the snow-packed wall? Frantically, he dug, his heart hammering in his chest. His mitten got stuck when the knitted fibres froze to the snow, and when he tried to pull his hand free, it came out. He tried to reach the mitten, but couldn't, so he continued to dig with the bare fingers of his right hand, ignoring the bitter cold biting into the flesh. Soon the fingers became numb. It made it hard to dig, not being able to feel his hand, unable to control it.

But he did dig, because Spencer was down there somewhere, and his mother had left him in charge. The more he dug, the farther down he got, the harder the snow seemed to be. The skin on his fingers cracked and blood seeped out onto the snow from them, but still he dug.

A chunk of snow gave way, revealing a small hole. Through it he could see the red rubber of one of Spencer's snow boots.

"Spencer!" he cried out. "I see you! I'm almost there!"

His brother didn't respond. His little red boot didn't move.

Graham couldn't reach the hole. He tried to shift his body, to get a better angle, but he was stuck, his right arm now pinned against his body, everything numb below his wrist.

"Kick, Spencer," he yelled. "Kick your feet!" If only his brother could widen the opening, help loosen some of the snow.

But the red boot lay still.

"Damn!" Graham yelled, frustrated at his brother just as much as himself. "Damn it all!"

That's when Graham began screaming at the top of his lungs. Buried in the snow in his front yard, unable to move, not able to reach his brother, he screamed his head off, hoping on the off chance that someone would hear him and help them.

And someone did come. His screams were heard and neighbours came running, some bearing shovels, and he heard them digging through the snow, calling out to him. Soon, the sun was beating down from an opening above, blinding him, and hands reached down pulling him out. As he did, he glanced back down into the hole and saw his brother's little red boot.

It was too late for Spencer. By the time they reached him and dragged his small, limp body from the bottom of the fort, he was no longer breathing. Maybe he hadn't been the whole time Graham had been talking to him. One of the neighbours began mouth-to-mouth while waiting for the ambulance, as Graham stood there wrapped in a blanket someone had thrown around him. But his brother's body did not respond, and he looked on helpless, thinking how disappointed in him his mother would be, because she had left him in charge.

Now, as he followed Clark's tracks away from the highway, he was fine letting his friend lead the way. Let Clark be in charge. Graham had been the one who'd decided to gather the others from their vehicles and bring them to the RV, but he had been too late for that young couple in the hatchback, just like he'd been too late for his brother.

So he bent his head and followed the trail Clark blazed through the snow, over the side of the highway and up the embankment. With the wind spitting snow in his face, he kept his head down and ploughed along, each step an exhausted effort, his slow pace unable to keep up with Clark.

Graham hoped this house would be the right decision. He could have easily stayed in the comfort of the RV with the others, but seeing Clark getting cosy with Shelby made him think of his own wife and how much he desperately wanted to get home to Natalie and his daughters. There had been too much discomfort tonight. He needed the warmth of their bed and his wife's arms around him.

When Graham realised he could no longer see Clark's tracks before him, he glanced up, using his right hand to shield his eyes from the snow. Clark was quite a distance ahead of him. How had he fallen so far behind? And why wasn't his friend waiting for him?

Clark also was veering off to the left. Graham scanned the woods, seeking the light from the house. He spotted it. Clark wasn't making a straight line for it. Could he no longer see it? It was difficult with the thick mist and snow.

Graham kept a direct line for the light, blazing his own trail toward the woods, dragging each step. He wanted to rest, needed to rest, but he didn't want Clark to get too far ahead. Would his friend leave him? Maybe he wanted to be the hero all by himself, impress Shelby with his act of heroism. Wouldn't that be a laugh? If only she had seen him when Graham practically had to drag him through the snow to get him to the RV. Clark would have died out there if it wasn't for him. So who was the real hero here?

Let Clark go off course, Graham thought. *I can see the light. I know which way to go. Let him end up catching up to me.*

The ground sloped, dipping down by a small evergreen tree before a clearing to the right of the woods, over by the river. Graham stumbled as the ground seemed to fall out beneath him and he lost his balance, pitching forward and ploughing headfirst into the snow.

The white fluff gave way easily as Graham's body barreled through it. He knew immediately what had happened based on his experience skiing and the safety lessons he had learned. He had fallen into a snow well.

How deep down he had gone he had no idea. It felt like he was entirely buried in the snow. He knew he was upside down at a steep angle, because he felt the blood rushing to his head. The snow compressed against his chest, making it hard for his lungs to fully expand and breathe. Graham tried kicking his legs to no avail. It didn't help having the snowshoes on as they were wedged in the snow.

When he fell, he had reached his arms out to brace the fall, and now they were impaled in the snow before him. He couldn't even see his hands. He felt that his gloves were still on, which was good, and he tried to work his fingers, wondering how far down the ground was. His fingers could barely move, but he felt his body sink a little farther as he struggled, like being in white quicksand.

As Graham sank, the snow pushed up against his face, squashing his nose. He swiped his face back and forth, trying to keep an air pocket before him. He sucked in some air. How much would he have? How long? *I need to get out of this*, he thought, pulling back on his arms, trying to create space in front of him so he'd have enough air to breathe.

The pressure on his head felt like it was in a tightening vise. The pain made it hard to think. The crushing snow against his chest made breathing difficult. The more he struggled, the harder it was to move. He wanted to call out to Clark, but he couldn't gather enough air in his lungs to holler. Had his friend seen him fall? Had he been looking behind to see what direction he went? Where was the hero now? He had to notice his tracks at least, see where they stopped. But with the snow still falling heavy and the wind blowing hard, would there be any trace left?

Help! Graham screamed inside his mind, jolting the pain already within his aching skull. *I need help. I need someone to come get me. Where are the neighbours? Where the hell are the neighbours? Where the hell is everybody? Can't they hear me? Wait! I'm not saying anything, that's why. They can't hear me because I can't talk because there's not enough air, I can't get enough air. Why can't they find me? Why can't I breathe? Why doesn't someone come for me? Why is this snow so heavy?*

His body growing numb, the shivering stopped as feeling left his body. Graham blinked his eyes. The snow seemed to push down on them, trying to close them. Before they closed, he thought he saw, through a hole in the snow in front of him, a little red rubber boot.

CHAPTER THREE

Clark was hesitant about continuing without knowing where Graham had gone. He constantly glanced back as he trudged through the woods, wondering if his friend was behind him or farther ahead. Or maybe he had turned around, daunted by the struggle through the storm, and gone back to the safety of the RV. Regardless, Clark felt he had to carry on, certainly while he could still see the light from the house. If that light went out, then he would be hopelessly lost in the woods.

At least the trees protected him from the worst of the snow and wind, providing a shield above and around him. The branches of the tall pines were weighted down with snow and bowed before him. The flashlight beam picked apart the shadows cast by the snow-covered trees. Branches of the trees laden with the heavy burden of snow groaned out, their creaks echoing in the silence of the woods like some hidden beast starting to stir. The sounds all around him caused him to periodically glance over his shoulder, always thinking something was sneaking up behind him.

Clark was desperate to get out of these woods. They had provided some protection from the storm, but little comfort. He kept on a straight course for the house that was beginning to take shape out of the mist on the outer edge of the woods.

One foot in front of the other, Clark thought, watching as he plopped each snowshoe before him. He kept a brisk pace, panting, the moist scarf over his mouth, knitted fibres clinging to his lips.

No matter what had befallen Graham, he was determined to continue. The others were counting on him. Shelby was counting on him. At the house where he grew up in Evergreen, his mother was anxiously waiting, wondering where her son was. He needed to get to her, so she would know he was all right. That made him determined, chugging along, forging his trail in the fresh snow through the woods. There were no other disturbances on the ground. No one else had come this way.

He kept his eyes on the light. Its brightness increased, signalling its closeness. *Not much farther.* He felt he could make it even as exhaustion sapped him of his strength. His legs and arms moved in rhythm, like he had no control over his body, as if his senses had gone numb from the cold. His body did what his mind told it to, even though he couldn't feel a connection, as if his muscles were independent of his brain.

As the mist thinned, the house beyond the woods took shape, emerging from the darkness, and the white edges of rooflines and corners became defined. Clark reached the edge of the woods and leaned against the trunk of a tree as he stared out at the clearing before him.

The house stood about fifty yards away. It was three storeys high and, with snow frosting its sides and roof, gave the impression of a tiered cake. A small roof extended over the front stoop and long icicles hung down from its edge, like long sharp dragons' teeth. Above that roof was a second-floor balcony, also covered, a tall narrow door leading to it. Farther up was the gabled room of the third floor, an oval window looking out like an eye. In one window, in a room on the first floor to the left of the front door, was a flickering flame, the light that had guided him from the highway.

That it was not an electric light dimmed his spirits, and he wasn't sure he'd be able to make it across the yard between the woods and the house. In front of the house was a maple tree, whose barren snow-covered limbs hung down, as if defeated by the storm as well.

Clark pushed off from the tree he leaned on, determined to make the final trek to the house. As he made his way into the clearing, he noticed the snow seemed to have stopped. The wind must have as well because the branches of the maple tree were still.

He had to practically drag his snowshoes across the yard, his weary legs barely able to lift his feet to take each step. Clark hoped the resident of the house wouldn't be too frightened to open his door to a lost traveller. He could smell smoke and noticed it rising from a brick chimney on the left side of the roof. Clark sniffed, sensing the warmth the smell of burning wood provided. He needed that warmth, and he tried to move quicker, anxious to get inside the house.

The night was quiet as he crossed the yard, only the crunching of the snow beneath his feet breaking the silence. The wind, finally still, had lost its voice.

Clark wondered if the occupant of the house was asleep and if it would be hard to wake him or her. Heck, he would break in if he had to, but he hoped it wouldn't amount to that. He just needed to get inside, and hopefully get help.

A soft plopping sound behind him after he passed under the maple tree stopped him in his tracks. He turned. A small pile of snow behind him had apparently fallen from one of the branches as its limb now revealed bare bark. He looked up at the tree, the branches towering above him. There was no wind. The branches didn't even sway in the night air.

Clark took another step toward the house and heard another plop behind him. He stopped again, looking over his shoulder at another bare branch. It was as if the tree were shaking off its blanket of snow, like a beast awakening from its winter hibernation. Given the odd occurrences of the night, Clark felt spooked and more than ever wanted to get out of the dark and inside the safety of the house.

A rumble like thunder drew his gaze up as the tree shook its limbs. Snow rained down on him. Thick chunks pounded him, trying to drive him into the ground. Clark tried to move forward under the shower of snow, but the awkwardness of the snowshoes slowed him down.

When he thought he was clear of the falling snow, something gripped his waist. He looked down to see a branch from the maple tree had wrapped its limbs around his stomach.

Before his mind could even register what was happening, his body was lifted off the ground. The flashlight dropped from his grip, the light winking out when it hit the ground.

Clark's stomach dropped as his breath was squeezed out of him. The thickness of his ski parka was the only thing keeping his midsection from being crushed. The limb pulled him up toward the other branches, which twitched with frenzied eagerness as he struggled.

This can't be happening.

But the hard wood wrapped around him said otherwise and he tugged on it, trying to release its grip while his mind struggled to understand his predicament. *God no*, he thought as the branch slammed him down onto the ground. If not for the thickness of the snow below, his bones would have shattered. His lungs expelled what little breath they held at impact. One of his snowshoes broke off from his boot.

Before he had a chance to catch his breath, he was lifted again. Another branch reached out and clawed at his face, knocking off his snow cap. Clark dug his hands under the branch gripping him, trying to pry it loose. He felt another limb tugging on his right boot.

The branch twisted him around and swung down. It felt like he was flying as he watched the ground rise up. He squeezed his eyes shut just before he felt his body punch into the snow. He tasted blood in his mouth, but also noticed the impact loosened the branch around his waist. He squirted out of its grip and scampered across the surface of the snow, away from the tree.

Once out of its reach, he rolled onto his back and looked back at the tree. It seemed angry, brandishing its branches. Clark exhaled, exhausted from the ordeal, unable to move. Pain etched across his right cheek and he pulled off a glove and felt the side of his face. His cold fingers followed the outline of the ridge of a gash and came away wet. He kicked off his remaining snowshoe and looked over at the house. On the stoop to the right of the front door, an old wooden toboggan leaned up against the siding. It reminded him of the one he laid his grandfather on to pull him out of the woods when he was dying. It couldn't be the same one. Could it? Anything was possible at this point, he thought.

Clark wasn't sure he had the strength to make the few remaining yards to the house, but he wasn't about to stop. He just needed to catch his breath while his mind tried to comprehend what had just happened. He had stepped into some unreal nightmare and now didn't know what to expect.

Clark tried to put his glove back on, but the stiffness of the frozen fabric wouldn't fit over his fingers so he tossed it aside. He was almost there. He could make it. He had to.

He rolled over onto his front and pushed himself up to his hands and knees. It was progress. But he had no energy to rise any farther, so he began crawling toward the house, still keeping his eyes on the flickering light in the window. The cold snow stung the skin on his bare right hand as he worked his way toward the house, his abdomen aching from the pounding the tree had given him.

Just before the front steps of the house, he collapsed onto the ground and rolled over onto his back. Clark felt dizzy, his head throbbing and foggy. *Can't make it*, he thought, reaching a hand up as if it could stretch up the steps and across the stoop to the knob on the front door. He dropped his hand, fingers clawing at the snow. *No use*, he thought. *I came this far, but couldn't finish.*

Clark closed his eyes, wishing sleep would just overtake him and end it all. That would be the best solution, the way he felt. *Sorry Shelby*, he said in his mind. *I tried. It just wasn't enough.*

With his eyes shut, he could hear the sound of a door opening and footsteps approaching.

It took great effort for him to open his eyes, even just a slit, and through them he saw a man peering down at him. The man wore a black coat over a red work shirt and had straw-coloured hair and a craggy face. The man looked familiar, but in Clark's dazed state he couldn't quite place where he'd seen him before.

Just before his eyes closed again, it came to him. This was the figure he had seen in the forest when he was dragging his grandfather on the toboggan.

Have you come to claim me? Clark thought just before passing out.

CHAPTER FOUR

Tucker Jenks sat upright in the sleeper cab of his truck, afraid to stir. He still had on his outerwear and boots, even his gloves. He didn't dare take anything off, even though the heater kept the inside of the cab so toasty that sweat dampened his forehead and the back of his neck. He kept still so he could listen for any sound coming from inside the trailer. Tucker also listened to the wind, wondering if it was calling him.

Can't just sit here, he told himself.

But sit he did.

He stared at the lights on his dashboard. He looked at the CB radio. It didn't work earlier, no reason it should work now. But how long would he wait? *Do something (stupid boy). Don't just sit here. They almost got you. They'll be coming for you.*

Tucker leaned forward and looked out the driver's side window. He couldn't see the snowmen on the edge of the highway. *Who would build snowmen out here, you stupid boy? They're here for you.*

He reached out and grabbed the mic of the CB radio and turned the power on. Static jumped out. "Breaker breaker," he spoke softly into the mic, as if afraid he would be heard by someone not on the radio. He felt like a child, scared and lonely, calling for help. But why shouldn't he feel like a child? It was Christmas morning after all. Didn't everyone feel like a child on Christmas morning? It was a time to be excited about opening presents.

There was a present waiting for him in the back of the tractor-trailer, waiting for him to open it, a surprise for him on Christmas morning.

But wait, it was already open. Open and waiting for him.

"Help," he called softly into the mic. "Please."

A barrage of static poured from the speaker, interrupted by a voice.

"Stupid boy."

It was his nana.

"Don't be a stupid boy."

The banshee howled outside.

Tucker switched off the CB. There was nobody out there. Nobody who could help him at least. Not even his nana. She was dead. The banshee had called for her a long time ago.

He turned his headlights on. The beam was dimmed by the snow covering the lamps, but what light spilled out illuminated a small stretch of the highway before him. The SUV was just ahead, the one that had spun out after passing him, causing him to hit his brakes and jackknife the truck. It was that asshole's fault he was stuck here.

But not really. What had stopped them all was what blocked the path farther down the turnpike.

The snowplough.

The beams from his headlights just caught the back end of it. Tucker thought about the missing driver and the blood they'd found inside the cab. But another thought formed in his head. He remembered seeing the keys still in the ignition in the plough truck.

Maybe it was time for him to try to get the hell out of here.

Tucker zipped up his coat, opened the door to his truck and stepped out into the night.

CHAPTER FIVE

It was much less crowded in the RV since the two men left, and Lewis Felker was glad of it. *Let the pretty boys try to be the heroes*, he thought, as he maintained his seat at the table. He doubted he would see either of them again. It didn't matter. At the moment, the only thing that mattered was the bottle on the table in front of him, and with two fewer people around, it decreased the chances anyone else would want some of it.

The only other person who seemed interested in the bottle was Mason Drake, sitting across from him, and every time the man reached for it, Felker shot him a glare. The man ignored it. His wife continued looking out the window.

"I can still see the light," Joy said, not moving from the glass.

"Any sign of them?" Shelby asked from her seat on the padded bench.

"No," Joy answered.

"I'm sure they're fine," Francine said, sitting beside Shelby. She reached out a comforting hand and caressed Shelby's shoulder.

Felker noticed the younger woman stiffening up at the touch. Tense. He didn't blame her. He eyed the older woman and her husband with suspicion. They seemed too calm about everything. Maybe it had something to do with the story the old woman had told about the Iceman. It couldn't have been a coincidence that he had seen the same man out in the storm with his bloody ice tongs, back down the highway where the road should have led, but didn't.

He wasn't sure what it all meant, but it must be bad. And if the pretty boys miraculously made it out of here somehow, they would be better off not trying to come back for the rest of them.

Felker glanced down at the bottle. It was more than half-empty. He slid the bottle toward himself, eyeing Mason as he did. If they weren't where everyone thought they were, and if this was some form of hell frozen over, then he would need this more than any of the others and he didn't care to share.

"Oh no," Joy said from her post at the window, and everyone looked over.

"What is it?" Shelby asked, sitting up from her seat.

"The light's gone."

CHAPTER SIX

Clark awoke to the sound of flickering flames. He opened his eyes to view the fire before him. He felt warmth from the small blaze in the fireplace, watching orange flames dance along blackened logs.

Where am I?

He remembered collapsing in front of the house. There was a man. Or was there?

Opening his eyes wider, Clark turned his head to take in his surroundings. He was lying on a couch in front of a fireplace. Someone had removed his jacket and ski pants, and even his boots, leaving his feet covered only in socks. He wiggled his toes, noticing the socks were dry.

How long have I been here? he wondered. Outside it was still dark, so morning hadn't come yet. Unless he'd been here even longer. He thought about the skeletons in the car on the highway.

The highway!

Clark sat upright, glancing around the room. At each end of the couch was a wingback padded chair with a dark floral pattern that matched the couch. They were positioned at an angle to face the fireplace. Along the outer wall to his left, between two windows, was another pair of cushioned chairs, facing each other with a small table between them. On the table was a large chess set. The pieces were situated as if a game were in progress.

As he moved his head around, he felt a twinge of pain on the right side of his face and reached his hand up to feel a wound along his cheek. He remembered the incident with the tree. What the hell was that? And where the hell was he?

At the front of the room, he spotted a lit oil lamp on a small table before a window that looked out onto the front yard and that nightmare tree. That was the light he had followed through the woods. But where had it led him? What was this house? And more importantly, who lived here?

Someone had brought him inside, removed his outerwear and placed him in front of the fire to warm. He had seen the man before he collapsed, the same figure he had seen in the woods as a child the day his grandfather died. How was that possible? Was that the man who had brought him inside? If so, he had saved his life. But for what?

There was a doorway that led to a foyer by the front door. He had the urge to get up and explore the house, rouse its occupants, but his body still felt too stiff and sore from his ordeal and the battle with the tree. His muscles throbbed throughout his body. The only blessing was he felt warm. The flames from the logs in the fireplace had driven off the cold that had settled deep into his bones, and it comforted him.

Clark stared at the flames, mesmerised by the flickering as they lapped the logs. He wanted to just sit and absorb the warmth and the soothing feeling it gave him. But because of the odd occurrences since he left the RV, he could not feel at ease. He looked away from the flames.

On the mantelpiece above the fireplace was a sole brass candlestick, long and tapered, but empty. Flanking the fireplace were two mahogany bookcases. But the shelves weren't filled with books. Instead, there were stacks of boxes piled on each of the shelves. He got up from the couch, stood on wobbly legs, and manoeuvered over to one of the bookcases.

The boxes were board games, stacks of them piled on top of each other. Most of them looked old, the worn boxes coated with a thin layer of dust. His eyes ran across them, reading the names. Some of them he recognised from his childhood, games he had owned or played with friends. Others were unknown to him. Snakes and Ladders, Scotland Yard, Bagatelle, Ludo and Haunted Mansion. There was a slew of war games on another shelf: Waterloo, Blitzkrieg and Shenandoah. There was a game called Transylvania that Clark had faint memories of playing when he was a small boy intrigued by spooks and goblins. Not so much anymore. Not after the things he had just experienced.

"Do you enjoy playing games, Mr. Brooks?" The voice came from behind him.

Clark turned around to face a well-dressed elderly man standing in the doorway. He appeared to be in his eighties, but with a full head of silver hair slicked back and a neatly trimmed white mustache and goatee. He wore a dark grey suit coat over a vest and white shirt adorned with a red-and-white striped ascot tie. His grey slacks were well-pressed. It looked like he was dressed for a formal dinner.

But it was almost morning. Why was this man dressed like this so early in the day? Or had he just returned from some late-night engagement, such as a festive Christmas Eve celebration? But in this storm?

The more important question was how did this man know his name? Clark felt the back pocket of his pants and noticed his wallet wasn't there. He figured that was how the man knew his name.

"Most people keep books on their bookshelves," Clark said.

The old man chortled. "These days, people don't read books much anymore," he said, striding into the room. "Of course, they don't really play board games either." He paused by the back of the chair to the right of the couch and scanned the bookshelves before him. "No, everything is all video games and e-readers nowadays. Such a sorry waste."

"I take it the storm's knocked out the power here, and phone lines," Clark said, changing the subject.

The old man walked over to the chessboard on the table. He stood over it, examining the pieces. "There's been no power here for a long time."

Clark's heart sank, thinking about the others back on the highway. He had come here looking for help, but it didn't look like he'd found any.

"I came from the highway. There are several people snowbound in their vehicles." He thought about the skeletal remains in the hatchback and shivered.

"It's a nasty storm out there. Not fit for man or beast." The old man picked up a black knight and moved it to a new position on the board.

"Are you in a game with someone?" Clark asked, thinking of the figure he had seen outside when he collapsed, still wondering if maybe that was only a figment of delirium.

The man turned to face him again. "Oh, I'm definitely in a game with someone."

"So you're not alone here?"

"No," he said. "I have a servant." He paused. "And then sometimes guests stop by."

"Not on a night like this." Clark felt the man was toying with him for some reason. All he could think of was the tree outside. Nothing seemed right about this place and this man's presence didn't make him feel any better.

"You'd be surprised who would stop by on a night like this." The old man smiled. He had a full set of bright white teeth. "You came, didn't you?"

Clark shrugged. "I didn't have a lot of choices."

Now the old man laughed. "No," he said. "Sometimes our choices are taken out of our control." He stepped away from the chessboard and closer to Clark and the fire.

Clark thought about Graham. "Have you had any other visitors tonight?"

"You're the first."

It seemed an odd response.

"You expecting others?"

The old man flashed his smile. "It's Christmas, Mr. Brooks."

Clark eyed the man. "You know my name, but I don't know yours yet."

"Oh, forgive my manners," he said, extending a hand, which Clark grasped, noticing its touch was cold. "My name is Thayer Sledge."

CHAPTER SEVEN

Tucker Jenks stood before the hulking mass of the orange state snowplough in waist-deep snow while he caught his breath. He surveyed the amount of snow built up on the road around the vehicle. It wasn't going to be easy to move it.

He spied a shovel sticking out of a snowdrift near the plough. *Time to get to work*, he told himself, striding forward and grabbing the shovel. The storm had lessened, flakes floating down lightly instead of being whipped in the frenzy of the blizzard.

Tucker started with the back of the truck, digging out around the large rear wheels. There was so much snow, he wondered if he'd even have the energy to complete the task. Shovelling out the back end wouldn't be too bad; he just needed to get around the wheels and create enough space so he could spread some of the sand from the truck for traction. The front of the plough would be the real chore. He would need to clear a lengthy path so he could get enough momentum going to plough his way to the next exit. And God knows what condition the exit ramp would be in. He would cross that bridge when he got to it. First things first.

He was glad the wind had mostly stopped. Tucker didn't want to listen to its howl. Maybe the banshee had fled.

That's what Tucker wanted to do now. Flee the scene. The others could stay in the RV and wait. No more waiting for him. He dug furiously, throwing shovelfuls of snow over his shoulder. After several minutes, he could see the rear tyres of the truck. Bending down, he reached under with the shovel, scraping and pushing snow out from the front of the tyres.

His back hurt, his arms and shoulders ached, but he still had a long way to go.

Standing up, he found the lever for the sand discharger on the back of the truck and banged it a couple times with the metal blade of the shovel to loosen the frozen handle. The clanging of the metal echoed in the still night, like a bell tolling.

Not tolling for me, Tucker thought. *I'm getting the hell out.*

He released the lever and sand began sifting out. He stuck his shovel under the flow, letting it fill, and then he spread the sand behind and in front of the rear wheels. Tucker put as much sand down as he felt necessary, making sure he saved some for the front.

Tucker moved to the front of the truck. The snow on the highway seemed to be piled even higher here. He took a deep breath, pausing to recharge his energy. As tired as he was, it was going to take sheer determination to get the job done.

He looked back down the highway, to where his own truck remained behind the SUV. He had left its safety and comfort to risk coming out here, and he hoped he'd made the right decision. It only took thinking about what had happened in the back of the tractor-trailer to convince him he was doing the right thing.

Tucker began digging. It was eerily quiet now that the wind had died down, the only noise the crunching sound his shovel made as it bit into the snow mounds piled in front of the plough and the grunts he sometimes uttered in his effort to toss the load off to the side. After only a few minutes he needed a break, feeling a burning sensation penetrating his shoulder blades and running down both arms to his elbows. He stood leaning on his shovel for support, catching his breath. He realised he had a lot more digging to do before he would have enough area to get a running start with the plough. Hopefully it would be enough to push off the rest of the snow that covered the highway ahead.

Now the only sound came from the deep breaths he took, puffs of mist with each exhalation. The morning seemed peaceful, belying the true state of his situation. He wished for daybreak to come and hoped things would seem better in the light.

He heard a crunch of snow coming from beyond the opposite lane of the highway. His eyes scanned the trees across the way.

Something moved through the woods. He heard what sounded like footsteps.

He strained his eyes, trying to distinguish shadow from tree. One of the shadows moved and he thought he could see horns.

A deer maybe, venturing out now that the worst of the storm had subsided?

The shadowy figure was just inside the tree line, moving to the left.

Tucker saw a dark shape appear in an opening between two trees. He only caught a brief glimpse, but what he thought he saw chilled him to the bone.

The animal figure walked upright on two legs.

Tucker frantically returned to digging, ignoring the pain in his shoulders and arms and the heavy weight on his lungs, as he was determined to clear a path for the plough.

CHAPTER EIGHT

Thayer Sledge's hand was cold, his grip tight as Clark shook hands with the old man. The chill went right up his arm, but that might have been because he recognised the name. It was odd because it had come up earlier in the night back in the RV. It was a strange coincidence, if indeed that's what it was.

"Sledge?" Clark repeated, as if making sure he heard correctly.

"Yes," Thayer said, a twinkle in his eye. "The name may be familiar to you."

It sounded more like a question.

"I went to school with a Sledge. Leroy was his name. His family owned the Sledge & Ferrin Game Co." Clark turned to look back at the bookshelves stacked with board games.

Thayer stepped over to the case to the right of the fireplace as if admiring its contents.

"That's right," he said. "I founded the company. With my partner, of course, Bernard Ferrin. But I sold it off to its parent company, now run by a board of directors. There are no family members involved any more. But I built it up to be one of the most successful game companies in the nation."

Clark stepped up beside him. "I'm familiar with many of these games," he said. "Played a lot of them when I was a kid."

"I'm sure you did," Thayer said. He grabbed a box off the shelf and blew dust off it. "How about this one?"

Clark read the title, *Snakes and Ladders*. Its box showed a numbered grid of squares crisscrossed with slithering serpents.

"I remember one like that," he said. "Although it didn't have that title."

"Oh yes, well this is the historic version, originated in ancient India. My company brought it to the United States based on a British interpretation."

"It was a rather simple game," Clark said. "Not much to it."

"Yes, well the Indian version was a morality lesson. You progressed up the board as part of a life journey, facing pitfalls, represented by the snakes, and merits, which were the ladders."

"Still seemed just a matter of chance," Clark countered.

Thayer faced him. "Sometimes, that's all life is, a matter of chance."

Clark thought there was something off about this man, and wasn't sure what he was talking about. He thought about the others back in the RV and Graham maybe wandering around outside.

"This talk of games isn't important right now. I have a friend who must be lost out in the storm. Would your servant be able to help me look for him since there's no way to call for help?"

Thayer shoved the game back onto the shelf, a puff of dust billowing out. "This night is not fit for wandering about," he said with a smirk. "Besides, you're in no condition to step back outside. You must still be chilled."

Clark had to admit that unless he was standing right in front of the fireplace, his body felt cold. "I'm just worried about my friend. I'd like to look for him, but you've taken my winter gear."

"Your clothes are drying. As for your friend, there's nothing anyone can do for him now. What you could use right now is a hot toddy. I will go see if my servant can warm up some hot buttered rum."

Before Clark could object, the man turned and exited the room. Clark stepped into the foyer and saw Thayer going through a door toward the back of the house. Clark looked around, noticing a grand staircase that wound its way up to the second-floor landing. An open door across from him led to a room shrouded in darkness.

On either side of the front door to the house were long narrow windows. Clark walked over to the door and peered out one of them. He could still see snow falling, though lightly. The maple tree out front remained still, no breeze shaking its menacing limbs. Clark tried the doorknob. It wouldn't move. Locked? He felt trapped.

A chill came over him, though he wasn't sure if it was from the predicament he found himself in, or the cool air that settled in the house. It seemed the farther away he had gotten from the fireplace, the colder he got, so he returned to the room and sat back down on the couch, trying to sort out this odd encounter. It felt like a dream, and he half thought maybe he was still lying outside in the snow delirious from hypothermia. Maybe that's why he couldn't stay warm. He wiggled his toes in his sock-covered feet, trying to keep the blood flowing to their numb tips.

A rattling sound came from above, drawing Clark's gaze to the ceiling. It sounded like the clinking of metal, and it was getting louder. He turned from his seat, looking over the back of the couch.

Something was coming down the stairway in the foyer. A shadow entered the doorway of the room, followed by the old man who cast it. He was short and stocky, balding with a round face and sagging jowls. The man's entire body was draped in chains, with several large metal padlocks connecting many of the links. The locks looked old and rusted, even in the dimness of the room, with a keyhole in the face of each one.

The man looked at Clark, no sense of surprise or curiosity on his face, and then grunted and moved over toward the chessboard. He sat in one of the chairs, behind the white chess pieces, and stared down at the board.

"Hello?" Clark said, curious, rising from his seat.

The man barely glanced up at him, uninterested, and returned his gaze to the chessboard.

Clark walked over. This wasn't the man he had seen outside, so who was he?

"Are you a friend of Mr. Sledge's?" Clark asked.

The man held up a hand, palm out. "Please," the man finally offered. "I need to concentrate. This is very important."

Clark remained silent, baffled by this man's sudden and odd appearance. The newcomer appeared in deep concentration, eyes locked onto the chessboard. After several moments, he sighed. His chains rattled as he reached his right hand toward the board and moved one of his knights. Once he was finished, he leaned back in his chair, the chains shifting around his body.

"Are you finished?" Clark asked.

The man grunted again. "If only. I fear there is still a long ways to go before the game is truly finished." He reached into a pocket on his waistcoat and pulled out a large keyring. On it were dozens of old metal keys.

Clark watched as the man went through the keys, selected one and inserted it into one of the many padlocks. He turned the key, face sagging as nothing happened, and removed it. After selecting another key, he tried it on the same lock, once again to no avail. He sighed, slumping back in his chair, his face a mask of frustration.

"Why are you in chains?"

The man's eyes rolled up toward Clark. "The question is, why aren't you?"

Clark looked at the man, bewildered. "Why? Am I a prisoner?"

The man gazed down at Clark's feet. "You have no shoes." He looked back up at him. "You don't think you'd be able to get anywhere like that, do you?"

Clark had to admit this was true.

The man fumbled with the keys before selecting another one. This one he tried on a different padlock, still with no success.

"But if you're a prisoner, why do you have the keys?"

The man looked at Clark with exasperation. "It's a game," he said in a disgruntled tone. "The right keys will open the locks in a certain progression. Only then can the chains be removed."

"Who chained you? Thayer Sledge?"

The man did not answer, only glanced back at the chessboard. "My move is made. I can only wait now."

He got up and shuffled toward the doorway, the chains weighing down his old frame, causing him to drag his feet. Once the man was out of view, Clark heard him on the staircase, the rattling of the chains dissipating as he ascended.

Clark had no idea what to make of this encounter, once again feeling everything had gone wrong from the moment he'd stepped out of the RV, from the skeletons in the hatchback, losing Graham in the snow, the attack by the tree and now this house of lunacy.

Maybe he was lying out in the snow somewhere, suffering some hypothermia-induced hallucination.

As he was pondering this, Thayer Sledge returned to the room.

"My servant will be bringing our drinks along shortly." He gestured toward the furniture in front of the fireplace. "Please, sit by the fire. You need to keep warm."

As frustrated as he was by his predicament, this was an appealing suggestion, so Clark took a seat in one of the high wingback chairs. Sledge sat in the other.

"I just met a man in chains," Clark said, hoping for some explanation.

"Oh yes, that would be Bernard." Sledge responded matter-of-factly.

"Friend of yours?"

"Bernard Ferrin was my business partner, of the Sledge & Ferrin Game Co."

"Your partner?"

"Yes. He and I built our gaming empire from the very beginning. It was a great partnership, at first. He was the thinker, I was the doer." Sledge smiled. "Bernard created many of our finest original games. I mostly oversaw acquiring games from Europe and the Far East."

"Like Snakes and Ladders."

"Exactly." Sledge snapped his fingers. "I handled the business aspects of acquiring the rights and all the legal contracts for the games we introduced in the U.S. I was good with figures, but Bernard was the creative one. He remained in his office night and day when working on a new game. He just didn't have much business sense. That was his downfall."

"Why is he in chains?"

Sledged frowned. "That's my fault, I'm afraid. Bernard used to be my conscience, but now he has become something of a burden to me. Those chains are almost as much mine as his."

Clark didn't understand any of this.

"He has keys to the locks."

"Oh yes. Puzzle games were another of our specialties. Back then we started with wooden puzzles. That's how our company originated. We founded this company in 1925, when I was twenty-seven years old."

Clark stared at the man in silence, looking at the lines etched in his face, the silver of his hair, his sturdy frame. He began doing the math in his head.

"But that would make you one hundred and twenty-one years old?"

"Not exactly," Sledge said, shaking his head with a smile. "I mean it would, if I were still alive."

CHAPTER NINE

Shelby couldn't stare out the RV window anymore. It was too nerve-wracking. Her insides churned, worry worming its way through her gut. Clark and Graham had been gone awhile. Surely they must have reached the house through the woods by now. *If they made it*, a voice in her head said. *No*, she told it. Of course they made it. They were young, fit and strong. They had rescued them all and led them to the RV. Besides, the storm wasn't as bad now. The wind had died down, the snow was falling much lighter. The worst had to be over.

But that voice in her head told her the worst had yet to come.

The children. She needed to check on the children. Shelby moved to the room at the back of the RV, opened the door gently and peeked in. Relief washed over her when she saw the two of them still asleep in the Volkmanns' bed. Luke lay with his head on Macey's chest, her arm around his shoulders.

She's comforting him, Shelby thought. As much as the two siblings squabbled constantly and got on each other's nerves, Macey was being protective of her younger brother in this time of distress. Shelby couldn't ask for a better Christmas moment than to see this scene. She just wished it didn't have to take place during a night of such anguish.

She closed the door softly and returned to the others. That ghastly Salvation Army man was drumming his fingers on the table again, swilling from the liquor bottle the old couple had brought out.

It reminded Shelby of her husband, Nelson, and his excessive drinking. Though they'd been divorced several years, it still had an effect on her. He was the whole reason she was here, snowbound in the storm, because he had been too drunk to drive the kids back to her house after his Christmas Eve visit with them.

Drinking had also put his job in jeopardy, with the ongoing investigation into the train accident that had killed a homeless man. Nelson was driving the train that night, and of course tests showed alcohol in his system. If he lost his job, which seemed highly likely, there went her child support. His stupidity and recklessness continued to make her life miserable.

And now he was probably happily sleeping off his drunken stupor with his new wife, while Shelby's night of suffering seemed to have no end. So Clark had to find help. She needed him to get to that house, call for help, and rescue them from this nightmare.

Please Clark, she said to herself. *Please be all right.*

Mrs. Volkmann glanced up at her from the bench seat, a smile on her face. Shelby looked away. How could anyone smile with all this going on? How could this old couple be so calm in the face of utter desperation?

Joy continued peering out the window, her husband beside her. But Shelby didn't want to look. She didn't want to see that the light in the woods was gone. She wanted to believe that Clark had found its source. It was the only thing she could hold on to right now, with her nerves on such an edge.

A crash of shattering glass made her jump. It came from the rear of the RV. It was followed by screams.

The children!

Shelby ran to the door and pushed it open.

Both kids were looking behind them at the shattered window and the hairy beast that stood outside it. She thought it was an animal, considering its hairy body, long pointed ears and pair of horns that sprouted from the top of its head. But its face looked human. Red eyes glared out at her and the mouth beneath its hooked nose opened, a long red tongue slithering out between its pointed teeth.

"Mom!" Macey screamed, frightened eyes locking with hers.

Shelby was too stunned by this bestial image to move, unable to comprehend what she was seeing.

In its right hand the beast had a birch switch, which it swept about, clearing the broken shards of glass from the rear window. Its left hand reached in and grabbed Luke, lifting him off the bed.

"*No!*" Shelby screamed. She lunged into the room and climbed on the end of the bed, as the beast shoved Luke into a wicker basket strapped onto its back.

"Help!" Luke's terrified voice echoed out of the container.

Shelby felt as if her body wouldn't co-operate, her muscles failing her as she tried to clamber across the bed, reaching out for Macey's outstretched hand. Her daughter was snatched away, just as their hands were about to connect.

Macey's eyes were wide with terror as the beast clutched the child to its hairy chest. Shelby reached toward the girl, but the beast swiped the switch across her face, the branches scraping her cheek and knocking her backward on the bed.

The beast's tongue protruded again, at least a foot out of its horrid mouth.

Shelby didn't know if the creature could talk, but it did seem to be laughing. It turned and ran off through the snow. Shelby leaped forward toward the open window, grabbing onto its bottom edge, not even feeling the shards of glass digging into her palms.

"Bring back my babies!" she screamed into the night, attempting to climb out the window before realising something was holding her back. There were hands grabbing her shoulders. She turned to see it was Mason Drake.

"Let me go!" she said, seething, her heart pounding.

"You can't go out there," Mason said, a firm grip on her.

"It's got my children!"

"You'll die if you go out there," he said, as if it mattered. She'd rather be dead than abandon her kids.

"I need to go after them," she pleaded, realising she was crying hysterically.

"Not like this," he said. "You don't even have a coat on."

She almost laughed. It seemed a silly thing to say. Something her mother would say: *Don't go out without a coat, you'll catch a death of a cold.*

Shelby did laugh, which quickly turned to wracking sobs. Mason pulled her forward and her face sank onto his shoulder. She closed her eyes, sobbing, feeling like everything had fallen apart in her world. When she opened her eyes, she glanced over Mason's shoulder at the others who stared back at her. They all seemed horrified or uncomfortable.

No, not all.

She pushed Mason aside and crawled off the bed. The others backed out of the bedroom into the living area of the RV as she came forward. She looked past Joy and Felker, to the Volkmanns.

"You!" she said, pointing at Werner. "You told that story about that creature."

"The Krampus," Lewis Felker acknowledged in agreement, coming along beside Shelby in support. "He knew all about it."

Werner opened his mouth, uttering an 'Uh', and then shut it, looking perplexed.

"It was just a story," Francine said in defence of her husband. "A European folktale. Who knew it really existed?"

Shelby turned to her. "You offered to put the children in the bedroom."

"We need answers," Mason said from behind her. He had shut the door to the bedroom, sealing off the cold air pouring in through the broken window. "We want to know what's really going on here." His face held a hint of disbelief.

Shelby turned to him. "You saw. We all saw."

"I'm not sure what I saw."

"Whatever it was took my kids." Shelby's fear had turned to rage. "And I need to go after them." She went to the closet where Francine had hung all their coats, grabbed hers and put it on.

"You can't go rushing off into the night, God knows where," Mason said. "You'll get lost out there."

"It'll be dawn soon," Joy said. "You need to at least wait till sunrise."

"If the sun ever comes up," Felker said.

This quieted everyone. Joy walked past the others to the front of the RV, but then stopped short.

The quiet was broken by the sound of a zipper as Shelby did up her coat. "I'm going. You can come with me to help," she said to Mason, "or get out of my way."

"Before anyone goes anywhere," Joy said. "I think you should look out the front windshield."

Everyone turned to look toward the front of the RV.

Beyond the windshield, in the beams from the headlights cast out onto the road, were three snowmen.

CHAPTER TEN

Clark was shaken by the old man's words as he looked deep into Sledge's steel-grey eyes.

"You're not alive?"

"Oh goodness no," he said. "Haven't been for quite some time."

Clark thought about the tree outside, the skeletal couple in the hatchback. Nothing made sense here. Had he wandered through the storm into some wintry version of hell? His head throbbed from trying to comprehend.

His thoughts were interrupted by Sledge's servant, who entered the room carrying two drinks on a tray. Clark stood to get a look at him. It was the man Clark saw when he'd collapsed outside the house, the man with the straw-like hair and craggy face. He wore a black jacket over a red shirt, and dark pants.

"Thank you, Everett," Sledge said, taking the drinks off the tray. "That will be all for now."

The man didn't speak, only nodding before turning and walking away.

Sledge handed Clark one of the glasses. "Hot buttered rum," he said. "Should warm your insides while the fire warms your outsides."

Clark took the glass with a shaking hand, careful not to spill a drop. He brought it to his lips, taking a gentle sip. It did feel warm, burning smoothly down his throat. "Your business partner, Mr. Ferrin, is he dead too?"

"Oh quite," Sledge said, after taking a sip of his own drink. "That of course was my fault."

"Your fault?"

"Yes." The old man grinned. "Only because I killed him."

Once again Clark was stunned by the man's words, maybe even more so because of his callous way of expressing them. "You murdered him?"

Sledge shrugged, taking Clark's arm and guiding him closer to the warm fire. "Killed, murdered, it's all how you look at it. You see, more than fifty years ago, when we were both alive of course, we had a chance to sell our gaming company to one of the larger corporations. A buyout that would have brought even greater financial rewards to the two of us than we already had. There was just one problem."

"And what was that?" Clark asked after another sip of his drink.

"Bernard didn't want to sell. Oh, he was a stubborn fool. He wanted the autonomy of our own company, without having to answer to a board of directors. Truth was, he just wanted the freedom to continue inventing games, and he felt that wouldn't happen with the buyout from a parent company."

"So you killed him."

"Not exactly." The man stroked his goatee. "I took him on a hike that winter, up Mt. Washington. Just a chance for the two of us to be alone and hash things out, try to get him to see reason."

"Up Mt. Washington? In the winter?"

"I was pretty fit even at my age," Sledge said with pride. "Couldn't say the same for Bernard."

"But he went anyway."

Sledge nodded. "It took some convincing, but I assured him I knew what I was doing." He winked at Clark. "And I did. Up the trail we went, beyond the tree line. The whole way up I explained the benefit of selling our company. He refused to listen. So, as a storm approached, which I was quite aware was coming, I abandoned him on the mountain, knowing full well he would not make it down." He didn't show any hesitation telling the story. "It took two days to find his body."

"And you sold the company?"

"The very next year." He polished off his drink and set it down on a table beside the couch. "Of course I sat on the board of directors for a while, a token assignment, more as a figurehead than anything. No real decision-making powers. And when it was time to step down from that and retire, I left with riches beyond my desires and lived to a ripe old age before passing from natural causes, in my sleep." He smiled. "Wonderful way to go."

"And no one ever suspected what you did?"

He smirked. "There were whispers of course. But my story of two nature lovers who bit off more than they could chew was believable. Mt. Washington has claimed many a hiker both experienced and amateur."

"And you got away with murder."

At that he laughed. "Well, I wouldn't quite say 'got away'. I ended up here."

"And where exactly is here?"

Thayer Sledge's expression shifted; his eyes seemed to withdraw as if searching inside himself for an explanation. He frowned, and then gazed around the room.

"I'm not sure you'd be able to comprehend," he finally said.

"Well, if you're dead, then is this the afterlife?" Clark pondered the meaning of what he was asking, thinking of his own mortality.

"There is no afterlife," Sledge said. "There is only after death."

"Then...." Clark hesitated, afraid to ask. His palms sweated, and not just because he was near the heat from the fireplace. But inside, around his heart and lungs, he felt chilled. "Am I dead?" He blurted it out, not sure he was prepared for the answer.

"Oh heavens no," the old man said. "You are very much alive, Mr. Brooks. That storm out there might have tried to kill you, but it hasn't. Yet."

Clark felt relief, his body almost shaking. He had so many questions. "Then what is this place? What are you doing in this house? Did you live here? Are you haunting it?" He couldn't imagine a man as rich as Thayer Sledge living in this home.

"What you see here," Sledge said, waving his hand around the room, "is not really a house."

More confusion. "It's not?"

"Sit down," Sledge said, gesturing to the couch. Clark sat and the old man took a seat in one of the chairs beside it. "I'll try to explain."

"Please do." Clark finished the rest of his hot buttered rum.

"On this side of death, there exist realms, places inhabited by those like myself. There are many realms, mostly of our own making. Think of it like a landscape, like one of my game boards." He pointed to the shelves beside the fireplace.

"So it's not really here, by the highway?"

Sledge chuckled. "I hate to tell you this, but neither is the highway."

Clark sat up straight. "The highway isn't here?"

"Afraid not."

"So those people I left are not trapped on the highway?"

He smiled. "They are trapped in a way, much like yourself."

Clark thought about the skeletal remains in the hatchback on the turnpike.

"And how long have we been trapped?" He was frightened at the thought of the answer. Maybe it would be best not to know, but he felt compelled to ask.

"Oh, time has no meaning on this side of the realm."

Clark felt faint. Maybe because of his exhausting trek, or the beating from the tree outside, or quite possibly the alcohol from the drink was intensified because of his weakened state. Or it could be that the unbelievable things this man was telling him made his head spin. He almost wanted to lie down again, but was afraid of what would happen if he fell back asleep. Maybe he would wake up from this nightmare. Or maybe he would not wake up at all.

"I know this is a lot to absorb," Sledge said. "Even by a man of your intelligence."

"How did you get here?" Clark asked. "To this – realm – or whatever it is?"

"There are entrances and exits to the realms. I sort of became stuck here, banished, I guess you could say."

"Because of what you did?"

He nodded. "My own fault I suppose. I reached too far."

At that point, the manservant entered the room. He was silent as he collected the empty liquor glasses.

"Everett," Sledge said, "can you take a look outside and see if you can't locate Mr. Brooks' friend, Mr. Sawyer?"

"My pleasure," the man said, his voice low and flat. He left the room.

"And what's his story?" Clark asked.

"I needed some help, and he was available."

"Who is he?"

The smile that came over the old man's face left Clark unsettled. "His name is Everett Wick."

Sledge offered no more, as if he expected Clark to comprehend. There was something very familiar about the name. He had heard it, fairly recently in fact. Then an image appeared in his head, of a little girl watching a man in black walking down a snow-filled street, a pair of bloody ice tongs in one hand. Clark's eyes widened.

"The story Francine Volkmann told."

Sledge nodded. "Everett Wick, known a long time ago as the Iceman."

Clark's stomach knotted. "What is he helping you with?"

"It's all part of the game," Sledge said, grinning.

"I'm thinking I'm not going to like this game." Clark could still feel the bumps and bruises from the thrashing the tree gave him and the sting from the scratch across his cheek.

"It's all a matter of perspective." Sledge rose from his chair.

Clark glanced up, wondering what the man's next move was. He didn't have to wait long.

"Let me show you something," Sledge said, extending a hand toward the hallway.

Clark looked down at his sock-covered feet, thinking even if he wanted to run, and could in fact get out of the house, he wouldn't get far like this. He needed something on his feet. With not much choice, he rose and followed Sledge. The old man exited the room, moving gracefully for a man over a century old, while Clark shuffled behind him, his body aching, his limbs stiff, his feet chilled. He followed Sledge to the room across the hallway.

The only light in the room was just a brief bit of moonlight coming in through the frosty windows looking out the front. The sun had to rise soon, Clark thought. The night had seemed to go on forever. But then Sledge's words about time came back to him. What if morning never came? Clark remained still, letting his eyes adjust to the darkness, which was soon broken by the strike of a match.

Sledge lit an oil lamp, much like the one in the other room, and placed it on a mantle over an empty fireplace. Clark wished this hearth was lit, as the room was numbingly cold. He looked around, now that the lamp cast its light, stopping short of the shadowed corners of the room. There was a hutch on the back wall, a dusty glass door revealing an assortment of small wooden boxes. A length of knotted rope lay coiled on one shelf. There was a wooden rocker in a corner, but no other furniture.

But there was something in the centre of the room.

Sledge stood on one side of it and Clark approached the other. It was a narrow wooden three-legged pedestal of dark pine about three feet tall that resembled a plant stand. On top of it, nestled in a black wrought-iron base, sat a glass globe about the size of a bowling ball. As Clark peered at it in the light from the oil lamp, he could see it was a large snow globe.

Inside the globe was a winter scene, with three snowmen standing before a group of evergreen trees. The middle snowman was taller than the other two and wore a black top hat and a red-and-white striped scarf. His carrot nose beneath his coal eyes was bent.

Clark stared in silence, watching the snow falling in the scene even though the globe hadn't been shaken. He stared at the snowmen as an awful feeling crept up inside him.

"I had this exact snow globe when I was a kid," he said, the words forced out through a dry throat. "My grandfather gave it to me the day he died." He stared into the globe. "I used to call it a snowball. Mine wasn't this big though."

"This is no ordinary snow globe," Sledge said, passing his hand a few inches over it, like a magician waving a wand over his magic hat. The globe darkened and then brightened again, like it was on a dimmer switch. The scene had changed. It now showed a brick building beside a playground. Clark recognised it as his middle school in Evergreen.

"What are you, some kind of winter warlock?" Clark asked, amazed and frightened at the same time. He could feel his blood thicken. "Is this your crystal ball?"

"Watch and see," Sledge said, as if this was some parlour trick.

Clark's eyes never left the globe as his vision seemed to zoom in on the schoolyard scene, on three young boys. He saw one boy throw a snowball at another, who ducked, causing the third boy to be hit with it. The third boy chased the snowball thrower around the schoolyard.

"What the hell is this?" Clark said, looking up at Sledge, knowing full well how the rest of the scene played out.

"Just taking a trip down memory lane," Sledge said. He watched the scene in the globe.

"I know what you're showing me, but I don't know how, or more importantly, why. That's Leroy Sledge. Your grandson, I presume?"

"Great-grandson," Sledge answered, casting his eyes upon Clark.

"And what role does he play in this game? Is he here too?"

"Not exactly," Sledge said, waving his hand over the globe again. It darkened.

All Clark could see was fluttering snowflakes, like falling stars in a night sky. Then the snowflakes grew dark, turning blood-red, floating around inside the globe.

"This is all that's left of him," Sledge said. "A little over a year ago, poor Leroy was run over by a train."

Clark swallowed hard, staring at the swirling red flakes inside the snow globe. He thought about Graham again, worried about the Iceman looking for him, hoping to hell he didn't find him. But whatever was going on outside, he had to deal with this madness inside first.

"I'm sorry about Leroy," he said, "but I don't see what this has to do with Graham and me. I haven't seen him since high school. I'm sure Graham hasn't either. It's a shame what happened to him. I hope he's resting in peace." He wanted to sound genuine, but didn't know if he had pulled it off. Clark truly was sorry, but felt so distant from it all he couldn't muster up much emotion.

"The dead don't rest. Sometimes the dead are angry." Sledge raised an eyebrow. "They resent the living."

"Is that how you feel? You resent me and Graham for being alive? And what about the others, back on the highway in the RV? You resent them too?"

Sledge started to laugh. "I don't resent them." He waved his hand over the snow globe and the scene changed, the red flakes turning back to snow, this time falling over a miniature replica of the RV Clark had left behind. In front of it were the three snowmen.

"They're already dead," Sledge said.

CHAPTER ELEVEN

"Don't you get it?" Shelby cried, her voice hysterical, as they stared at the snowmen out in front of the RV. "Someone's playing a sick game with us."

Mason stood beside his wife, both hunched over Werner Volkmann, sitting in the vehicle's driver's seat as they stared outside. Someone was out there, he thought. Someone who built these snowmen. But why? He turned to look at Shelby over his right shoulder. Her eyes were wild. *She's losing it,* he thought. *She lost her kids and now she's losing her mind.*

"What are you talking about?" he asked, not really wanting an answer.

Shelby was pulling on her mittens. "There's a sick fuck out there screwing with us." She pulled a pink snow cap out of a pocket and pulled it over her head, tucking wisps of brown hair inside, out of her face. "They dressed up in some Crumpus costume—"

"Krampus," Francine corrected from behind her.

Shelby spun around. "I don't give a fuck what it's called!" she screamed at the old woman, spittle flying from her mouth. "Whoever it is took my kids, and they think it's such a big joke, that they build some stupid snowmen to mock us. They're fucking mocking us!"

"And what do you plan to do about it?" Mason asked, wishing she would just shut the hell up.

"I'm going out there," she said, grimacing through gritted teeth. "And I'm going to find these bastards and get my kids back."

"You can't go out there," Felker said, the only one seated at the table now. "It isn't safe." He wasn't looking at Shelby, nor was he looking out the windshield like the others. He just stared at the less than half-filled bottle on the table in front of him.

"Then maybe one of you brave men would like to go out there with me." Her tone stung with sarcasm.

Mason resented her insinuation, but he didn't want to go out there. There was something dangerous outside. "No one should rush out there just now," he said.

"Then screw you all." She pushed past Francine, heading to the side door. "The only real men have already left."

Mason stepped forward and grabbed her arm. "Just wait," he said, pulling her back.

Shelby spun around, trying to jerk her arm away. "Let go of me!"

What Mason did next he'd seen a hundred times in old movies, but it seemed warranted. He slapped her face. Wasn't that what they always did to hysterical people in motion pictures?

Her face turned red, part from the impact of Mason's open hand, part from rage seething inside her. He sensed she was about to explode and braced himself for it. Mason had dealt with a lot of angry parolees, but they were mostly men and he knew how to handle them. This was different.

Shelby raised a hand, ready to strike him back, but hesitated. Her eyes burned into his. He saw a conflict of emotions in those eyes: anger, confusion, helplessness, but mostly what he saw was fear. Yes, there was a lot of fear in those eyes.

"Let her go," Joy said, coming to her husband's side. "If she wants to go, so be it."

Mason watched Shelby stare down his wife, and then turned to go.

At the same time, Felker rose slowly from the table. He picked up his Salvation Army cap and placed it on his head. For a second, Mason thought the man was going to go with Shelby, which he thought odd.

"Take a look," Felker said, pointing out the windshield. "One of the snowmen is missing."

Everyone turned to look outside. The headlights of the RV cast their dim beams on the snow-covered highway and the two snowmen before them. They were the two shorter ones, their branch arms outstretched, twitching in the wind in a taunting manner. The taller one with the top hat was missing.

"It can't be," Mason said, taking a step forward as he looked out over the top of Mr. Volkmann's grey head.

"Where did it go?" Joy asked, clinging to her husband's right arm. He could feel her nails digging in as she tensed.

"Now do you get it?" Shelby asked, her voice suddenly calm.

Mason removed his wife's grip from his arm, as gently as possible, and moved toward Shelby. "I think you need to stay here right now," he pleaded.

A knock came.

It appeared to come from the driver's side door.

Werner looked back at Mason. "I think we have a visitor." The old man was grinning.

"Don't open it," Felker said, his voice raised.

Werner paid no attention, reaching for the door handle.

"*No!*" Mason screamed, trying to lurch forward to stop him, but Joy was in his way.

Werner pushed the door open, and then swivelled his chair to look back at the others, still smiling a twisted grin. "Company's here," he said, and began laughing.

Mason stopped when he saw the snowman's head appear in the doorway, ducking down as it entered to fit its top hat through the opening. The snowman extended one of its branch arms toward Werner, who seemed surprised. Two fingers on its branch hand plunged into the eye sockets of the old man, who let out a roar.

Mason heard Francine screaming behind him as her husband was lifted out of his seat, the snowman gripping his head like a bowling ball, blood streaming out his punctured eyeballs. The snowman backed out, pulling Werner with him, and flung him out into the snow like a rag doll, the man's screams muffled.

"Oh my God," Joy said in front of him, as Mason backed up, not thinking to pull his wife back with him.

The snowman moved forward into the front seat, turning its head to look at them, its coal-black eyes boring through his. *It sees us*, he thought. *This unearthly thing is looking at us, sorting through its prey.* He couldn't move. His mind went numb; his limbs felt detached. The temperature inside the RV dropped, the cold raising the hairs along his arms and legs.

Out of the corner of his eye he saw Felker grab the whiskey bottle and thought the man was going to smash it on the edge of the table to use it as a weapon, but instead Felker bolted for the side door, past a stunned Shelby and a whimpering Francine. He flung open the side door and left.

After watching Felker's escape with surprise, Mason turned to see the snowman lumber forward with surprising grace, pushing its wide round shape around the seats and toward Joy.

His wife turned to look at him, reaching a hand toward him, but before she could move, the branch arms of the snowman wrapped around her. Her eyes widened in horror.

"Mason!" she screamed.

He hesitated, looking at her outstretched hand, fingers grasping air, and he thought about reaching out to her, moving forward to try and save her.

Instead he backed up.

Her eyes turned from fear to puzzlement, her mouth agape in confusion.

Mason continued backing up, watching the snowman's head lean forward, its black mouth opening, exposing jagged teeth inside. The jaws clamped down on his wife's neck and her open mouth emitted a piercing scream above the sound of flesh, sinew and bone giving way with a tearing crunching noise as blood shot out from the wound.

Mason turned to flee, shoving aside a shell-shocked Francine and knocking a bewildered Shelby to the floor. He flung himself out the open side door and into the frigid night, the sound of his wife's screams following him.

CHAPTER TWELVE

Tucker Jenks leaned on his shovel, exhausted. He looked back toward the lights of the running snowplough. It had been an exhausting effort, but he had managed to clear about fifty feet of the roadway in front of the truck. That should give him a good running start for the plough to push through the thick snow in the roadway and clear a path to get the hell out of here.

The wind started picking up again, and he worried if it got strong enough it would blow the drifts back into the roadway he'd just cleared. There was no time to waste. At least it had stopped snowing.

He started back toward the truck when he heard something that made him stop.

Was the wind blowing hard? Or was the banshee howling again?

Not going to get me, he thought, hustling back to the truck. He opened the door and flung the shovel across the seat. As he began to climb up, he felt ice on the seat of the truck. In the illumination from the dome light, the ice looked red. That's when he realised it was frozen blood. The plough driver's blood.

He smashed the ice with his gloved right fist, breaking it up into chunks. Then he brushed the red pieces off the seat and into the snow outside. He climbed up into the seat and leaned out to grab hold of the door.

Time to leave, he told himself.

Before swinging the door shut, he heard the scream again.

Just the wind, he assured himself. *There's no banshee out here. It's only the wind.*

But he hesitated, listening. The wind wasn't that strong to howl like this. That's when he realised what he was hearing was a woman screaming.

CHAPTER THIRTEEN

Clark no longer thought of Graham. Nor did he think of the others. His only thought was of Shelby as he stared at the snow globe and watched the first snowman enter. After that, the globe became just a swirl of white snowflakes and the scene was gone. The snowflakes then turned red.

His stomach tightened.

He felt despair and helplessness, which soon turned to anger, his skin tingling as he looked up at the old man.

"What have you done?"

Sledge's eyes held their composure. There was no emotion behind them, not a hint of excitement or even satisfaction. His lips were tight. "Just finishing what I started." His eyes shifted to lock on to Clark's.

"Why?" Clark asked. "Why are you doing all this?" He looked at the globe, wishing the scene hadn't faded out, wanting to see more, trying to will the vision to return, even though he was afraid. And there was no doubt about that. Fear had boiled up inside him and his whole body felt like it was in a pressure cooker. More so than when he'd struggled out in the blizzard, and even more than when he'd been in the grips of that absurd maple tree's branches. He wished this were all a nightmare, that he was still lying delirious in the snow in a state of hallucinatory hypothermia.

This can't be real, he told himself. *This house can't be real, this man can't be real. None of this can be happening. Am I mad?*

But no. Thayer Sledge stood before him, a man long dead, who had somehow concocted this place and these circumstances.

"I did this for my great-grandson, despite the lowly miscreant life he made for himself."

"I don't understand," Clark said.

Sledge held up a finger and walked over to the hutch, opened the glass door and retrieved an object. He brought it over to Clark and held it in his open palm. It was a wooden cube. Lines showed it was constructed of multiple pieces.

"This was one of our first games," Sledge said. "A puzzle box. They were quite popular at the turn of the century. My century, I mean, not yours."

Clark stared at the object, confused. This was no answer.

"When I started my game company, we sold lots of these. Bernard Ferrin designed it, as he did many of our early puzzle games. It's fairly simple by today's standards. The cube is made of several interlocking pieces, each of a different shape." He reached up with his left hand and used two fingers to extract one of the pieces. He slid it partially out, pausing before removing it completely. "The pieces go together in a particular way. Once all the wooden pieces are connected, they form the solid wooden cube. But the pieces can only go together in one certain way; otherwise, the cube can't be formed and the puzzle remains in pieces, unsolved." He slid the wooden piece back inside and handed the cube to Clark. "I was never good at it. Bernard was the puzzle master."

Clark looked at the cube in his hand, still not understanding. "I don't get it."

"Of course you don't," Sledge said. "You don't know how to play games. Take that apart and put it together, and I'll show you more." He started to walk toward the door to the foyer, then stopped to turn back. "I believe it's my move in the chess game. I shall return. And don't think you can just pretend to solve the puzzle and give me back the solid cube." He pointed at the snow globe. "I'll be watching."

With the old man gone, the sense of loneliness swarmed over Clark. He felt lost, helpless. He didn't know where he was, or even when he was, for that matter. He took the puzzle box to the chair and sat down, placing the box on his lap. He wanted answers, but Sledge just played games with him. He thought about Shelby and her kids.

They can't be dead, he thought. The old man was playing tricks with him. He shouldn't trust what he said. The puzzle box on his lap beckoned. *Solve this stupid thing*, Clark thought, and maybe he'd get some answers. Maybe. He couldn't even be sure of that.

He pulled the first wooden block out of the cube. As soon as he removed the second piece, the cube fell apart, all the pieces separating. There were only ten pieces; it shouldn't be too hard. He tried to keep them together and remember the order they went. But as soon as he began sliding pieces together, he was already confused. He was unable to find a third piece that fit the other two. How could something with so few pieces be that difficult? It looked like a child's toy, and here he was, an intelligent man.

It was hard to concentrate. His mind drifted all over the place, but mostly back on the highway, worrying about Shelby. If he could find his boots and coat, he'd bust out of this place and head back. As long as he could get by that damn tree. He'd need to be careful about that. Without the snowshoes it would be tough. He remembered the toboggan he saw leaning up against the front stoop. It was mostly downhill to the highway. He could use that to get over the snow. (Just like the one he used to drag his grandfather's body to safety. Only he didn't make it in time. Time ran out on him. Was it running out on him now too?)

If only he could solve this damn puzzle.

Clark wished the fireplace was lit, because he felt chilled again. Of course, if there was a fire, he'd probably have thrown the stupid wooden puzzle pieces in it. *Solve that!*

He looked at his two interlocked pieces and began trying different blocks that would connect. Finally he found one that fit and slid it into place. With three pieces done, it was much easier finding a fourth to fit. Clark got excited. Somehow the puzzle coming together pushed aside the despondent feelings of his predicament. Somehow, solving this was the only thing that mattered to him right now.

A fifth and a sixth piece went into place. He grinned, a mad grin of a lunatic happy to be putting wooden blocks together. He didn't care. He wanted to one-up Thayer Sledge and right now this was the only way he could.

Finding a seventh piece to fit was tough. *Come on*, he yelled at himself. *Only a few more pieces. It should be getting easier, not harder.* Frustration was returning, along with tension. *So close. Can't fail now.*

A piece clicked into place and his nerves relaxed. The last two pieces were obvious, and once inserted, he held up the wooden box before him and smiled. *Take that, you bastard!*

A tapping sound came from the front window.

Clark looked up, startled, dropping the wooden cube onto the floor with a clatter.

A man looked in the window at him, face covered in frost, icicles clinging to his hair.

It was Graham.

CHAPTER FOURTEEN

Shelby looked up from the floor of the RV at the mayhem before her. She stared in horror as the snowman used its branch claws to tear Joy Drake apart. Thank God her screams had stopped, Shelby thought. The sound had been maddening. But Shelby felt dazed staring at the blood and flesh that covered the walls of the RV.

She looked up and saw Francine, who also looked on in shock. There were blood splatters on the old woman's white knit sweater, face, and even speckling her grey hair. The snowman in the top hat raised its head now that it was finished with Joy, blood dripping from its sharp white teeth and the tips of its branches, forming red streaks down its white bulbous body. It was grinning, leering at the two of them, before beginning to slide toward them.

Shelby pushed herself up, realising she had to get out of here, glancing at the open door through which both Mason Drake and Lewis Felker had fled. Mason had bolted like a coward, leaving his poor wife to her fate. Now Shelby realised she had to get out the same way. As Shelby got to her feet, Francine must have thought the same thing, for the old woman snapped out of her stunned state and moved to the door as well, knocking Shelby aside before disappearing outside, the door banging in its frame as she fled.

Shelby went down on her backside hard. When she looked up the snowman had crept closer. She sat up, glancing once more at her avenue of escape when the side door to the RV opened and its frame was filled with white.

Another snowman stood in the doorway, this one shorter and fatter, a red Santa cap with a white furred edge perched atop its head. Beneath its coal eyes was the plump butt end of a broken carrot stick; below that a beak-like opening of a mouth that began laughing.

The other snowman in front of her was grinning, blood dripping from its jaws.

Her way out was blocked.

She screamed.

Fear rippled through her as she knew she was trapped by this insanity. What she saw before her was so crazy she felt like capitulating rather than dealing with the madness of it all. But she thought about what they did to Joy and then she thought of Macey and Luke. She wasn't about to give up.

Shelby crawled backward, toward the back bedroom, screaming the whole time. Somehow it helped her move faster as she reached up and grabbed the doorknob to the bedroom, turned it and pushed the door open. She scampered back up onto the bed as the taller snowman followed her into the room, the shorter one right behind.

She couldn't take her gaze off those black coal eyes of the tall snowman. They seemed to sear right through her, as if she could feel the burning heat from the coal. She crawled to the back of the bed, by the headboard. The room was immersed in cold and she wondered if it was emanating from the snowman's body.

The creature leaned forward, reaching out its branches, the finger-shaped twigs at the end grasping the material of the comforter. It pulled the blanket forward, dragging her with it, toward that drooling grin with the sharp teeth.

Her mouth gaped open in mute horror.

Something grabbed her from behind and Shelby screamed again.

She turned her head to look behind her, trying to fight off the hand that had reached in the busted window and grabbed onto her jacket. She gazed up at this new adversary and saw a large black man's face.

"Come on!" he yelled. "This way!"

Before she could register comprehension, the man was dragging her out the broken window. As she was pulled out, she glanced back at the snowman in the top hat as it climbed up onto the bed after her.

The man set her down on her feet in the snow.

"We got to get out of here," he said, grabbing onto one of her hands. In his other hand he held a snow shovel.

Shelby didn't know who this man was or where the hell he'd come from, and her mind didn't have time to sort it out before she was whisked forward, glad to have the strength of the stranger's hand holding onto hers. He led her around to the left side of the RV and ahead she saw a sight that made her want to pull back.

A third snowman, this one wearing a black pork-pie hat, bent down over the prone body of Werner Volkmann, or what was left of him. Pieces were everywhere, splattering the white snow with gashes of red. The thing looked up, its jaws dripping red.

The stranger was pulling her along toward it, but she didn't have the strength to resist.

"Damn!" the man said, as they approached it, before swinging his shovel and lopping off the snowman's head. The round head went rolling along the snow-covered road, the hat flying off in the other direction. "Keep going!"

She still hadn't spoken a word to him, still too stunned to speak. She had been immersed in a nightmare, sure that a horrible death was imminent, and then suddenly whisked away by a man who appeared out of nowhere. Where had he come from? And more importantly, where was he taking her? She couldn't think, only kept moving to keep up with him, glad he hadn't let go of her hand.

He dragged her through the snow. Fear must have made her immune to the cold, because she couldn't feel it, even though the snow was up over the top of her boots. She spotted her minivan as they passed it, buried in the snow. It seemed so long ago that Clark and Graham had rescued her from it. Now she was being rescued a second time. Always the damsel in distress.

As they passed the hatchback, she thought about the couple inside that had died. At least they went peacefully, spared the horrors that followed, unlike Joy Drake and Werner Volkmann. And as for the others, who knew what fate had befallen them? She glanced back to see if the other snowmen were following. There was no sign of them.

When she turned back to the man in front of her, he helped her manoeuver around the jackknifed tractor-trailer. Where were they going? She soon found out when she saw the snowplough truck ahead, its lights on and engine running.

"Are you the snowplough driver?" Shelby asked.

"No," he said. "That's my rig back there." He pointed at the tractor-trailer. "But that ain't going anywhere. This is our ride out. I've cleared a path." He huffed, trying to catch his breath. He moved quickly for a large man. "We should be able to plough our way out of here."

Shelby stopped, pulling her hand free from the man's tight grip. He turned and gave her a puzzled look.

"We can't go," she said.

"What?" His face was masked in confusion.

"What's your name?" She kept her voice calm and even, concentrating on her breathing.

"Tucker."

"Well Tucker, my name's Shelby, and I'm ever so grateful for you saving my life." She paused to catch her breath. "But I also have two young children, a boy and a girl, and they were taken by this—" She didn't know how to explain it. "This horned creature or something. And I have to get them back."

"You do realise," he said, pointing in the direction they had just come, "that there was a fucking snowman back there eating some guy?"

"I know."

"And another one was about to eat you?"

"This thing took my kids," she said, as calmly as she was able to manage under the circumstances. "Do you have kids, Tucker?"

The man paused. "No," he finally said. "But I have nieces and nephews."

"I'll do this on my own," she said. "But I'd rather have some help."

"Damn!" he said, throwing the shovel down in frustration.

She smiled.

"Do you have any idea where they were taken?" he asked.

Shelby shook her head. "No, but a couple of guys with us spotted a house through the woods with a light on and they headed there to get help."

"And did they get help?"

She shook her head again. "They haven't come back."

"Oh my Christ!" He threw up his hands. "And that's where you want to go?"

"If we can find them, and whoever else is at that house, maybe we can get some help to find my children." She stammered, on the verge of tears, trying to hold them back. "I-I don't know what else to do."

"Okay," he said, palms out in a calming gesture. "We'll go look. Let me just shut this damn truck off before it runs out of gas and we don't get nowhere." He went to the plough and climbed up into the driver's side. The engine's rumbling stopped and the lights went dark. When he climbed back down he had a flashlight in his hand. "Let's see if we can find your friends and this house."

"Thank you." She smiled. "It was this way." She pointed toward the woods beyond the west side of the highway.

Tucker led the way. "I must be crazy to go traipsing through the woods with man-eating snowmen and horned creatures running around out here."

CHAPTER FIFTEEN

Clark scurried to the front door, heart racing like a kid on – huh – Christmas morning. He grabbed the knob on the door, praying it would open this time, which it did. The cold pushed its way in. He leaned out, looking left.

Graham shuffled over, arms wrapped around himself, body hunched, shivering.

"Jesus!" Clark exclaimed, ushering him inside. "Get in here quick."

He closed the door and immediately led his friend to the living room, bringing him to one of the wingback chairs beside the fire and easing his stiff body into it. He hadn't noticed if Sledge's servant, Wick, kept stoking the fire, but the blaze somehow was still roaring, throwing off its warmth.

Graham's face was iced over, casting a deathly white pall, his hands were bare, the flesh on his curled fingers a bluish hue. His teeth chattered.

"What the hell happened to you out there?" Clark asked, rubbing the frosted fabric of his friend's winter coat. His shoulders and arms felt tight. "I looked for you."

"F-f-f-freez-ing," Graham managed to utter with great effort.

"I'm not surprised," Clark said. "You've been out there quite awhile." In actuality, he had no idea how much time had passed. (*Time has no meaning here*, Sledge had said.) "I'm surprised you're even alive." He continued to rub Graham's back and shoulders, trying to massage warmth into him. At least the fire was hot.

"I f-f-fell into a sn-sn-snow well," Graham strained to say. "I was b-buried. I couldn't move."

"Well, thank God you got out." Clark looked around for a blanket of some sort, but saw nothing like that in the room. He needed to get his friend thawed out. He looked at his boots, which were caked in snow. His toes must be frozen. But Clark was more concerned about his fingers, surprised the tips hadn't turned black.

"I saw S-Spencer," Graham said. "He was just below me in the snow. But I couldn't reach him."

He must be delirious, Clark thought, *bringing up the brother he lost*. He ignored the reference.

"Even after all these y-years," Graham went on, "I still couldn't reach h-him."

"Don't think about that," Clark said. "You're here now. You're safe." He almost had to laugh at the thought that Graham was no safer in here than he was outside. How to explain to him everything he'd seen and learned since he'd gotten to this house? Clark still didn't understand it himself.

But he couldn't think of that now. His biggest concern at the moment was getting Graham warm. He must be suffering from hypothermia. Clark needed to help him, even if it meant getting Sledge.

"Stay right here by the fire and thaw out, buddy," Clark said, patting his friend's shoulder. "I'm going to see if I can get you a blanket or something, maybe a change of clothes." *There must be something in this house I can find*, he thought. There were three men living here. He thought about that, realising it wasn't quite accurate. They weren't really living.

"I'll be right back," he said, before leaving the room.

"I'll b-be here," Graham uttered through chattering teeth.

Clark crossed the foyer into the other room, thinking Sledge might have returned there, but it was empty. He looked at the snow globe glowing in the centre of the room. The scene inside had changed to an image of the very house they were in now, snow falling down over it. There was one light in the window to the left of the front door.

He turned to go, but something caught his eye. It was the wooden cube puzzle he had solved. It was on the floor where he'd dropped it earlier. Clark reached down and picked it up. Sledge had promised answers if he solved it.

Back in the foyer, Clark glanced up the winding staircase. Darkness saturated the top of the landing. Past the stairway was a doorway leading to what must be the back end of the house. Clark bypassed the staircase, headed for the door, and pushed through it.

Beyond it was a dining room with a long trestle table surrounded by a dozen chairs. Two long candles in brass tapers on the centre of the table were lit, casting a dim glow throughout the room, but leaving its edges in shadow. There were two doors in the room, one at the back and one to the right.

Clark went through the one to the right and found himself in the kitchen. The room was dark. Silhouettes of pots and pans hung from a rack suspended over an island countertop. On it was a wooden knife-holder block, the handles of half a dozen assorted knives poking out. It reminded him of the one in Benson Read's kitchen, the one the old man used to… no, he didn't want to remember that day.

Clark thought about grabbing one of the knives to at least have a weapon, but were knives any use against dead men? He couldn't imagine.

A door at the back of the kitchen led outside. He glanced around. There was another door to his right and he opened it. It was a pantry with empty shelves. Dead people don't need to eat, he thought. (*But they drink hot buttered rum?*) At the end of the kitchen was another staircase leading up. Beside that was another door, which upon opening revealed a staircase descending into a basement.

Clark felt like he was in a maze. He went back into the dining room and tried the other door. He found himself in some kind of solarium along the back of the house, with glass walls looking out into a garden of snow-covered hedges. Moonlight streaked in through the windows, illuminating plant stands of green ferns, hollies, poinsettias and a tall robust balsam tree in one corner. There was a round patio table surrounded by wicker chairs. A cornucopia centrepiece overflowed with bright ripe fruit. *Maybe Sledge sits out here and plays with his board games*, Clark thought, chuckling to himself. An image of Sledge, Ferrin and Wick sitting at the table moving tokens around a game board came to mind.

He was getting nowhere and realised he needed to get back to check on Graham. Clark returned to the dining room. A familiar cracking sound came from down the hallway. He stepped out and saw another doorway he hadn't noticed. It was open a crack and Clark leaned close, putting one eye to the opening to peer in.

Sledge and Wick stood around a pool table playing billiards. Clark pushed the door open and stepped in.

"Lost?" Sledge asked, leaning over the table and taking a shot.

"You could say I've been lost all night," Clark said, watching the eight ball roll across the green felt and drop into a corner pocket. Clark seethed at the calmness of the man. He slammed the puzzle box down on the pool table. "I've solved your damn puzzle!"

The old man looked down with disappointment. Clark enjoyed the moment, however brief. Sledge picked up the box, turning it over in his hand, examining it as if Clark had pulled some deception.

Wick stood by silent, tapping his cue stick against his open palm.

"Mr. Wick," Sledge said, "I believe you have some unfinished business to take care of."

"Yes, sir," Wick said, returning his cue stick to the rack on the wall. He brushed past Clark on his way out of the room, a mad grin on his craggy face.

"Never send a snowman to do an Iceman's job," Sledge said. "Bumbling buffoons." He laid his own cue stick down on the table. "Well done." Sledge set the puzzle box down on the table beside his stick. "Though it was designed to be solved by a child."

"What does it mean?" Clark asked.

Sledge sucked in a breath. "The pieces of the puzzle fit together in an intricate pattern. That's the beauty of the box. Each piece has to go in place exactly right for the puzzle to be put together. One piece out of place, and the whole puzzle falls apart."

"So?"

"One thing I've learned since I've passed on and ended up –" he looked around, "– here, is that our lives are made up of pieces. And if the right pieces don't fall into place, it can all fall apart."

This felt like a brainteaser and it hurt Clark's head. "What the hell are you talking about?"

"On that schoolyard playground more than a quarter century ago, your friend threw a snowball at you."

Clark's mind drew up the image he had seen in the snow globe of that distant memory.

"So?"

"When you ducked and that snowball struck my great-grandson Leroy, it set off a chain reaction. A snowball effect that ended with him dying on that train track a year ago."

CHAPTER SIXTEEN

Francine Volkmann wandered through the woods, the numbing cold freezing out the thoughts of the horror back on the highway. It wasn't supposed to happen this way, she thought as she stumbled along. That wasn't what *he* had led them to expect.

She had fled the RV and when she saw what had been done to her husband, she kept running, or at least what one could call running considering the waist-high snow she had to blunder through. She was without a coat and at first terror had prevented her from feeling the elements, but now an icy grip sank its talons into her, clawing into her bones. Francine tucked her hands under her arms to keep her bare fingers warm. It didn't help much and made it awkward to walk. She stumbled often, falling several times, but she always got back up, knowing if she just lay in the snow, death would sweep right over her.

Her only hope now was to find the house. That's why she was heading through the woods, grateful that the snow wasn't as deep here, making it much easier to walk. There was no feeling below her knees, but she kept her legs moving. At least the wind wasn't blowing.

There was no sign of the light at the house the others had spotted through the woods. She hoped she was heading in the right direction. Morning had to come soon. Regardless, she was putting distance between her and the highway and those horrible things that had emerged from the storm.

Francine didn't understand everything that had happened. It had all gone wrong and now Werner was gone and she was alone. Alone in the woods on a stormy winter day. This was not how she'd expected to spend Christmas.

Francine emerged from the woods and found herself on…

…a street?

It was daylight.

Oh my, she thought, *morning has broken fast.*

There were houses along both sides of the ploughed street, the snowbanks high along the edges, mailboxes poking out of the piles. The scene looked familiar. She marvelled as she looked around. She knew this place. This was Charron Street in Berlin, New Hampshire, where she grew up. Down below was Main Street and downtown nestled along the Androscoggin River.

But how could that be? She was nowhere near there. This couldn't be right.

Francine walked down the street, looking up at the hillside above and the bare trees dotting it. Down the end of the road was Hill Street. She remembered walking down it on her way to Bartlett School. She recalled sledding down the road during that terrible winter.

Of course, that was before the bad things had begun to happen.

She continued down the snowy street till she got to the house she knew very well, the one she'd grown up in. She brought her hand to her mouth in awe, forgetting how cold and raw her fingers were. She stood at the end of the driveway looking at the house, not daring to walk up to it.

Francine's trance was interrupted by footsteps and she turned to see Calvin, the mailman, walking down the street toward her, mailbag slung over one shoulder, fur-lined flaps of his cap down over his ears, framing his round red face. She saw the smile beneath his walrus mustache when he saw her.

"Hello there, Francine," Calvin said with a toothy grin.

She looked at him in silence.

This was all wrong, but it felt so good to see a familiar face after all she'd been through.

"Hi," she said, still stunned.

"Some storm last night, eh?" He stopped before her.

Francine looked up. The sun shone down from a bright blue sky, glaring off the crusty snow covering.

"Yes, it was," she agreed. She looked at his mailbag. "Anything for me?"

"I believe there is," he said, bending his head down and digging through his mail pouch. "I think there's a Christmas present in my bag for you."

Francine smiled with glee. "I can't wait to see what it is."

Calvin continued to rummage through the bag, digging down past the envelopes.

Something occurred to Francine. Something wasn't right.

"Calvin," she said. "How come you're delivering mail on Christmas?"

His hand stopped moving, as if it had found something in the pouch. His head tipped back to look at her. His face had changed, the mustache gone, the skin craggy, straw-like hair poking out from under his mail cap.

"Because I have a special delivery for you today." He grinned with crooked teeth as his hand withdrew from the mail sack, pulling out a pair of black ice tongs.

Francine stepped back, her mouth opening. Before she could utter a sound, or comprehend what she was seeing, Everett Wick raised the tongs in both hands.

She was about to scream when he plunged the sharp points of the tongs into the sides of her neck. Her scream was drowned in the rush of blood that flooded her throat from the punctured jugular vein and carotid artery.

Francine collapsed to the ground by her mailbox, raising her head as she gurgled on her own blood. She looked up one last time at the back of the Iceman as he walked away, blood dripping from the ends of the ice tongs, staining the snow on the road.

CHAPTER SEVENTEEN

"You're crazy," Clark exclaimed, incredulous. "You blame that schoolyard incident on what happened to your great-grandson? That's insanity."

"I'm not saying that one indiscretion caused everything." Sledge leaned forward, both hands gripping the edge of the pool table. "It was just the catalyst that set everything in motion."

He may be dead, Clark thought, *but worse than that, he's mad*. Maybe that's what a place like this did to you. Maybe being wherever they were distorted your mind after so much time. If so, Clark needed to find a way out.

"Whatever happened to Leroy Sledge, he chose his own path."

Sledge chuckled. "Not quite. Let me show you what I mean." He stepped over to the wooden cabinet against the side wall and opened one of the bottom drawers. He extracted a large wooden box, but as he did, Clark noticed something else in the drawer, a revolver. He took note of which drawer it was in, in case he got a chance to get back to this room.

The old man set the wooden box on the pool table and Clark peered closer. It was a tabletop labyrinth. He remembered having one as a child. There were knobs on each side of the box to control the surface of the maze. Sledge took a round silver marble out of a slot and placed it on a spot at the starting line of the maze.

"More games?" Clark asked.

"Our lives can follow different paths," Sledge said, turning the knobs that tilted the surface and manoeuvered the ball through the labyrinth and around the holes. "And along the way, obstacles intervene and alter our course, and if we're not careful –" the ball dropped through a hole, "– we get lost." He stepped back from the table and looked across at Clark.

"And that's what happened to Leroy?" Clark asked. He had never been able to get to the finish line in the labyrinth game those many years ago, no matter how many times he tried. Close, but never to the finish.

"You and your friend Graham were the first of many obstacles that hindered my great-grandson's life."

"You base a lot on games."

"My whole life was built around games," Sledge said. "It's what got me everything I had."

"And what got you here? You finally played a game you lost?"

Sledge chuckled. "I played a demon in a game of Snakes and Ladders. I had a chance to go up –" he held his hands in the air – "but I ended up down in this realm. Of course it didn't quite look like this. I built this place, well, in a manner of speaking. Not with my hands, but with my imagination."

"So you finally lost at a game." Now it was Clark's turn to chuckle. He could tell from the look on the old man's face that he didn't appreciate it.

"But who's losing now?"

This infuriated Clark. "Those people on the highway aren't just token pieces on a game board," he said, his voice raised. "They're real people with real lives."

"That's where you're wrong."

"They're just innocent people," Clark pleaded.

"You're quite mistaken," Sledge said. "Follow me."

He led Clark out of the billiard room and down the grand foyer to the room with the snow globe. On his way by, Clark peered into the open doorway to the living room and saw Graham still warming himself by the fire.

Sledge waited for him by the snow globe. The scene inside it as Clark approached was the house they were in. Snow still fell inside the globe.

"I told you that you and your friend were just the beginning. There were others who affected the course of poor Leroy's life." He passed his hand over the globe. A series of faces floated inside the glowing orb. "His expulsions from school, beginning with the incident with your friend led Leroy to meeting and befriending another troubled youth, Evan Hodge, who ended up introducing Leroy to drugs. He was the son of Toby Hodge."

"Who the hell is Toby Hodge?"

"He was the snowplough driver," Sledge said as another face appeared in the globe. "You don't want to know what happened to him."

Clark glanced up at the man's expression. He was revelling in this, he thought. He could see it in his eyes.

"Of course Leroy ended up dropping out of high school as you may recall. His father tried to help him, got him a position at the Sledge &

Ferrin Game Co. A low-level job of course, something made up to help keep him off the street. But it was a start, and Leroy worked toward his GED in the meantime. There was opportunity to grow in the company. But then the parent company I sold the business to brought in a consultant to scale down the firm and eliminate any dead weight."

Another face materialised. Clark didn't recognise it.

"Dean Hagen was his name, and of course Leroy's meaningless position was jettisoned, with little deference to the fact that he carried the Sledge name. Mr. Hagen was the man who ran naked into the storm. I'm sure his body is nicely preserved somewhere out there." The old man smiled.

Out in the hallway, Clark could hear the sound of rattling chains approaching. He imagined it must be Bernard Ferrin's move in the chess game. More games, he thought. What significance could that one have, he wondered?

"Once unemployed," Sledge continued, "poor Leroy slipped back into his bad habits. His father sent him to live in a drug rehab facility down south. It was only a few months before he slipped out one day. He probably would have been caught fairly quickly, since he wasn't familiar with the area or anyone down there, but he managed to hitch a ride with a truck driver on a run back up northeast."

Clark saw the brown face of the truck driver appear in the globe. "Tucker Jenks shared some pot with Leroy, and that's all it took to unravel all the work the rehab centre had accomplished. Jenks dropped Leroy off in Manchester, and my great-grandson began a life living on the streets. It wasn't long before drugs led to other crimes, and soon he was committing burglaries. That led to a stint in the state prison. Even his father and all our family money and lawyers couldn't help him."

"Another hole in the maze," Clark said, staring into the globe.

"Indeed," Sledge responded. "Once Leroy was out of prison, the family again tried to intervene and help get him on the straight and narrow. But a simple parole violation sent him back, something that could have been easily overlooked by his parole officer...."

"Mason Drake," Clark finished, seeing the man's image pop up in the globe.

"Yes. Leroy bounced between jail and the streets, living the transient life when he wasn't in a cell, scoring drugs when he got the chance. When last winter set in, he was able to get shelter at the Salvation Army homeless facility. But he was ratted out picking another transient's pocket by Lewis Felker and kicked out." The face of the Salvation Army worker floated in the globe. "There was no place for Leroy to go, except the streets. The last day of his life, last November, he was panhandling and a couple of young college kids felt pity for him and gave him some money.

The image of the dead young couple in the hatchback appeared in the snow globe and Clark felt his blood stir.

"They were just trying to help him," he said through gritted teeth.

"And do you know what he did with the money they gave him? He bought heroin and shot himself up under a bridge beside the railroad tracks." The old man leaned forward so the glow from inside the globe cast a light up under his face, a glow highlighting his expression. "That was the last day of his life."

Wait a minute, Clark thought. Something was missing. Shelby. Her face hadn't appeared. Nor her kids. His heart had been racing anticipating her image before him and he had dreaded it, trying to block out what horrible fate might have befallen her inside the doomed RV.

"Shelby," he uttered softly. He raised his eyes to look at Sledge. "Shelby and her kids. They had no part in this, did they?" He wanted an answer. At least he thought he did.

"Sometimes," Sledge said, "you can move pieces around on a game board, but you can't necessarily control everything."

"You fucked up, you bastard." Clark clenched his fists by his side.

"Not exactly," Sledge said with a sigh. "Shelby Wallace was not supposed to be out in the storm tonight. Her husband was supposed to bring the children home to her, but he got drunk and couldn't drive, so she went and picked up the kids."

"So her husband?"

"Nelson Wallace was the engineer driving the train that killed Leroy Sledge."

"So Shelby didn't deserve what you've done." Clark felt the urge to throttle the man if he only thought it would do any good.

"Unfortunate circumstance," was Sledge's response.

Something else occurred to Clark.

"And her kids? You were willing to sacrifice them too?"

"Hell no," Sledge said. "I'm not a monster. I wouldn't hurt the children. I had them brought here with me."

"What?" This shocked Clark, trying to fathom the thought that they were somewhere in this house all this time. In the distance, the rattling of chains made their way up the staircase. Were Shelby's kids in chains somewhere in the house?

"It gets lonely here," Sledge said. "I wanted the children for companionship. Seems a fair trade for the loss of my great-grandson."

"Did you even know Leroy that well?" Clark asked.

"Not really. I died two years after he was born."

"He wasn't a nice kid."

"That doesn't matter," Sledge said. "He was family." The man turned to go. "And now I believe Mr. Ferrin is done and it's my move."

"You didn't show me the Volkmanns in your snow globe," Clark said, almost forgetting about the couple who had rescued them, though it all seemed a moot point now.

Sledge stopped in the doorway and turned back.

"Oh yes, the Volkmanns. You'll get a laugh out of this."

"I doubt that." Nothing was remotely funny to Clark this evening. Or this morning rather. It had been a long night.

"They are actually Leroy's grandparents on his mother's side of the family." The old man chortled. "I sort of recruited them for their help."

Clark couldn't believe it. They seemed like a typical nice old couple. "So they were dead too?" he asked, wondering if they inhabited this realm like Thayer Sledge.

He laughed again. "Well, I hope so now," he said, his grin wide. "Useless pawns are usually sacrificed after serving their purpose." He strode out of the room.

Clark turned back to the snow globe. Its image had returned to the house he was in. He wished it would show him something useful, something to help him get out of here. Or at least maybe where Shelby's kids were. Since he hadn't been able to save her, he wished he could at least save her kids.

He waved his hand over the globe, like he'd seen Sledge do. Nothing happened. Snow still fell on the house inside. He had the urge to pick the damn thing up and smash it on the floor. He moved his hands toward it, feeling static electricity as his fingers got close to the glass, like some kind of energy was emanating from it. What power did this thing have? He was afraid to touch it.

Clark suddenly thought of Graham.

He hurried from the room. Across the hall, in the other room, Graham still sat by the fire. Clark looked over at the chessboard, but neither Sledge nor Ferrin were there. Sledge must have already made his move. Clark wondered what it could be.

He approached Graham.

"How you doing, pal?"

"Still cold," Graham said, nodding.

Clark looked at his friend. Something was odd. Even though Graham was sitting by the fire, which threw out tremendous heat, his face was still covered over in an icy frost. Nothing had melted even after all this time.

"What's wrong with you?" Clark asked.

"Funny thing happened when I fell in that snow well out there," Graham said. He was grinning.

"What happened?"

"I died."

CHAPTER EIGHTEEN

The screams of Mason Drake's wife reverberated in his skull as he fled up the highway away from the RV. He wanted the wind to pick up and drown out the sound and as if on cue it did, blowing snow in his face.

Shame nagged at him as he clambered through the snow heading for his car. He had a chance to stay and save Joy, but instead he had turned coward and ran. He should have been her protector. The fear in her eyes as that thing grabbed her was imprinted in his mind.

And then the screams.

Mason had stood in horror as the branch arms of the snowman shredded her sweater and started stripping the flesh from her bones. He had fled to save himself the same fate. There was no honour in that. He had failed her, but at least he was alive. How would he explain this to their kids?

The only important thing now was to survive. Without a winter coat he wouldn't last long. That's why he was trying to get to his vehicle. He wasn't sure what he'd do when he reached the SUV; start it and get warm for starters. He still wouldn't be able to drive it out, but it would give him time to think.

Then it dawned on him.

The keys!

They were in his coat pocket back in the RV. Dammit! *Need a new plan.*

Mason looked around. On the opposite side of the highway were the woods where Clark and Graham had gone to find the house they had seen. He searched through the trees, trying to spot the light, but there was no sign of it.

He turned to look on the northbound side of the highway, also bordered by snow-covered trees. But there was something else. Mason climbed through a snowdrift until he bumped into the guardrail buried beneath. He looked down below where the ground sloped to a gap in the trees. It was a frozen river under the highway, cutting a path through the woods. He tried to recall what river it was, trying to remember where on the highway they had been. Driving in the storm it had been hard to decipher at what spot they had ground to a halt. He remembered passing an exit, but wasn't sure what number, only focusing on the road ahead.

But wherever he was, rivers usually flowed through towns, so if he could just follow this one, maybe it would lead him to safety. Mason scrambled over the snowbank at the edge of the road, lost his footing and pitched forward. He cried out as he tumbled down the embankment, rolling like a snowball. He came to a stop when he slammed into the base of a small tree, banging his hip.

"Damn!" he yelled, pain searing up his side. He lay still, puffing out white breaths of air. At least he was still breathing, he thought as he got to his feet, brushing snow off his clothes as best he could.

He walked to the edge of the river, his left side aching. Light was beginning to break and it allowed him to see the frozen river winding through the woods. He should be able to keep fairly close to its edge, he thought, and follow it. He hoped it wasn't too far to a town or maybe some homes where he might seek help. He prayed he would last that long. He was already shivering.

But he also felt a shot of adrenaline that produced a burst of energy to help keep his mind off the cold. He was taking action at least, instead of sitting around in that RV feeling helpless. Maybe he should have offered to go with Clark and Graham, or even with Shelby to find her kids. But he hadn't wanted to leave Joy's side.

Ironic how that'd turned out, he thought, and erupted with a mad chuckle. He chalked it up to the stress of what he'd just endured. But as he followed the river's edge, weaving around the trees, the echoes of Joy's screams in his head grew fainter.

Push on, he told himself, *or it's the end for you.* His path was serpentine as he dodged each tree keeping his eyes to the left, making sure not to stray too far from the river. It was important to keep close to it. It was his lifeline. Otherwise he would get lost out here. He turned the corner around a tree and stopped in his tracks.

A snowman stood a few yards in front of him.

Or at least a part of a snowman. It had the round base and a middle ball, but its head was missing. Out of its midsection, two branches extended, hanging limply by its side.

Mason stared at it for a moment, thinking of the snowman in the RV and wondering if this one was like that. It was smaller than the one that had attacked Joy, and without a head it had no teeth.

It can't see you, he thought. *It has no head, no face, no eyes. Just walk around it.*

But what was it doing out here?

Maybe it wasn't like that other diabolical creature. It could be that someone had started to build it but never finished. That might mean there was a house nearby. He looked beyond the snowman, scanning the woods for some sign of a dwelling.

There was nothing.

But he might be close, he thought. Excitement spurred him on, and he walked around the snowman. Something gripped his arm, pulling at his sleeve. He thought he had gotten it snagged on a branch and turned. He was right, but the branch belonged to the arm of the headless snowman. It had reached out and grabbed him with its twiggy claw.

Mason reeled back, heart jumping into his throat, the sleeve tearing. Once free, he turned and ran, not looking back to see if it was following. He ducked under the branch of a tree in front of him, but not quick enough and it lashed across his eyes. He screamed, putting his hand up to his face and feeling blood on the bridge of his nose. His eyes watered, blurring his vision.

He stumbled through the woods, pulse pounding at the thought of that thing behind him. Through his blurred sight he spied a clearing ahead and staggered between two trees toward it.

Mason looked back to see if the thing was following. His feet slid out from under him and he went crashing to the ground. A thud sounded as he landed and pain shot through his whole body. He had landed on something hard.

It was ice. He had inadvertently run out onto the middle of the frozen river.

Slowly, he got to his feet, steadying himself. He looked to the edge of the shore closest to him.

Two snowmen stood on the shoreline. One was the snowman in the top hat and scarf that had killed Joy. The other was a shorter one with a Santa hat on. That one raised one of its branch arms and waved, the twigs of its fingers flapping, its mouth opening in a silent giggle.

Mason turned to look at the opposite shoreline. It was farther away, but he began taking slow strides toward it. *It's not that far*, he told himself.

A crack sounded and he stopped.

He glanced down at his feet, keeping still. Behind him, he saw the snowmen weren't approaching. They were standing on the riverbank watching him. The ice groaned beneath his weight. Holding his breath, he took another step. More groans from beneath, and he even thought the surface of the ice moved.

The shoreline was no closer. *I can make it*, he thought. *I can get there.*

Mason took one more step and the ice opened up beneath his feet, plunging him down into frigid water, the pain from the cold sucking the breath out of him. He gripped the edge of the hole, holding himself up. The water was up to his chest. He had never experienced such pain in his life. His chest felt like it was being squeezed by a burning vise. Everything below that point was numb. He tried kicking his legs, to keep himself up, but he couldn't even tell if they were moving.

A glow emanated from the icy water below him and he looked down.

A body floated below him, drifting up toward his feet. As it turned in the clear water, its head tipped back, face coming into view. He recognised him, Selden Crockett, his friend from high school, who had drowned when they'd crashed their car into the lake.

This can't be.

He looked just like he had that day the police divers pulled his body from the frozen lake – hair iced back, face white, eyes closed (thank God), arms raised and fists clenched. He hadn't been able to pound his way through the ice, Mason thought. It was too thick.

Up here, Mason's mind called out. *There's a way out up here. Here's a hole!*

Selden's eyes opened.

Mason felt his fingers slipping on the edge of the ice, losing their grip.

Selden's lips spread in a grin and his arms pushed his body up toward Mason's. When he reached Mason's feet, his fists unclenched, and he grabbed onto his ankles.

Mason felt himself being pulled under and he frantically clawed at the ice, digging his fingernails in, trying to reestablish his grip. The force below was strong, and Mason didn't think he could hold on much longer.

I tried, he thought, thinking of his children. *It just wasn't enough.*

His grip released and he sank down into the frigid water.

Before the numbing cold overtook him completely, he looked up at the hole in the ice in time to see the heads of the two snowmen peering down at him. The one in the Santa hat raised its branch hand and waved goodbye.

CHAPTER NINETEEN

"What are you talking about?" Clark asked, coming around to stand before Graham.

His friend sat in the chair with his frosty head bowed. He held his hands clasped, rubbing his white fingers slowly.

"When I was in the snow well, I couldn't breathe." His head stayed down. He wouldn't look up at Clark. "The snow was heavy and…I suffocated." He looked up, and Clark could see all the colour had drained from his irises and his eyes were pure white.

Clark took a shuddered step back, banging up against the bookcase beside the fireplace. He reached his left hand out to grab the edge of a shelf to brace himself, looking at the games stacked on it. He saw the one titled Haunted Mansion, with the picture of a creepy old house on the cover, a game he remembered having as a child. The object was to move your token through the mansion, being wary of spooks and goblins that would thwart the player's attempt to escape. There was something familiar about the house on the cover with its lone circular window looking out from a gabled third-floor dormer. It dawned on him after picturing it with a layer of snow. It was the house they were in.

"You're delirious," Clark said, ignoring the sight of the frozen man before him.

"I saw him," Graham said through bluish lips.

"Saw who?" Clark wondered if he was talking about Thayer Sledge, or maybe Everett Wick.

"My brother," he answered. "I could only see his boots, but I knew they were his."

Clark stayed silent.

"And you know what?" Graham continued. "I couldn't reach him. I still wasn't able to save him."

"Don't think about that." They had to get out of this house, or whatever this place was. It wasn't real. None of this was real. He had to help his friend up, and he needed to find Shelby's kids and get the hell out of here, back to the highway, back to some kind of reality.

If it was still there.

"You shouldn't have ducked," Graham said.

"What?" Clark looked around the room, wondering where the hell his boots could be. He certainly couldn't go running around in the snow in his stocking feet. He'd never make it, not without losing a few toes along the way.

"That day on the playground, when I threw the snowball at you. You should have taken the hit and not been such a wimp."

"You're talking gibberish."

Clark looked out the window. It was light out, dawn breaking. That would make it easier to find their way back.

"This is all your fault. If you hadn't ducked, none of this would be happening."

Had Sledge gotten to him, brainwashed him? The old man had been in here recently to make his chess move. Where the hell had he gone to now?

"I have something for you," Graham said, his voice ominous. He reached his hand into his jacket pocket. "I found it out in the snow and brought it for you."

Clark looked at him.

Graham pulled his hand out of his pocket. In it he held a snowball. Jagged shards of ice stuck out of it. Graham compacted it with his palms, compressing it, the sharp points of the ice cutting into the flesh of his hands, drawing blood that oozed onto the snowball, the red soaking into the ball like flavoured syrup onto a snow cone.

Clark didn't like the look on Graham's face, or the madness he saw in those damned eyes.

"You're going to take this one," Graham said, rising up out of the chair. "And we're going to end this now."

Clark shot a glance toward the foyer and the front door. Could he reach it in time? He sprinted toward it, knowing he had to get away from whatever his friend had become. He grabbed the knob, turned it, pulled on the door frantically, but it wouldn't budge.

"It's no use," Graham said, gripping the snowball in a bloody hand and lurching toward him like some ghoul. "There's no way out of here." He had reached the entryway to the foyer.

Clark eyed the staircase and the dark landing above. He ran for it and leaped up the stairs two or three at a time, his heart racing as fast as his feet, but still feeling slow.

"You killed us all!" Graham yelled as he began mounting the staircase. "Now it's time for you."

At the top of the stairs, a hallway stretched in both directions. Clark turned right, but he guessed it didn't matter which way he went. He tried remembering where the back staircase he had seen in the kitchen was in relation to this part of the house. If only he could get to that and out the back door before Graham caught up to him.

Closed doors lined both sides of the hall as he ran by. He wondered if the kids were locked up behind one of them. He couldn't leave without trying to find them. And some boots.

He stopped, hearing something. It was the rattling of chains. It came from behind one of the doors. Maybe the kids were chained up in one of the rooms.

"Stop!" Graham yelled.

Clark looked back down the hall where the ghastly image of his friend stood, still clutching the snowball.

"You can't escape this," Graham said. "There's no use running."

Clark backed up against a window at the end of the hall. Maybe the staircase was behind one of these doors. He opened one as Graham moved down the hall toward him. There was a staircase behind the door, but it went up to the third floor.

This house felt like a maze.

"Hey, Clarkie boy!" Graham yelled, winding up his right arm like a baseball pitcher. "Catch this, pretty boy!" He hurled the snowball.

Even in the dim lighting of the hallway, Clark could see the object hurtling toward him, jagged ice poking out of the red-stained ball.

Clark ducked.

Like all those many years ago on that school playground, the snowball sailed over his head and broke through one of the panes of the window behind him.

"You *fucker!*" Graham screamed, his frozen mouth spitting saliva.

Clark straightened up just as Graham reached him.

"Why did you do that again?" Graham asked, his face pained. "Now look what you've made me do." He looked behind Clark at the broken window, cold air and flakes of snow blowing in. "Mr. Sledge is going to be furious with us." His eyes fell on Clark. "This is all your fault." He reached out and grabbed Clark by the throat, squeezing icy fingers into his neck.

"Graham!" Clark yelled hoarsely as his throat tightened. "This isn't you." He tried reasoning with his friend as the breath was being squeezed out of him. The dead white eyes bored into his with wrath. He remembered something Sledge had said. *The dead resent the living.*

But this was his childhood friend, his best friend.

"Please," Clark said, trying to pull the stiff arms off him with no luck. "You don't want this."

Graham's eyes softened and his grip relaxed. He looked down at his gashed bloody white hands. "Oh my God," he said, amazement on his face. "What am I?"

"You're Graham Sawyer," Clark said. "You're my friend. You're a husband and a father."

Graham's eyes met Clark's, full of sadness. "I'm dead." It was as if it had just occurred to him. "And I'm very cold."

Clark didn't know how to respond.

"I'm so tired of being cold," Graham said, taking a step back. A trickle of water ran from his temple down his right cheek. The frost on his skin and hair was thawing out. "What's happening to me?" His eyes looked confused. Steamy mist dissipated from his flesh, as if his whole body was vaporising. "Say goodbye to Natalie and the girls for me," he said with pleading eyes.

"I will," Clark said. He tried to reach out and grab hold of his friend, but it was too late.

With one last look from those white eyes, Graham's flesh turned to mist and his whole body collapsed, the vapour sucked out through the opening in the broken window, leaving behind only a jumbled bundle of clothes and boots.

Clark knelt down, wanting to scream. Instead, he composed himself and grabbed Graham's coat and boots and put them on, finally glad to have something on his feet. They were a little tight in the toes, but they'd do in a pinch. He glanced at the broken window. *That might be the only way out,* he thought, striding over to it. After removing some big shards of glass, he peered out.

There was no ground below, only a white void. He thought about what Sledge said about this place, what it represented. Maybe there was no way out.

The clinking of metal drew his attention back to the hallway. Chains, he remembered. Someone was behind one of these doors.

But which?

Clark ignored the one that led to the stairs to the third floor and tried the one just past it down the hall when he noticed a dim light from under the bottom of the door. It opened when he turned the knob and he peeked in warily.

Bernard Ferrin sat in a heap in a wooden chair before a rolltop desk. He was trying a key in one of the padlocks on his chains, but stopped when he noticed Clark.

"Lost?" he sighed.

Clark entered, closing the door gently behind him. The only other furniture in the room was a four-poster bed covered in rumpled sheets. An oil lamp on the desk illuminated Ferrin's face, but little else in the room. Was there no electricity here? Clark wondered. Did a place like this even need electricity?

"You could say I'm lost," Clark said.

"Join the club." Ferrin continued trying the key in a lock.

"My best friend is dead." Clark sighed. "And he just tried to kill me." Saying it out loud sounded ludicrous.

"We're all dead here." Ferrin did not look up, concentrating on his keys, sorting through the choices and selecting another one.

"I'm not," Clark emphasised, still afraid to raise his voice. He didn't know where Sledge or his henchman, Wick, was.

"Some fates are much worse than death." Ferrin tried a key unsuccessfully.

Clark walked over to the desk. "Why are you here?"

Ferrin looked up. "Do you see these chains? It's not me that's fettered. It's him. I'm bound to him."

"I don't understand this place, or what it is."

Ferrin looked cross. "You haven't figured that out?"

"He talked about realms. I don't know anymore."

Ferrin exhaled a frustrated breath. Whether it was because of him or the locks, Clark wasn't sure.

"This realm is just a landscape he's concocted. Think of it like a game board. And we're all just pieces moving around."

Clark thought of the Haunted Mansion game on the shelf downstairs, the one he had as a child. Playing it as a kid, he remembered moving his token around the board, trying to avoid the spooks and traps throughout the house. Wasn't that what he was doing now? He looked down at Ferrin.

"Can't you help?"

"What the hell do you think I've been doing all this time?" He huffed. "I've been challenging him from the beginning."

Clark was confused. "I don't know what you mean."

"That damn chessboard!" Ferrin shouted. "How do you think he's put all his pieces in place? And I've been trying to dodge him every step of the way." He sank back into his chair, the chains rattling as they shifted on his pudgy frame.

"Pieces?"

"That's all you are to him. Pieces in a game. I've been playing against him ever since I ended up here." He shook his head, disgusted. "Every move I make on the chessboard, he counters. I always thought I could outsmart him, but he's damned determined."

"There must be a way out," Clark pleaded.

There was a glint in Ferrin's eyes. "Maybe for you. No real way out for me, but hopefully someplace better than this."

Clark thought about the highway and how they had ended up on it. Was that really all Thayer Sledge's doing? Did he really put everything in place to make them end up there? It was mind-boggling.

And now he had no idea where that highway was, or even where he was.

"The world," Clark said. "The real world. It has to be somewhere."

"Sure," Ferrin said. "Somewhere outside of that damned snow globe of his."

CHAPTER TWENTY

Lewis Felker buttoned up his Salvation Army jacket as he staggered through the woods, a single expression sticking in his thoughts. It was an oft-heard phrase: A snowball's chance in hell. And now he understood what it meant. Because he knew that was about the same chance he had of getting out of this alive.

· That's if he even was alive. After what he saw back at the RV, he was even more convinced he was in hell. And it had surely frozen over.

One gloved hand clung to the neck of the whiskey bottle and he raised it to his chilled lips. He drained the last swallow before tossing the bottle aside, where it landed in the snow with a soft *plop*.

Felker had no idea where he was going, just moving forward away from the highway. Light flakes still fell and morning had broken so his path through the woods was lit. The snow wasn't as thick, so it made his steps easier.

He never looked back. No, he didn't want to see if anything was following. What good would looking do anyway? He was in no condition to outrun anything. As it was, he felt he could collapse at any moment. The whiskey filtering through his thin blood oiled his joints and greased his gears as he kept going forward.

He did not worry about any of the others, was not even bothered by the fact he'd left the women alone, especially the one screaming. No one had cared to listen to him. No one considered anything he said. They all looked at him like some kind of monster. But now they all saw the real monsters. If any of it was real.

Felker still wasn't sure.

It seemed to be brighter ahead and he saw why as he came to a clearing in the woods.

He stood at the edge of the trees, staring with disbelief at what lay in the clearing. But why shouldn't he believe? Nothing should surprise him anymore.

It was a bar.

Oh, not your average dark wood bar that Felker was used to in most of the dismal dives he could afford to drink in.

It was an ice bar.

The morning sun glared off the smooth ice of the bar, nearly blinding him. It stood in the middle of the clearing, long and clear like smooth carved glass, its edges sharp. A bartender stood behind it, and behind him were shelves carved of ice holding bottles of liquor.

This isn't hell, Felker thought. *This is heaven.*

He sauntered up to the bar, half expecting it to disappear as he approached. But it didn't. He stood before it and placed both gloved hands on its surface, fingers splayed. It was solid.

Felker smiled. Even though he could feel the cold chill thrown off from the bar, the sight of it made him feel warm inside.

There was another customer, a man standing down at the far end of the bar. The bartender set a martini glass made of ice before the man. The bartender wore a black jacket over a red shirt, a craggy face beneath straw-like hair. Had he seen him somewhere?

The bartender took no money from the man (open bar?) and walked over to Felker.

"What can I get you?" the bartender asked.

Felker thought a moment. He took his Salvation Army cap off and set it down on the bar. "Well, since it is morning, how about a Bloody Mary?"

"Good choice. Coming right up, sir." The bartender turned his back and grabbed some bottles.

Felker glanced down at the end of the bar, watching the other man lift his glass. There was something familiar about the man's face. He stared at him through bloodshot eyes. When the man turned to look at him, Felker saw the scar running down one side of the man's face, under his chin and back up the other side.

Oh my God, Felker thought. *It's Brodie Kane.* His old friend. He hadn't seen him since the aftermath of the snowmobile accident. In fact, he had made sure to keep clear of the guy all these years, guilt-stricken by what had happened.

What the heck was Brodie Kane doing in his hell?

He hoped the man wouldn't recognise him. Felker suddenly didn't want to be here, but he needed a—

The bartender turned back around and placed an ice-carved glass in front of him filled with a pinkish liquid.

Felker looked at his drink, and then back at Brodie Kane.

His old friend smiled at him and then raised his glass.

"Bottoms up," Brodie said, and then reached one hand to the bottom of his chin, grabbed hold of the flesh there and pulled up, peeling his face off the front of his skull to his forehead, revealing red sinewy muscles. He brought the drink up to the opening of his mouth and tipped his head back, pouring it in.

Felker turned away with a shiver, looking down at his drink.

"Something wrong, sir?" the bartender asked.

Felker stared at the drink, not daring to look back at the haunting sight at the end of the bar. He didn't want his drink, but oh how bad he needed it.

"It's just," he said, looking at the glass on the bar in front of him, "it doesn't look right." That was true. The drink didn't quite look like a Bloody Mary. It wasn't very tomato-like. That's probably because it had more alcohol than mixer in it, and maybe that was just what he needed right now.

But still…. "I don't think there's enough tomato juice in it. It looks kind of pale. It should be much redder."

"Of course," the bartender said. "Let me take care of that." He reached down beneath the bar and pulled out a large pair of ice tongs.

That was when Felker remembered the man he had seen when he was lost in the blizzard. But he had remembered too late.

Damn! he thought.

Everett Wick brought the prongs of the ice tongs up to either side of Felker's neck and punctured both sides of his throat in one quick motion. The blood shot out of his carotid and jugular simultaneously, pouring in a stream onto the surface of the ice bar and filling his glass with the rich red fluid.

Felker pitched forward against the bar, gloved hands reaching up, trying to stem the stream from his throat. He saw the blood pooling around his Salvation Army cap and that was the last sight his eyes beheld before his life force drained out of him and he tumbled to the snowy ground, immersed in a red puddle.

CHAPTER TWENTY-ONE

Morning light filtered through the trees, and Shelby was grateful as she followed the trail behind Tucker Jenks. It was much easier walking now that they were under the cover of the trees, not like before, tramping through the waist-deep snow. She was relieved she had convinced the trucker to accompany her, frightened by the thought of doing this alone. Of course she would have gone by herself if he had decided to stay behind. Her kids were out here somewhere, and they needed her, and she needed them. They were the only thing that mattered now. They were all that always mattered. Not their father, not Clark. Just Macey and Luke.

Who knew what that horrible creature had done to them? If they weren't alive, she didn't care if she ever got out of here. Let it take her too. She didn't want to be alone.

She wondered if the creature lived here in the woods, maybe in a den or hollow. She cast her eyes around. The woods looked just as forbidding in the light of dawn as they had in the dark with only the beam from Tucker's flashlight to illuminate the shadows. Now as she gazed at the pine trees, green limbs drooping, bowed under by the weight of clumps of heavy snow, she felt more frightened. The trees creaked and groaned, calling out to her, warning her…or were they toying with her, mocking her? She couldn't tell.

Was the creature lurking behind those trees, stalking them? It had her children, did it want her too? *Over my dead body.* Of course, that might be what it took. If she had to die, she would die for her children.

A birch tree ahead bent over so its tip touched the ground, forming an arch. Tucker had to duck to get his large frame under it. Shelby didn't. On the other side, there seemed to be more light ahead.

They reached the clearing at the edge of the woods and saw the house. Her toes inside her boots stung from the frigid cold and the muscles in her legs throbbed. She didn't think she'd be able to go on much farther.

If not for Tucker leading her along and the thought of finding Macey and Luke, she might have collapsed back in the snow somewhere.

The house in the early morning light shimmered from the snow coating its sides and roof and gables. Long pointed icicles hung down from the eaves along the edge of the roof and from the porch over the front stoop.

Leaning up against the wall beside the front door was an old wooden toboggan. It reminded Shelby of the one she and Kirby Decker rode down Tobin's Hill that disastrous night so long ago. A chill ran through her body.

Light glowed from one of the windows on the left side of the house. Was this the light Clark and Graham had followed, she wondered? If so, what had they found? And why hadn't they returned? She feared the worst.

But most of all, she worried about her kids, wondering what that beastly thing had done with them. If it harmed them, God help them all.

Though it was light enough, Tucker still held the flashlight and cast its beam around something in the snow in the shadows beneath a tall maple tree in the front yard. It was a broken and bent snowshoe. The trucker glanced at her with a grim gaze but didn't utter a word. He stepped into the clearing and she quietly followed, heart pounding in her chest.

Tucker stopped beside the snowshoe, bent down and picked it up, examining its twisted frame.

"Do you think it belonged to them?" she asked in a whisper, as if afraid someone in the house would hear them. An aching creak drew her eyes upward at the massive branches of the maple tree. There was something odd about it, and she realised it was because there was no snow on the tree. She glanced backward at the woods, noticing that their branches were covered. Strange that this tree was bare.

"I don't know," he said, quiet as well. He looked down. "What about that?"

Embedded in the snow was a flashlight that Shelby recognised as the one Mr. Volkmann had loaned Graham. Her heart sank. Everything kept getting hopeless. She looked up at the house with the lamp burning in one lone window. The rest of the house was dark.

"Should we try the door?" she asked.

Tucker raised one eyebrow. "I don't like the look of this." He dropped the snowshoe onto the ground. "That is one uninviting-looking house."

She had to agree.

"Those icicles look like a set of jaws that want to eat me," he said. "And if you haven't noticed, I've got a lot of meat on me. Let's go around back, see if we can find a different way in. I'd feel a lot better about that."

He took her hand and led her around the side of the house, keeping a safe distance from it. *If someone's in there*, she thought, *they've probably already seen us*. She kept watching the dark windows as she walked, trying to penetrate their emptiness. There seemed to be nothing behind them, like soulless eyes.

On the backside of the house she saw a glass extension that looked like an attached greenhouse, the glass frosted over by ice. A couple of panes were shattered. Tucker walked up to a wooden door and tried it. Locked. He poked his flashlight into one of the broken windows, peering in.

"Do you see anything?" Shelby said behind him.

"Someone definitely doesn't have a green thumb," he said, looking back at her. "Mostly dead plants and sticks in pots." He reached an arm in between two jagged shards of glass.

"Careful," she said, nervous.

She heard a click and he pulled his hand out and then opened the door. He looked back at her with a worried grimace.

"Let's be awfully quiet in here," he said. "Okay?"

She nodded, almost holding her breath. *Please God*, she said. *Let them be in this house and let them be all right.* She was almost too nervous to enter, but followed the big man inside.

It was dark. He shone the beam from his flashlight around.

There were tiered black wrought-iron shelves on either side of the door. Wilted plants in terracotta pots lined the shelves. Shelby noticed poinsettias, their leaves brown and shrivelled, and some Christmas cacti, brittle and emaciated. Climbing up a black trellis by one wall was a holly bush, its leaves crisp, its berries a deep red. In one corner stood a tall balsam, leaning in its stand, its needles brown and drooping.

"Guess nobody's been watering the plants," Tucker said. He grabbed something off a shelf. It was a small piece of lead pipe about a foot in length.

"Might come in handy," he said. "Come on."

The floor of the solarium was tiled, and their boots clicked on it with an echoing sound. Shelby heard a creaking noise and looked up at the glass ceiling. A layer of snow covering the glass screened out what sunlight tried to filter into the room. She worried the weight of the snow would cause the glass to cave in on them, raining shards down like knife blades.

To her right was a small kidney-shaped artificial pond. It was frozen over, the head of a turtle embedded in the ice, its mouth agape in a silent gasp. She shook. She'd always thought of solariums as warm, comforting rooms, not so much like this place.

A glass table was surrounded by white wicker chairs. On the table was a cornucopia, with fruit spilling out from it. Grapes, clinging to their vines, were shrivelled and well on their way to becoming raisins. Maize displayed rows of crooked kernels, like misshapen teeth in an old man's mouth; several gourds were blackened and split open with rot.

If this was an indication of what this house offered, Shelby thought, heaven help them all. She wanted out of this room, but dreaded what awaited them farther in the house. They reached a door at the end of the room, and Tucker gripped his piece of lead pipe tight before opening it and stepping through.

They were in a dining room; empty chairs surrounded a dining table shrouded in shadows. They crept quietly into the nearby kitchen. Dark pots and pans hung from a rack over a central island counter. Shelby spotted the knife rack at the same time as Tucker and he briskly walked over to it. She stayed right behind him. It was amazing to watch how lightly such a big man could step. She imagined an old house like this would be full of creaky floorboards. He pulled a knife out of the rack and handed it to her.

"Take this," he said. "Just in case. And don't be afraid to use it."

"What about you?" she asked.

He brandished the lead pipe. "I can do a lot of damage with this."

They scanned the room and the several doors leading in different directions.

Shelby looked at Tucker and shrugged, as if reading his mind. He shrugged back and started toward one of the doors. He opened it slowly and they saw steps leading down into a dark cellar. The beam from the flashlight showed dusty steps. It didn't look like anyone had been down them in a very long time. Tucker closed the door just as softly and walked toward another. This time it opened on steps leading up. The big man let out a worried sigh.

"Shall we see what's up there?" he asked.

If the kids were being held here, upstairs was just as good a place to look as anywhere. She nodded, afraid to speak. Her heart was in her throat. Her hands in her gloves felt sweaty, but she didn't want to take them off. Last night had been the longest night of her life, and this morning things didn't feel like they were coming to an end.

She followed the big man up the enclosed staircase, holding the knife tightly.

His large frame blocked out the stairs as she ascended behind him, the glimmer from his light causing shadows to dance along the walls. The top ended at a long hallway.

The air felt chilled up here and for the first time she realised the house held no warmth. They hadn't tried any light switches for fear of alerting whoever resided here, and she now wondered if the power was out. Probably, she thought. And that meant Clark hadn't been able to send help.

So where was he?

CHAPTER TWENTY-TWO

Clark heard footsteps down the hallway when he left Ferrin's room and thought it might be Sledge or Wick searching for him. He tried another door and ducked inside.

At first he thought he had stepped outside, there was so much white, but that couldn't be since he was on the second floor of the house. He realised that the walls of the room were painted white and the contrast from the room he'd just vacated had overwhelmed him. As his eyes adjusted, he was jolted by a shocking sight.

Benson Read, his divorce client from California, sat on a white leather couch. He was holding a kitchen knife coated with red. Droplets dripped from the end of the blade, staining the couch.

"Good of you to drop by," the old man said, looking up at him with a crooked grin.

Numbness ran through Clark's brain as he tried to comprehend this insane vision. The room looked like the inside of Benson's house in California, the one Clark visited that horrible day.

"What the hell's happening?" He didn't mean to direct the question at Benson, didn't even realised he had spoken aloud.

"I've been waiting for you, Clark."

"What the hell are you doing here?" Clark took a step back, leaning against the door he had closed behind him, too dumbfounded to go out the room's only exit. "You're supposed to be—"

"Awaiting trial?" He nodded. "Yes, I should be. But I was able to make bail, my new attorney made sure of that. He was a good attorney, the best that money can buy, not like you."

"I'm not a criminal lawyer." Clark felt the need to defend himself. "I'm a divorce attorney." It sounded outlandish to say it like that. It was downright embarrassing.

"I killed myself." The old man rose up from the couch in a slow, graceful movement. "I wasn't going to risk the chance of going to jail for the assault on my wife." His tone was acidic. "They were going to charge me with attempted murder. Didn't they realise I wasn't trying to kill her?"

"Of course not," Clark said, trying to appease the deranged man.

"I just wanted back what was mine." He took a stride forward. "What I paid for."

Clark thought about Audrey Read lying naked on their bed, her chest sliced open.

"I know you didn't want to hurt her." Clark reached a hand behind him, fumbling for and finally grasping the doorknob.

The old man cocked his head. "Do you want to know how I did myself in?"

"Not really."

"I used carbon monoxide from the exhaust on one of my cars in the garage at my old house. You remember, the house you couldn't get back for me in the divorce settlement." He leered. "But I still had the goddamn garage door opener!" Spittle flew from his mouth as he spoke. "I parked in the garage in what should have been my house and ran a hose from the exhaust. I wanted to die in that house so I could haunt that bitch forever and all her fucking lovers." He cackled. "But somehow I end up in this fucking place!"

Clark tried turning the knob without the old man noticing.

"And do you know why I'm here?" Benson asked, taking another step closer.

"No." Clark shook his head.

"Because you ducked from that damn snowball!"

Clark was bewildered by the old man's reasoning.

"And somehow I got caught up in your stupid game." He lurched closer and Clark smelled the rotten stench from his breath. "So now I'm going to carve *your* chest open."

Benson lunged, knife raised high above him.

Clark pulled the door open and backpedalled into the hall, bumping into something, or someone.

Benson let out a cry of rage as he followed him into the hall, knife flailing. In a whir, a dark hand brought a lead pipe crashing down onto the bald dome of the old man's skull, caving it in down to his eyeballs. That's when Clark noticed he had bumped into Shelby Wallace.

Benson's body stood upright, shuddering, the pipe still embedded in his skull. His head turned to face his attacker, eyeballs barely visible under his crushed forehead. Then his eyes shifted back to Clark.

"Where'd the fuck the black guy come from?" Benson said, before falling backward into the room.

"What the hell was that?" Tucker said, eyes wide.

Shelby clung to Clark. "Oh my God, are you all right?"

He was still shocked by the sudden appearance of the duo, but relieved by their timing.

"Shut that door," he commanded Tucker.

The big man retrieved his lead pipe, kicked aside the form of the old man lying on the floor and closed the door. Clark grasped Shelby and pulled her close in an embrace.

"Thank God," he said. "I thought you were dead."

"I would have been," she said, holding tight, "if it wasn't for Tucker saving me."

Clark looked at the trucker and nodded. The man returned a half-hearted smile. He didn't exactly look glad to be here.

"You won't believe what happened," Shelby said, looking up at him with moist eyes. "It's all so crazy."

"You'd be surprised what I'd believe. This ain't exactly Wonderland." He noticed the knife in her hand. "What are you doing here?"

She told him about the Krampus stealing her kids and how she and Tucker had come here looking for them.

"Well, you came to the right place. They're supposed to be here."

"You've seen them?" Her face lit up with hope.

"Not exactly." He tried to explain as briefly as possible about Thayer Sledge and his twisted games, leaving out the details about the snowball incident. He told her he had seen the snowmen attack the RV in the snow globe.

"I think the others are all dead." She frowned.

"Can't worry about that now."

"Where's Graham?" she asked, as if just remembering.

Clark looked down at his friend's boots on his feet. "He's dead too."

"Listen," Tucker said. "I hate to break up all this reminiscing, but what the hell do we do now?"

"How'd you two get in here?" Clark looked from one to the other.

"Came in the back," Tucker said, jerking a thumb toward the rear staircase.

Clark nodded. "We'll keep that in mind when it's time to go."

"Have you seen that Krampus thing around?" Shelby asked.

Clark shook his head. "But maybe there's someone who can help. Come on."

He led them down the hall to Ferrin's room. When they entered, the old man turned to face them with a big smile.

"At last!" Ferrin cried.

At first Clark thought Ferrin was glad to see them for some strange reason. But then he noticed opened padlocks discarded on the floor by the man's feet. He held the keyring in one hand, a rusty key gripped in his fingers. He inserted it into the last padlock on the chains across his chest. With a click, the lock popped open and the chains slithered down his body like metal snakes, curling up around his feet.

"I'm free," Ferrin said. He turned to go, ignoring the others.

"Wait," Clark implored, stepping forward. "We need your help."

Ferrin stopped and looked back. "I've helped you all I can. You're on your own now."

"We're looking for my children," Shelby pleaded.

"Some big horny thing took them," Tucker added.

"The Krampus? You'll want to keep away from that one." He stepped over to a door.

"We're not leaving without them," Shelby said, on the verge of tears.

"Can't you do anything to help?" Clark asked.

"My game is over," Ferrin said. He opened the door, revealing a closet. A pull string dangled from the ceiling.

"You can't just leave us here."

He was reaching up to the drawstring but stopped. "It's up to you now. I can't do any more for you. Good luck with that madman."

"How can we stop him?" Clark was getting pissed.

"Beat him at his own game." He pulled the string and a drop set of stairs came down. Ferrin scurried up them like a rodent and drew the stairs up behind him.

"This is one fucked-up place," Tucker said.

"What now?" Shelby asked, turning to him with desperate eyes.

"We keep looking," Clark said. "Search the other rooms." He hesitated, thinking about what could be lurking behind any of those doors – maybe the Iceman or some other horror. But at least he had some company. It felt better than being alone. He took the knife from Shelby's grasp and grabbed her hand. "Come on."

Clark went to the door opposite the room they had just been in, clutching the knife in one hand and Shelby's in the other, not wanting to relinquish either even for the second it would take to open the door. She had instantly become a security he wanted to hold onto for as long as he was able. He looked at the big man behind him.

"You did pretty good with that thing," he said to Tucker, nodding at the lead pipe in his hand. "How about you go in first?" He didn't intend it as a question and he could see from the expression on the man's face it wasn't received that way.

"Of course," Tucker said, moving to the door. "And my nana told me not to be stupid." He turned the knob and pushed the door in. It swung slowly on straining hinges.

The big man stepped inside the room. Clark followed, craning his neck to see around the man's shoulders. The room held only two twin beds and a dusty lamp on a nightstand.

Shelby shuddered beside him. "Looks like a kid's room," she said, sadness in her voice.

Clark thought about what Thayer Sledge said about keeping her kids for companionship. Was he preparing this room for them? He decided not to relay his concerns to Shelby.

"Let's move on," he said.

They went to the next room down the hall. It was empty, with the exception of a large cardboard box in the middle of the room. One flap of the box's top was open.

"I've seen this movie before," Tucker said before closing the door.

"Thayer Sledge needs some home interior design help," Clark said, trying and failing to break the tension. It made him think. Where the hell was the old man and why wasn't he after them? Or his psychopathic sidekick? It was as if Sledge was toying with them. Maybe he was watching them in his snow globe, getting a kick out of their helplessness.

They backed out of the room. There was only one more door they hadn't tried. As Clark approached it, something stopped him. An icy chill seeped through the wooden door. He shivered. He glanced back at Shelby, releasing her firm grip so he could push open the door. When he did, he received a blast of frigid air. He could see his breath as he stepped into the room.

It felt like walking into a freezer. In the centre of the room was a bed made of ice, a fur blanket draped over it. Large blocks of ice were piled up along either side of the bed. On the wood-panelled walls of the room hung a variety of rusty ice-cutting implements: saws, picks, chisels and tongs.

"Damn, it's cold in here," Tucker said, clenching his teeth.

This must be Everett Wick's room, Clark thought. It was more than the cold that gave him the chills in here.

Shelby came up alongside him. "I remember reading about a hotel in Canada made entirely of ice." Each word from her lips was followed by a puff of white vapour. "They have to rebuild it every winter, because they let it melt when the summer comes. I always thought it'd be a romantic place to spend a night."

"Not like this," Clark said, shaking his head.

"I don't want to wait around for the dude that sleeps in that bed," Tucker said.

Clark agreed, glad to be out of the chill of the room, even though there was no comfort in the hallway.

"What next?" Shelby asked, her brow creased with tension.

Clark pointed to the ceiling. "Next floor." He led them to the door he had discovered earlier that opened onto a staircase. He flicked a switch inside the doorway, but no lights came on. Tucker handed him his flashlight.

Directing the beam of light, Clark saw the staircase spiralled up to the left. He took the first steps, soft and slow, and the others followed. Behind him came an aching creak on the treads, and he looked back at the anguished face of Tucker Jenks, who only shrugged. If that thing were up here, Clark thought, it knew they were coming.

The top of the staircase dumped them off at the head of a narrow hallway. Down at the opposite end was the large circular window Clark had seen from the front of the house, the one that looked like a giant eye. Some light spilled into the hallway, catching floating dust in its ray. The dust reminded Clark of the snowflakes floating in the snow globe.

On either side of the hallway was a door. He led the trio down the hall and stopped before them. His eyes looked left, then right, as he wondered which to try first. He leaned toward the one on the left, putting his ear up against the cold wood. He thought he heard a whimper from the other side.

He looked at Shelby, not wanting to acknowledge what he had heard. He adjusted his grip on the knife and tried the door. It was unlocked. Either Sledge had a lot of trust, or he was welcomed into the room. He didn't like either possibility. Clark opened the door and crept inside.

CHAPTER TWENTY-THREE

Shelby's pulse quickened as she followed the two men up the stairs, wincing with every step Tucker took and the alarm it heralded. And when they got to the top, she could tell Clark felt something was behind one of the doors. The look on his face as he had listened to the door said it all.

Please God, she thought, as she entered the room with them, *please let me find them and let them be all right*. During this whole ordeal, she had never been more frightened than she was right now. Not even when the creature had taken her kids. At least then she knew they were alive. It was the not knowing that left her wrenched in anguish.

The room was dark, with no window to let in even the stingiest amount of light. Tucker shined his flashlight beam over the rafters. Stringy cobwebs linked the dark timbers. From what Shelby could see, the room was spacious, but crammed with stuff. As the trucker's light played over the contents of the room, unknown dark shapes revealed themselves.

The light caught the face of a white wooden rocking horse, dark mane flowing back, nostrils flared wide. Its painted blue saddle bore a chipped yellow star. Next to it was a large wooden steamer trunk, its lid up, overflowing with toys. A large stuffed teddy bear sat atop the pile, its brown fur ragged, one button eye missing. Other stuffed animal shapes emerged from the pile in the trunk: a green frog, a cat wearing a cap, a bespectacled white rabbit in a vest and an elephant wearing a sweater emblazoned with the letter *A*.

A stack of books teetered beside the trunk, a striped rubber ball beside it. Next to that was a large bongo drum. Beside it was a wooden toolbox. Dust covered a hammer, screwdriver and monkey wrench sticking out of it. Tucker continued shifting his light around the room. A nearby table held a toy train set, its engine and the first few box cars derailed. In the middle of the circular track was a phalanx of vintage toy soldiers, muskets and bayonets thrust forward, ready to engage.

Did these toys belong to all the children the Krampus snatched? Was the creature some kind of Grinch that robbed the innocent of their Christmas? When Volkmann told the story back in the RV, he said the Krampus came after the bad children. So why did it come for hers? That wasn't fair. But then, nothing about this night was fair.

A scratching sound came from the right and Tucker's light swung over to catch sight of something small and furry scurrying into a hole in the wall.

Just a rat, Shelby hoped. Nothing more.

But the flashlight beam caught something else. It looked like a metal crate for a large dog. She heard a whimpering sound and something moved inside.

Shelby's breath hitched, almost choking on dusty air, as she caught sight of brown hair draped over sleepy eyes as a head rose.

It was Macey.

Oh God. Shelby felt a rush of joy as she ran over to the cage, overwhelmed by excitement. She dropped to her knees, reaching her hands to clasp her daughter's.

"Mom," Macey said in a sleepy voice. It sounded like she had been drugged. Had Mrs. Volkmann put something in those cookies she had given the kids? Is that why they'd slept so deeply in the RV's bedroom? Shelby's eye caught the snowflake pendant still around her daughter's neck. She looked upon the wretched necklace with revulsion at just the thought of that snowflake and what it represented, the storm that stranded them on the highway and the nightmarish things it had brought forth. She wouldn't care if she never saw another snowflake again.

"I'm here, honey," she said, frantically scanning the interior of the cage till she spotted Luke.

"I'm so scared," Macey said.

"We'll get you out," Clark said, coming up behind her.

"Is your brother okay?" Shelby asked, worried her son hadn't stirred.

Macey looked back and kicked him with her foot. The boy groaned and shifted on the floor of the cage. Shelby smiled, thinking her prayers were answered. But they still had to get out of this madhouse.

There was a padlock on the gate to the cage.

"Give me a hand with this," Clark said to Tucker.

Shelby reluctantly let go of Macey's hands and stepped back to let the two men have some room to work. She started to wonder if they'd be able to get them out. Worry sank in again. Nothing came easy.

Tucker set his flashlight down and inserted his piece of lead pipe behind the padlock to pry it off. Shelby backed up some more as the big man strained, leaning back and pulling with all the force of his big arms. He relaxed, unable to break the lock. Shelby's heart nearly broke.

"Let me get a better grip," Tucker said, adjusting his hands on the pipe. He pulled back again, groaning. There was a metallic pop and the padlock broke open and dropped to the floor with a clatter.

Shelby's heart thundered in her chest, a smile breaking over her face.

Hot breath brushed against the back of her neck as something wet and rough slithered up the flesh on her right cheek. Repulsed, she turned to see a long pointed red tongue retract into the jaws of the Krampus. She wanted to scream, but as she stared into those burning blood-red eyes in that wicked face, all the breath felt sucked out of her throat and her mouth opened in soundless terror.

"Mom, look out!" Luke yelled from behind.

Shelby wiped the saliva off her cheek as she backed up.

"Get out of the way, Shelby," Clark said, stepping forward, the knife gripped in his hands.

Shelby stumbled on something and she toppled over backward onto the floor, pain shooting up her tailbone. She clenched her teeth.

Krampus took two steps forward, his cloven hoofs thudding on the wood floor. How had she not heard his approach before? She must have been too enthralled with the release of her kids from the cage.

"Stay back," Clark said to the beast, brandishing the knife back and forth.

In Krampus's right hand he held a switch of birch and waved it back and forth in a mocking gesture. Shelby swore the creature was smiling, its tongue flicking out between its pointy teeth. The beast stepped forward and Clark raised his knife.

With one swipe of its free hand, Krampus smacked the knife from Clark's grip, sending it sailing across the room. It stuck in the wall of the attic with a vibrating thud. Before Clark could react, the creature gripped his face in its clawed hand and shoved him back. He landed across the floor in a heap.

Tucker charged forward with a grunt, lead pipe raised menacingly over his head. Krampus dodged him like a bullfighter, stepping aside quickly. It slammed its hand across Tucker's shoulder, knocking the big man off balance and sending him tumbling to the floor. The boards shook under his weight. The lead pipe dislodged from his hand as he landed, rolling across the floor into the shadows.

Macey crawled out the open door of the cage and ran to her mother's side. Shelby clung to her, relieved to feel her daughter's embrace, but terrified at the scene playing out before them.

Krampus stood in the middle of the room. It glanced back and forth at the two men lying prone at opposite ends of the room. Clark got up first and the beast turned to face him. Tucker scrambled to his feet with tremendous effort and charged its back.

The beast spun, catching Tucker's throat with its left hand, choking him. Clark pounced on his back, trying to wrestle the grip away. Krampus shot back its right elbow, caught Clark under the chin and flung him off as easy as shooing away a fly. Clark fell to the floor in a daze.

Krampus lifted Tucker up off the floor by his throat, continuing to choke the trucker, whose eyes bulged as his breathing strained. His arms hung limply by his sides.

"Stop!" Shelby yelled, and the beast turned its red eyes on her, its grin spreading. It was enjoying the torment. If the creature could easily dispatch these two strong men, what hope did she and her children have? She looked over at Luke, who crawled to the opening of the cage, but stopped, as if fearful to leave the security of his prison.

Krampus slammed Tucker's head up against one of the rafters and the big man's eyes rolled up. The creature let go and he dropped into a heap on the floor with a groan. He reached up to rub the back of his head.

Still conscious, Shelby thought. She saw that Clark wasn't moving though.

Krampus loomed over Tucker, raised the birch switch and began beating the man with it, pounding lash after lash upon his helpless body.

"No, Nana!" Tucker cried out, holding his arm over his face for protection. "No, please! I won't be stupid anymore!"

Shelby thought the man must be delirious. She couldn't say she blamed him. Krampus cackled as it continued raining lashes down on him. The sound of the creature chilled her. She let go of Macey, rushed toward the creature and began pounding on its back with a clenched fist. It swept her aside with its free hand, sending her crashing to the floor. Macey rushed to her side, wrapping her arms around her mother. Clark started to stir and Shelby tried willing him to his feet.

Krampus stopped whipping Tucker and bent down over him. Its free claw reached menacingly toward his throat. Shelby squeezed her eyes shut. *I don't want to see this*, she thought. She'd seen too much horrible death already.

"Stop!" yelled a small voice. It was Luke.

Shelby opened her eyes to see her son on his feet, approaching Krampus.

"Luke! Get back!" she cried helplessly. She wanted to get up off the floor, but Macey clung tight to her, arms wrapped around her neck, weighing her down.

Krampus turned away from Tucker and cast its eyes upon Luke, who approached the creature with slow steps.

"You're supposed to take the bad kids," Luke said to Krampus, his tone strong. "But we're not the bad ones. We're good. We're not the ones who deserve this." He continued toward the creature.

Shelby looked on, half with fear, half with pride at how brave her son appeared. Krampus stood still, its face full of puzzlement. Clark began to stir, rising up to his knees, shaking his head to clear it. He looked up at Luke confronting Krampus in the middle of the room.

"You need to leave us alone," Luke told the creature. "You need to let us go home. It's Christmas."

The boy now stood before Krampus, who looked down upon him. Shelby saw the expression on the creature's face change, from bewilderment, to embarrassment, to sadness. Its grin faded, replaced with a pout.

Luke turned and walked over to Shelby, and she couldn't have felt more proud as the boy – no, young man – helped her to her feet. Macey released her grip but grasped her mother's hand. Luke held the other, leading her toward the door.

Krampus stood in the middle of the room, head turning, following them with its red eyes. Clark got up and went around the creature to where Tucker lay. He helped the big man stand. Then Clark pulled the kitchen knife out of the wall and led Tucker toward the door, where Shelby waited with her kids.

Luke opened the door, but before they left, Macey released Shelby's hand and walked over to Krampus.

"Macey, don't," Shelby said, afraid to raise her voice too loud and startle the suddenly docile creature. Clark started forward, but Shelby stopped him, not quite sure why. Maybe after seeing Luke's effect on Krampus, she trusted Macey's sudden bravery.

She watched from the door as her daughter removed the snowflake pendant from around her neck and held it out for Krampus. The creature looked down at it, eyes unsure, and then dropped the birch switch and held out its hand, unfurling its fingers. Macey dropped the pendant onto its palm, and the fingers curled around it.

"Everyone deserves something for Christmas," she said to the creature, before turning on her heels and joining the others at the door. When everyone was safely in the hallway, Clark closed the door behind them.

"How are you feeling?" Clark asked Tucker, who was rubbing his head.

"I'll feel a whole lot better when we get the hell out of this place."

Clark grinned and looked at Shelby and the kids.

"Do you think that thing will come after us?" she asked him.

"Let's not stick around too long to find out," he answered. He banged the hilt of the knife against the doorknob, breaking it off. "Come on."

"You don't have to tell me twice," Tucker said. He took the lead and headed for the stairs. For a big man who'd just taken a vicious beating, he moved quickly. When he reached the door at the bottom of the stairs and stepped out into the hall, the floor fell out from beneath him and he disappeared into the hole.

CHAPTER TWENTY-FOUR

As soon as Clark saw Tucker drop through the trapdoor in the floor, he rushed down the stairs past the others. He feared the worst, but when he sank to his knees beside the opening and peered down, he saw him clinging to the edge of a metal chute that extended down into the darkness.

Fright gripped Tucker's face, his teeth clenched, knuckles on his dark hands white from the strain. Clark set the knife down, reached into the opening and grabbed onto his left arm.

Clark was reminded of the laundry chute in his grandparents' old house, but that was in a bathroom closet, not in the middle of a hallway. He had a feeling this chute didn't lead to a laundry room in the basement.

"Hold on," Clark said, trying to get a good grip on the man's arm.

"What the hell do you think I'm doing?" Tucker said, his voice high-pitched.

Clark felt Tucker slipping as the weight dragged him down. The man was heavy. He didn't know if he could keep holding on or pull him up out of the hole, but he didn't dare let go.

He didn't have to. Shelby dropped down by his side, reaching down to help grab hold of Tucker's other arm. The two began pulling him up.

"Help us out!" he cried to Tucker, who immediately began pushing his feet up along the metal chute. Once they got him halfway out of the hole, he gave a final shove and collapsed beside them on the floor.

"Oh, Christ!" Tucker said, rolling onto his back, wheezing. "That scared the shit out of me."

Before getting up, Clark looked down the hole, wondering what lay below in the darkness.

"Can we get out of here?" Shelby said, rising and gathering her children in her arms.

"I want to go home," Macey whined, almost on the verge of tears.

"Soon," Shelby said, stroking her daughter's hair.

Clark thought about that, wondering about the likelihood of getting back to where they'd come from. But he wasn't even sure where they were. Clark had seen too many things he couldn't begin to explain. A realm, Sledge had called it. He didn't know how easy it would be to escape it. Ferrin had found a way out apparently, but he was already dead so it didn't matter. They were still very much alive. For now.

"This way," Tucker said, not afraid to take the lead again despite his close encounter. He strode down the hallway and the others followed. Clark kept close to Shelby, who stood between her children holding their hands.

When they reached the rear staircase, Tucker was about to descend.

Clark grabbed his arm. "Stop!"

Tucker tossed him a confused look. "What gives?"

"What's the matter?" Shelby asked.

Something gnawed inside Clark's mind. Something Ferrin had said.

"This just has a bad feel to it," he said.

"This whole house has a bad feel to it," Tucker said.

Clark peered down the stairs, thoughts spinning in his head. He recalled pieces of conversations he'd had today with both Sledge and Ferrin. What had Ferrin said about this place? Sledge created it as a big game board. Clark looked back down the hall to where he could still see the opening in the floor from the trapdoor.

"Snakes and Ladders!" he said.

"What are you talking about?" Shelby asked.

She hadn't seen what he'd experienced since he'd woken up in this house, nor heard the things Sledge had talked about. What else had the man said? *Games have rules.*

"We can't go down."

"Why?" Shelby asked.

"It's like a Snakes and Ladders game. Going down is bad, like that chute back there." He pointed down the hallway. "And who knows what'll happen if we go down this staircase." He thought about what Sledge said about the game, about its roots in morality, where the game board represented a life journey with virtues going up and vices going down, depicted by the snakes and ladders. He tried explaining it to the others.

"You're not making sense, man," Tucker said.

"This guy Sledge, who lives – I mean inhabits this place. He was a game manufacturer. This whole time he's been playing games with us."

He looked from Shelby to Tucker and then down at the kids. They all looked at him as if he'd gone mad. "I know it all sounds absurd, but you haven't seen what I have. You have to trust me."

"I know I've seen enough to believe you," Shelby said.

"So what do we do?" Tucker asked.

"We go up." He heard a *thunk* from the other end of the hallway that quieted them all. They stared down the darkened end. He realised the sound was the closing of the trapdoor in the floor, as if the house knew they were coming that way and was resetting its obstacles. "Come on."

Reluctantly they followed him, Shelby holding tight to the young ones' hands. Each step heightened Clark's nerves as he searched the surroundings for any other surprises. He imagined they were walking along a game board: roll the dice, take a step, lose a turn. The hall seemed to go on forever, as if the actual floorboards had stretched out like an accordion.

As the group passed each closed door, Clark tightened his grip on the knife, anticipating something springing out at them. His head swivelled from side to side as he prepared for a response from the rooms beside him. When he was close to the opened door to the third-floor stairs, he stopped, holding his hand out to prevent any of the others from inadvertently stepping too close to the spot on the floor where the trapdoor lay like a hungry mouth waiting to swallow them whole.

"Careful here," he whispered, guiding them all along the wall to keep away from the spot.

He signalled each of them to head up the stairs, starting with Tucker, followed by Shelby and her kids. She gave him an anxious look as she passed. He kept right behind them as they ascended.

At the top, the others awaited his direction.

Clark glanced at the two doors, the one with the missing knob and the one leading to the room they hadn't checked out. He pondered what to do now as the others looked at him for guidance. One room they definitely couldn't go in, the other....

So far they hadn't had much luck in this house. They needed to find a way out. They had ascended to the top – where else was there to go?

He looked down the end of the landing to the light that came in from the large circular window. "There!" he said, pointing.

Clark rushed to the window, followed by the rest. He looked out its frosted glass onto the front yard and the maple tree that had attacked him.

His eyes scanned down to the roof that he remembered covered a second-floor balcony. Beneath that balcony was the roof of the front stoop.

"We get out here," he said, glancing over his shoulder at Shelby.

"What?" Tucker exclaimed. "Are you kidding?"

"We can do this."

"In what world?"

"I thought you said going down was bad," Shelby reasoned.

"We got as high as we can. Now we get out and off the game board." He turned around. "We can make this work."

Shelby nodded.

Clark faced the window. "We just need to smash out this window."

A thunderous thud came from behind, drawing their attention. It was the door that led to Krampus's lair. Clark's pulse quickened and he saw the harried looks on the others' faces. The kids moved behind their mother.

"You better hurry," Tucker said.

Clark turned back to the window. He began pounding on the glass with the hilt of the knife. It should have shattered, but it didn't. Was this another trick? A tease? A window on the floor below had been broken by an icy snowball, but he was pounding with all his might on this glass, the impact reverberating up his arm to his shoulder, and it was no use.

A loud crack and splintering of wood erupted behind him and he turned to see the Krampus burst through the attic door. The creature stood in the hall looking at them, its red eyes burning.

"Mommy!" Macey whimpered, clinging tight to her mother's side.

Clark moved in front of the others, brandishing the knife as the Krampus took several steps toward them. He could see the glittering snowflake pendant now around its neck. He had thought the gift had softened the creature's heart and appeased it somewhat. Now he had doubts.

Krampus shifted its eyes from one to the other, as if surveying his victims. It raised one clawed hand and waved it to the side. Clark was puzzled, not sure what he was seeing.

"Get out of the way," Shelby interpreted. She moved the kids to the side of the circular window. Clark understood, and he and Tucker backed up against the side wall.

Krampus charged down the hall toward the big round window. Clark watched as the creature leaped and burst through the glass, sending shards scattering, and landed on the roof of the balcony below with a thud.

Clark stuck his head out the broken window, cold air blowing against his face. Krampus sat on its haunches on the roof below. It craned its neck to look back up at him. It grinned and then its powerful legs launched itself off the roof to the snowy ground below. It bounded up in a spray of powder and scampered off into the woods.

After watching it disappear from sight, and hoping the creature had found its own escape, Clark looked back at the others.

"We now have an exit," he said.

Tucker came up beside him and peered down, shaking his head. Then he looked at Clark with an eye roll. "I ain't looking forward to this part."

"You want to live," Clark said, "we get through this."

Clark used the hilt of the knife to smash out the jagged remnants of glass in the window frame. Then he tucked the knife into his belt and helped the big man up onto the edge of the window and eased him out, lowering him down onto the pitched roof of the balcony. Tucker secured his footing in the snow on the roof, managing to remain steady. He gazed up at Clark, a dubious expression on his round face. Clark smiled back.

"Easy as pie," he said.

"I could go for some pie right now," Tucker replied.

Clark ignored the comment. "How's the footing?"

Tucker dug his feet down into the snow. "Seems fine."

Clark worried about him slipping off the roof. "I'm going to lower the kids down first."

"Okay."

Clark turned to Shelby and brushed a loose strand of hair from the side of her face. "Are you ready?"

She nodded, her half smile contradicting the worry lines on her forehead.

He bent down to eye level with Luke and Macey. "Who wants to go first?"

"Me," Luke exclaimed with excitement, the drowsiness long purged from his system.

Clark helped the boy out the window and lowered him into the waiting arms of Tucker, who set him down on the roof beside him. Clark then turned to Macey. "Are you ready?"

She looked to her mother. "I'm afraid."

Shelby knelt down beside her, stroking her back. "You've been brave this far. You'll be all right. None of us will let anything happen to you."

Macey bit her lower lip and nodded.

Clark picked her up, but as he brought her to the open window, he felt her arms tighten around his neck and he was afraid she wouldn't let go. Tucker stood below, waiting.

"It's going to be okay, Macey," Clark said. He felt her arms release, and he lowered her down.

Clark was relieved once the kids were secure on the roof with Tucker, and he helped Shelby down before following behind. He was glad the snow had stopped and the morning sun warded off most of the daylight chill. It was a good thing since the kids had no coats. They would need to keep warm for the trek back to the highway.

They began the process of climbing down onto the balcony, shimmying down the column supports. They repeated the same order, with Tucker going first, and then Clark lowered the kids to him. The distance was shorter, which made the task much easier.

On the balcony, Clark cast a wary eye to the glass door that led inside, wondering where Sledge and Wick lurked. It struck him as odd that neither of them had made an appearance in a while. He could imagine Sledge in the study watching their every move in that cursed snow globe.

Clark went to the railing to look over the edge of the balcony. There was a wooden trellis that ran down the side of the front stoop. A vine snaked its way up from the ground through the slats in the trellis.

"We can climb down here," Clark said.

The others peered down.

"I don't know if that will hold me," Tucker said.

"Then I'd better go first," Luke said and climbed over the railing.

"Luke!" Shelby cried in surprise.

"That's the initiative," Clark said, watching the boy climb down the trellis like a monkey. Before he even reached the bottom Luke jumped down into the snow and looked up at them with a smile.

"Great job," Clark called down to him.

"I can't do that," Macey said.

"I'll help you," Clark told her. "We'll do it together."

He climbed over the railing, and then helped Macey over, showing her where to grip the trellis, making sure she held on to the openings in the slats and not the thin stems of the vines, for fear the fragile plant would rip away from the wooden structure. He guided her step by step as the two of them descended the trellis. He could hear it creak, and he was afraid the slats would crack beneath each foothold. When the ground was in sight, he dropped down, and then reached up and pulled Macey off into his arms. When he set her down in the snow, he realised both her and her brother's feet wouldn't last long in the cold. They needed to hurry.

He looked up at Tucker and Shelby.

"You better go next," Tucker said to Shelby. "I should go last."

"Okay," she said with a smile.

Clark watched her descend, slow and careful, and was glad when she was safely on the ground.

"I'm cold, Mom," Macey complained, and her mother scooped her up in her arms.

Clark took off his jacket and draped it over Macey's shoulders. He brushed the snow off her socks and rubbed her feet to keep her blood circulating. "Better?"

The little girl nodded.

"Come on," Clark called up to Tucker, trying not to be too loud.

Tucker looked at the trellis doubtfully, shook his head, and heaved his body over the railing. The wood screeched from the burden. Tucker looked awkward and clumsy trying to climb down, having trouble getting the tips of his boots into the holes in the slats. The vines shook as he struggled, almost as if they were alive.

The vines began to curl themselves around Tucker's body, and that's when Clark realised that they were alive.

"Watch out!" Clark yelled, his incident with the maple tree fresh in his mind.

One long piece of vine wrapped itself around Tucker's throat. His left hand released its hold and grabbed the vine that was choking him. Clark could hear him gagging, struggling to breathe.

"Oh God," Shelby cried.

Tucker's feet kicked in his struggles, both released from their footholds. His body hung free, solely in the grips of the vines that had now wrapped around his entire body. He used both hands to try and loosen the vine's grip around his throat, but the thickness of his mittens hampered his efforts.

"Hang on!" Clark yelled. He pulled the knife from his belt and began climbing up the trellis. He reached Tucker, who was gagging and gasping, and began cutting at the vines around his large waist.

Clark frantically slashed with the blade, slicing into the man's coat in an attempt to cut the vine's hold, trying to be careful not to cut Tucker. He worked his way up the man's torso, hacking and slashing, till he reached his shoulders. Clark grabbed on to Tucker with his left arm while he continued cutting vines with the knife in his right.

Tucker's eyes bulged wide and white, his mouth open, his thick tongue hanging out. The vine around his throat sank into his flesh. Clark didn't dare try to cut it off. He hacked away at the vines around Tucker's shoulders, trying to find the source of the one wrapped around his neck. Tucker appeared to be losing consciousness.

With a loud crack, the wood on the trellis split under their weight and Clark felt himself leaning backward. He held tight to Tucker and the two of them fell. The vine around Tucker's neck snapped and they landed in the snow with a soft thud.

Clark took most of Tucker's weight on top of him, the air squeezed out of his lungs like a bellows, the knife loosened from his hand. He couldn't breathe. Once the wind had been knocked out of him, he couldn't suck any more back in. He tried pushing Tucker off him, but the man's weight was too great. If the snow hadn't cushioned his fall, Tucker's body would have crushed his rib cage.

Clark struggled beneath Tucker, feeling like he was drowning, thinking he was going to black out. All he could see was the pale blue dawn sky above him, with just a few wisps of white cloud.

Tucker rolled off him, and Clark felt a rush of air into his lungs. He gasped, sucking in air. His lungs felt as if they were about to burst, and then he exhaled and felt relief. Shelby's concerned face loomed over him as he panted. And then Tucker's smiling face appeared.

"You gonna be all right, man?" Tucker asked.

Clark was glad the man was alive.

"Yes," he said between gasps. "I – just – need – to catch – my breath."

"Well, don't take too long," Tucker said. "We want to get the hell out of here."

Clark could see the edge of the house beside them, and the windows that looked into the room with the snow globe. *Yes*, he thought. *They needed to get away from here.*

"Help me up," he said. Tucker extended a hand.

There was a loud crack and Clark saw movement above. The long pointed icicles on the roof's edge broke free in one section and dropped down like a guillotine blade, heading right for Tucker.

"Watch out!" Clark yelled. He found the sudden energy to scramble to his feet and throw himself at Tucker, knocking the big man to the side.

Four sharp icicles slammed into the snow where Tucker had just been standing. Clark looked back over his shoulder.

"Damn," Tucker said, realising what had almost happened. "Now you better help me up."

When they got on their feet, they moved away from the side of the house. Clark glanced up at the roof, wondering if the house was still trying to stop them.

"Can we go now?" Shelby asked, still holding Macey, worry etched on her face.

Clark looked at Macey's sock-covered feet. The kids wouldn't get far walking without any boots. Then he remembered something he'd seen when he first got to the house. The toboggan on the front stoop.

He ran to it and pulled the wooden sled out of its mooring in the crusty snow at the edge of the stoop. He brought it over and set it down before the others.

"Get on this, kids," he said.

"Here," Tucker said, removing his jacket and putting it on Luke before helping the boy onto the front of the toboggan. He had a heavy grey sweatshirt underneath and didn't seem to miss the coat. He took his big mittens off and put them on Macey's feet, like socks.

If Clark thought his coat was big on Macey, Luke got lost in the big trucker's jacket. At least they would help keep the kids warm, and the toboggan would be able to keep their feet out of the snow. He helped Macey on behind her brother.

"Hold on to him tight," he told her, and without a fuss she wrapped her arms around the bulky jacket that encompassed Luke's waist. "You two should be able to get them back to the highway okay," he said to Tucker and Shelby.

"Wait a minute," Shelby said. "What about you?"

"There's something I still need to do," Clark said, not having time to explain.

"I'm not going without you," Shelby said.

"Let's all just go now," Tucker pleaded.

"You don't understand," Clark said. He thought about the snow globe and the image of the highway on it. He thought about the realm they were in and how Thayer Sledge had brought them here. He thought about the skeletons of the young couple in the hatchback. Wherever they were – whenever they were – they were still not yet out of this.

"Make me understand," Shelby said, her eyes pleading.

"This Sledge guy," he started, searching for the simplest explanation to something he still didn't quite comprehend. "He's got us trapped here, and even if we got to the snowplough and got it going, I'm not sure we'd be able to get out." He paused. "I have an idea of what might help, but I don't want you wasting any more time waiting around. Get to the highway, and I'll be right behind you as soon as I can."

"I'm afraid," Shelby said, her eyes moist.

"I'll catch up with you." He reached out and brushed a tear away that had loosened from the corner of her eye.

"Promise?"

"I promise."

She leaned up and kissed him on the lips, and he thought he'd never felt a kiss so soothing and comforting in his life.

"You better, damn you," she said, strength in her voice.

"Now go," he said, waving them off.

Tucker nodded. "I'll have the engine revved and ready for you. Just get your ass there."

"Watch over them," he replied. "Keep them safe."

Tucker grabbed the reins of the toboggan and began pulling it through the snow toward the woods, looking exhausted but grateful. Shelby stood still for a moment, staring back at Clark longingly. He smiled in an attempt to reassure Shelby that he would be okay, but wasn't sure if the silent message found its target. But he knew as she turned to follow the toboggan that he wanted more than anything to be by her side right now, and that he'd do everything in his power to make that happen.

CHAPTER TWENTY-FIVE

Shelby kept silent, trying her best to keep up with the toboggan and not fall behind as Tucker pulled the kids on it through the woods. Just seeing the toboggan brought back memories of that fateful night on Tobin Hill with Kirby Decker. God, how that one incident had changed her life so dramatically. If that tragic mishap hadn't happened, she wouldn't even have these kids she loved and was trying desperately to protect.

She noticed how cold and fragile they seemed sitting on the sled, bundled up in the adult coats, holding onto each other for warmth and security. In the woods, they lost some of the warmth the rising sun had provided, the shade casting a chill around them.

She needed to get them safe, but she still didn't feel right about leaving without Clark. She kept looking over her shoulder, hoping to see him emerging from behind a tree. He said he'd be along as soon as he could. She just wished he would hurry.

At least she had Tucker. She was grateful for his help. He could have refused to come along, but he risked his life to help her and they had succeeded in getting her kids away from that creature, and all the other horrors in that decrepit house or whatever it really was. She didn't quite fathom what Clark was spouting about, but then nothing much made sense during this whole ordeal. Still, she didn't know what other horrors might lie ahead. Those things that attacked the RV were still out there somewhere.

Shelby couldn't wait to get out of the woods. Besides the swooshing sound of the toboggan being dragged through the snow, the only other noise was the occasional cracking of a tree branch giving way under the weight of the snow. The sound echoed in the woods, as if it was all around her, giving her the feeling something was out here with them. *It's just the trees*, she kept telling herself, *nothing more*. But she couldn't help but look around, just in case.

She concentrated on one step after another, trudging through the snow. It was draining; each laborious step felt like a dozen. Up ahead,

Tucker pulled the sled with little effort, just quick puffs of breath and some beads of sweat on his forehead. He didn't seem affected by giving up his coat and gloves. But she could tell he was as anxious as any of them to get out of here.

They reached the edge of the woods and stopped. Shelby felt like she was about to collapse from exhaustion. She looked down the slope to the highway. In the daylight she could see the buried vehicles, misshapen mounds of snow. There was also the RV, and she shivered at the thought of the bloodbath that took place inside it. She wondered, but didn't really care, what happened to the others.

She could also see the snowplough, their means of escape, its orange hulk standing out among the other vehicles. God, she hoped this worked. She glanced back into the woods for some sign of Clark. There was nothing. She turned to Tucker.

"I need to rest a minute," she managed through strained breath.

"No time for that," Tucker said.

"I just don't know if I can go on just yet – my legs." At the mere mention, her legs buckled and she sank down into a sitting position in the snow.

"That's okay," Tucker said. "From here on, we ride."

"What?" Before she realised what he was talking about, he climbed onto the back of the toboggan, right behind Macey. He looped the reins over the kids' heads and turned to look at Shelby.

"Climb on," he said with a toothy smile.

"Yes, Mom," Macey said. "Come on."

Shelby eyed the toboggan, thinking about that last ride. But seeing the faces of Macey and Luke, with their desperation mingled with excitement, she overcame her reluctance and climbed on behind Tucker. She tried to put her arms around his large waist, but couldn't even make it halfway around.

"Hang on," Tucker yelled, "it's going to be a bumpy ride." He pushed off with his feet and hands till gravity grabbed hold of the toboggan and pulled it down the slope.

Luke shouted out with glee as the toboggan picked up speed, icy wind rushing past them. Shelby buried her face into the thick back of Tucker's sweatshirt to protect it. She clung tight to his body, gripping the folds of the sweatshirt.

As the toboggan careened down the slope, Shelby felt a sense of exhilaration, as if she were a kid again and this was a fun winter excursion, forgetting the misery of everything that came before it.

Shelby felt arms around her own waist, holding tight onto her.

Her eyes widened and cold sank deep down inside her gut. She pulled her face away from Tucker's back and turned to look behind her.

She stared into the dead face of Kirby Decker, the top of his head split open, dried blood caked in the crevice.

"How about that kiss?" his dead lips said.

His arms pulled Shelby off the back of the toboggan and she had no air to even scream as she watched the sled continue down the hill.

CHAPTER TWENTY-SIX

Clark watched Shelby and the others leave and hoped they would be safe. He remained where he was till they were no longer in sight. He felt guilty about letting them go off by themselves. If something happened to them, he wasn't sure what he'd do.

But he had business to take care of.

He turned to head back into the house, but stopped at the foot of the front stoop when he heard the door open. Sledge and Wick came out.

"You surprise me, Mr. Brooks," Sledge said.

Wick stood by, grinning in silence. Creases at the corner of his mouth extended his smile, exaggerating it. He held his hands behind his back.

"Why is that?" Clark asked.

Sledge gestured toward the woods with his right hand. "Your friends have left, but you didn't go with them."

"I have unfinished business here."

The old man chuckled. "That's quite an understatement." He stepped to the edge of the stoop. "Makes no matter. Your friends won't get very far, I assure you."

Clark's spirit sank, but he kept his face rigid, not wanting to show it. "Leave them out of this. I'm still here."

"I can't do that," Sledge said. "Games have rules."

"Were you this mad before you died?"

He scowled. "You'd be surprised what this place will do to you. But you'll find out soon enough." He snapped his fingers.

Wick stepped forward, bringing his hands out from behind his back. In one hand he held a large pair of black ice tongs, their pointed tips stained red. The Iceman descended the steps toward him.

Clark stepped back, unsure what to do.

Wick grinned a sadistic smile, grasping the handle of the ice tongs with both hands and raising the tool up.

Was this the last thing all his victims saw, Clark wondered, this madman coming at them with his instrument of death? He looked around for something to defend himself with, and taking his eyes off the Iceman for just that brief second was all it took for the maniac to spring on him with sudden swiftness.

Clark raised his hands in defence, and grasped the tongs in both hands as they lunged toward his throat. Wick gritted his teeth and pushed the tool toward Clark's neck. Clark strained to keep the tool at bay, digging his boots into the snow to maintain his leverage.

Wick was taller and bore the strength of his arms down on him. The pointed tips inched closer. Clark could smell the coppery scent of blood on them and wondered whose it was. Wick's eyes were wide and mad.

Clark pulled the tongs to the side, knocking Wick off balance, but not off his feet. Clark lost his own footing in the process and slipped in the snow, relinquishing his grip on the tongs, and fell to the ground. He looked up in time to see Wick looming over him, once again lifting the tongs above him.

Clark saw the broken icicles that had fallen from the roof. He scrambled through the snow toward them, plucked one up from where it lay in the snow and jumped to his feet, holding it waist-high like a spear, its sharpened tip pointing at Wick.

The Iceman's grin shrank, and he looked confused.

Can you kill a man who's already dead? Clark wondered. He thought about Graham and what had happened to him upstairs in the house. What did he have to lose?

Clark charged forward with the icicle, surprising Wick, who stumbled backward up against the newel post of the front stoop. Clark thrust forward with the icicle aiming for where Wick's heart would be, if a monster like him was even capable of having one.

The pointed icicle plunged through the material of Wick's shirt and whatever flesh was beneath it, and continued through till it hit the wood of the post behind Wick's back with a hollow thud.

Wick made no sound. No cry of pain (*can the dead feel?*), no shout of anger. His eyes drained of any colour, his pale skin became even more pallid, and his hands trembled, dropping the ice tongs into the snow at his feet. His body grew motionless.

But his grin remained.

The Iceman looked like a frozen corpse, like the one the authorities never found at the bottom of Jericho Lake, preserved in his winter grave.

Thayer Sledge began clapping, slow and drawn-out. "Score one for your side," he said.

Clark looked up at him, seething. But he knew he was far from finished. And hopefully, Shelby and the kids were in the plough with Tucker and heading down the highway.

CHAPTER TWENTY-SEVEN

Shelby felt herself being dragged down into the deep snow, the cold arms of a long-dead corpse gripping tight around her waist. She wanted to scream, but maybe it was the hold squeezing the air out of her, or maybe it was just the mind-numbing shock of seeing the ghastly thing her former boyfriend had become, but the only thing that she was able to get out was a strained squeal.

She struggled in the thing's grasp as it pulled her farther into the snow, almost up to her chest.

It's going to drown me, she thought, panicking. She knew it was a mistake to get on that toboggan. The last ride had been the worst winter memory of her life, until now that was. She couldn't believe she had almost reached the highway, almost made it out.

Though she felt helpless, like a swimmer caught in a riptide, she hoped Tucker and Clark would at least get her kids out. That was the only thing she wished for now.

Shelby stopped squirming and craned her neck around to look Kirby in his dead white eyes.

Why are you doing this?

She studied his face, visualising the happy man he had been when he was alive and how much she'd adored him, thinking of the life they could have had together had they not taken one last ride down Tobin Hill. It was so unfair. Everything about this was unfair.

I don't want to die.

She could breathe better. The pressure was eased now that Kirby's arms loosened a bit. His face moved toward hers and she kept her eyes open as dead lips pressed onto hers, cold and lifeless. He ended the kiss, and she saw a smile spread across his face, and colour even came back into his eyes.

And then Kirby's corpse released her and sank under the snow and was gone.

Shelby sat there, half-buried in the snow, reflecting on the passion she had once felt for the man Kirby used to be. Warmth filled her body.

Someone was calling her.

She looked up to see Tucker sprinting up the hill toward her. Down at the bottom she could see her kids standing by the toboggan.

"Christ!" Tucker cried out. "What the hell happened?" he asked when he reached her, huffing and puffing, bending over with his hands on his knees. "I turned around and noticed you'd fallen off."

"Yeah," she said, smiling. "Just lost my grip."

Tucker extended a hand and pulled her out of the snow. They made their way back down the hill. Macey and Luke embraced her when she reached them.

"Let's get to the plough," Tucker said, "and get everyone warm."

"And then wait for Clark," Shelby said, nodding to make sure he understood. "Because we're not leaving without him."

"Right," he said.

Tucker scooped up one kid in each arm and climbed through the deep snow along the side of the highway till they reached the plough. He helped them into its cab.

"I'm waiting out here," Shelby said, standing beside the vehicle. "I want to watch for him."

Tucker was about to argue with her, but just nodded. "I'm just going to get this thing started, so the heater can warm up." He climbed into the driver's seat.

Shelby noticed the cleared path of roadway in front of the plough. She had a queasy feeling that the vehicle wouldn't start after all their effort to rescue the kids and get here, but with a rumble the engine roared to life and she hoped they would finally emerge from this nightmare.

She looked back to the woods, scanning the spaces between the trees for any movement, some sign that Clark was on his way. There was nothing. *What could be keeping him*, she wondered? He'd said he needed to do something to help them escape, but she didn't understand. They had the plough and a cleared path, all they needed now was him.

Please, she cried. *Please get here.*

The driver's side door of the plough's cab opened, and she turned. Tucker climbed out.

"The kids are hungry," he said, smiling. "I've got some snacks in my truck. I'll just be a second."

She watched him go off through the snow toward his rig. He disappeared after he passed the buried SUV that had belonged to the Drakes. Her gaze returned to the woods as she hugged herself to keep warm.

What was taking Clark so long?

Her stomach was knotted. Maybe she was hungry too, but more likely it was the frantic state of her nerves. She wanted this to be over.

Shelby looked over toward the eighteen-wheeler. She glanced at the cab of the plough. From her vantage point she couldn't even see the kids. She was glad at least they had a chance to get warm.

She kept shifting her gaze from the plough to the woods to the tractor-trailer truck. She realised why her stomach was in knots. She felt all alone right now, standing in the middle of the snowbound highway, unable to see her kids or Tucker and with no sign of Clark. The warmth of the morning had passed and she hugged herself tighter, rubbing her hands up and down her arms.

Or was that fear creeping back in?

This isn't over yet, she felt.

The rumble of the plough engine was the only sound.

Crunching steps in the snow joined it and she looked down the highway.

Tucker emerged from around the SUV, his arms cradling bags of chips and crackers, and she breathed a sigh of relief.

"Thank goodness," she said as the smiling man approached. "I was getting worried."

"Just tried the CB one more time," he said. "Still nothing." He looked at her. "No sense waiting out here in the cold. Come sit in the truck, keep warm while we wait."

She nodded. "Ok. I could use some warmth. I'm sure he won't be much longer." (*Please.*)

She took some of the snacks from him, and he helped her into the truck, where she sat in the middle, next to Macey. Tucker climbed in and sat behind the wheel. It was cramped with the four of them. It already felt warmer, the hot air pouring out of the truck's vents filling the cab. She handed the snacks to Luke and Macey, who ripped them open with glee.

It was harder to watch the woods from the truck's cab, but she did, Tucker also keeping his eyes peeled for any sign of Clark.

"Mom?" Luke said.

"Yes, honey?" she asked, turning to look at him, noticing the trembling sound in his voice. "What's the matter?"

Luke didn't say another word. His eyes were wide. Macey sat still beside him. Her mouth hung open. Luke pointed toward the windshield.

"Oh no," she heard Tucker say before she looked up.

Three snowmen stood in the clearing in front of the plough. The tall one in the front wore a black top hat, a red-and-white striped scarf draped around its neck. Behind it stood two shorter ones; the fatter one wore a Santa cap. The other one had no head.

The tall snowman's black mouth opened, revealing sharp teeth.

CHAPTER TWENTY-EIGHT

Clark approached the stoop, not taking his eyes off the figure of Everett Wick pinned to the porch post by the icicle, not sure if the twisted killer was dead (*but he's already dead*) or just frozen (*frozen in time?*). Still, he didn't want to get too close as he ascended the steps to where Sledge stood, a deep scowl on his face.

"Now what's your next move, Mr. Brooks?"

"This is where I go to the head of the class," he replied, brushing past the toy tycoon and entering the house. Sledge made no attempt to prevent him, but followed close behind. Clark hoped he knew what had to be done.

Once inside, Clark entered the study to the right of the hall, to where the snow globe rested on its pedestal. He paced around the object, keeping one eye on it as well as a close eye on Sledge in case the old man tried to stop him.

Clark stopped and stared down at the globe. Inside it he saw the orange plough in the midst of the snowdrifts on the highway. They had to be there by now, he thought, they had enough time. But what was time to this place, this realm?

It didn't matter. He had run out of it.

"I wouldn't do anything rash," Sledge said, stepping into the room.

He looked up at the sinister eyes of the old man. "Just making my final move," he said.

Clark picked up the snow globe, hefting its weight, before glancing once more at Sledge. He could feel a warmth and vibration in the orb, as if it was a compacted energy cell.

"You don't know what you're doing," Sledge said, his face cross.

"Don't I?" Clark spun and with all his might heaved the snow globe into the empty fireplace. The glass shattered against the cold bricks.

"Do you realise what you've done?"

Clark turned to look at Sledge with a smile. "Game over."

CHAPTER TWENTY-NINE

"We can't wait," Tucker said, gazing out the windshield at the ominous snowmen in the road before them. "We've got to go." He revved the engine.

"But we can't leave without him," Shelby cried frantically, looking helplessly toward the woods.

Macey was tugging on her sleeve. "Mommy, let's just go."

Shelby looked down at the panicked expression on her daughter's face. She glanced over at Luke staring outside, terror in his eyes. She followed his frightened gaze out the windshield to the snowmen.

"But he said he'd be here," Shelby said, not directing it to anyone but herself.

"He's going to have to find his own way out," Tucker said, putting the truck into gear and lowering the blades of the plough.

Shelby felt hopeless as she put her arm around Macey and looked forlornly at the woods in the distance.

"Go," she finally said, tears in her eyes.

Tucker released the clutch and pressed down on the gas pedal. The truck lurched forward and then picked up speed, Tucker raising the plough blade slightly just before they slammed into the trio of snowmen, sending chunks of snow flying.

Shelby could have sworn she saw the tall snowman's sharp-toothed grin turn into a frown just before the plough hit it. The black top hat spun in the air and landed on the hood of the truck, danced around and then bounced off the side. The red-and-white striped scarf got caught on the driver's side mirror, clinging to it.

Tucker kept the gas pedal pressed down and lowered the plough blade to the road as they reached the end of the cleared path. The plough hit the pile of snow covering the road beyond it with a lurch that almost threw Shelby into the dashboard. She grabbed onto Macey with one hand, reaching over to clutch Luke's shirt with the other.

"Hang on!" Tucker yelled, firming his grip on the steering wheel as the truck's tyres spun in the snow. Then they dug in, making the back of the truck sway. The plough blades pushed the snow to the side, clearing a path. The truck slowed under the burden before it, but Tucker kept his foot heavy on the pedal and struggled to keep the wheels straight.

Soon the truck cut a path through the snow with less effort.

Up ahead was a snow-covered road sign before what looked like an exit ramp. Tucker veered the truck toward it, bursting through the snowbank built up across it. Shelby thought she heard the sound of breaking glass.

"Where does this exit go?" she asked Tucker.

"I don't know," he said, shaking his head. "Anywhere but here."

CHAPTER THIRTY

"Now you've done it," Sledge said, staring down at the broken glass in the fireplace. He turned and walked out of the room, crossing the foyer into the living room opposite it, where Clark had awoken what seemed like ages ago. Clark followed him. A fire still roared in the fireplace, warming the room.

"Is that it?" Clark asked, wondering why the man seemed to be giving up so easily.

Sledge walked over to the chairs by the chessboard, sat down and silently rearranged the pieces on the board.

"No more games?" Clark asked.

Sledge chuckled. "There are always more games." He motioned to the chair opposite the chessboard. "Please, come sit."

Anger seethed up inside Clark as he approached the table. After everything this man had put them through, it enraged him that he could calmly sit down to play a game. The deaths this man had caused. He thought of Graham and his girls, who were now fatherless. He thought of the nameless young couple in the back of the hatchback.

"I'm not sticking around," Clark said. "I've had enough."

"I don't think we'll be going anywhere anytime soon," Sledge said with a smirk. "For me, it's of no concern. For you, that's an entirely different matter." He motioned to the seat opposite him.

A sinking feeling overcame Clark, a sense of despair as his insides knotted up. He thought about the smashed snow globe and the realm they were in. He thought about how breaking it had given Shelby and the others a chance to get out, but he knew it meant a different consequence for himself.

He collapsed in the chair on the other side of the chessboard, looking down at the white pieces on his side.

"I believe it's your move," Sledge said, leaning back in his chair. "It's going to be a long winter."

ACKNOWLEDGEMENTS

I owe a lot of appreciation to those who helped make this winter nightmare possible. I especially want to thank Flame Tree Press and my editor, Don D'Auria, who saw the potential in this story, and for his guidance, and that of copy editor Imogene Howson, for seeing it to its finished form. I am grateful for artist Nik Keevil and Mike Spender for the terrific cover art.

I have a special thanks to Karen Hendrickx for introducing me to the legend of Krampus, and Tamara Vachon for giving me a tour of her RV. I also appreciate JetPack Comics owner Ralph DiBernardo and Water Street Bookstore owner Daniel Chartrand for their overwhelming support of a local author.

I thank my parents for keeping the spirit of St. Nicholas alive as long as possible in a young boy's imagination. I have so many joyous memories of Christmas past with Jenna and Casey, and look forward to Christmas future with them and Brett, Bailey, Jacoby, Brady, Brooks, Erica and Jace. And Rhonda fills my Christmas present with so much love.

What's my worst winter memory? That I will share at a time when the heavy snow falls and the cold wind howls on a lonely dark night.

FLAME TREE PRESS
FICTION WITHOUT FRONTIERS
Award-Winning Authors & Original Voices

Flame Tree Press is the trade fiction imprint of Flame Tree Publishing, focusing on excellent writing in horror and the supernatural, crime and mystery, science fiction and fantasy. Our aim is to explore beyond the boundaries of the everyday, with tales from both award-winning authors and original voices.

•

Other horror titles available include:
Thirteen Days by Sunset Beach by Ramsey Campbell
Think Yourself Lucky by Ramsey Campbell
The Hungry Moon by Ramsey Campbell
The Influence by Ramsey Campbell
The Haunting of Henderson Close by Catherine Cavendish
The House by the Cemetery by John Everson
The Devil's Equinox by John Everson
Hellrider by JG Faherty
The Toy Thief by D.W. Gillespie
One By One by D.W. Gillespie
Black Wings by Megan Hart
Hearthstone Cottage by Frazer Lee
Those Who Came Before by J.H. Moncrieff
Stoker's Wilde by Steven Hopstaken & Melissa Prusi
The Playing Card Killer by Russell James
The Siren and the Spectre by Jonathan Janz
The Sorrows by Jonathan Janz
Castle of Sorrows by Jonathan Janz
The Dark Game by Jonathan Janz
House of Skin by Jonathan Janz
Dust Devils by Jonathan Janz
The Darkest Lullaby by Jonathan Janz
Will Haunt You by Brian Kirk
We Are Monsters by Brian Kirk
Creature by Hunter Shea
Ghost Mine by Hunter Shea
Slash by Hunter Shea
The Mouth of the Dark by Tim Waggoner
They Kill by Tim Waggoner

•

Join our mailing list for free short stories, new release details, news about our authors and special promotions:

flametreepress.com